MURDER, EH?

A Belle Palmer Mystery

by Lou Allin

D1246572

RENDEZVOUS
PRESS

Cover art: Alan Barnard

Le Conseil des Arts | The Canada Council
du Canada | for the Arts
depuis 1957 | since 1957

We acknowledge the support of the Canada Council for the Arts for our publishing program.

Napoleon Publishing/RendezVous Press
Toronto, Ontario, Canada

Printed in Canada

10 09 08 07 06   5 4 3 2 1

Library and Archives Canada Cataloguing in Publication

Allin, Lou, date-
          Murder, eh? / Lou Allin.

(A Belle Palmer mystery)
ISBN 1-894917-27-8

          I. Title. II. Series.
PS8551.L5564M87 2006   C813'.6   C2006-900034-4

PROLOGUE

The Sudbury Star, August 26, 2006

"Second Murder Rocks City"
A concerned neighbour found the body of Selma Atler, 42,
Sunday morning after she failed to answer the door at her
home on Bloor Street in the Donovan area. An accountant
at the Taxation Centre, Ms. Atler appeared to have been
strangled, then placed nude in the bathtub.

June Reymond told police that they always drove to
church together. "I just went on in. The door wasn't locked.
That wasn't like Selma."

There was no sign of forced entry, but missing were a
plasma television, a Sony laptop, and an assortment of
jewellery, according to Norm Atler, her son, a lawyer in
Lively.

"We're the Nickel Capital, not the Murder Capital. The
person responsible will be found and prosecuted to the full
extent of the law. That's a promise," said Nan Martin,
Police Public Relations Officer, in a press conference
Tuesday afternoon. She was referring to a local newscast
stating that the latest death had bumped the annual
homicide rate to 5.5 per hundred thousand, passing the
leaders, Saskatoon and Regina. "With only 165,000 people
in the City of Greater Sudbury, small numbers can skew

the data. We were only .6 last year. Why doesn't anyone mention that?"

The shocking killing echoed the death of Jennifer Spark the week before, also found under similar circumstances by her sister, Marge Blake. A divorcee, the 40-year-old Spark lived alone in an apartment on Teele Street in Lockerby. Mrs. Blake noticed the absence of a collection of Georgian silver, a Bose radio, a bottle of Courvoisier and several hundred dollars collected for a cat shelter.

Take Back the Night, a local activist group, will march tomorrow to Tom Davies Square to demand more police patrols. Meanwhile, single women are being advised to lock their doors and report any stranger. Anyone with information is urged to call the TIPS hotline at 705-226-7821.

The tragic deaths have touched many parts of the community. Belinda Jeffries, manager of the City Pound on Douglas Street, reported that most of its larger dogs had been adopted. Dick Derro, manager at Blue Steel Protection, said, "We've doubled our rate for installations of home security systems. No one wants to take chances."

ONE

The stink of gas exhaust announced an unwelcome presence long before Belle Palmer heard the distant, guttural chug of an ATV. Twenty minutes earlier, she'd squinted in suspicion at a rusty white Ford 100 truck parked at the schoolbus turnaround at the end of her remote road along Lake Wapiti. A cleated metal ramp on the tailgate meant that a rider was already on the Bay Trail. Freya, her German shepherd, had given the bottom of the steep hill a thorough sniff, squatting to pee proprietorially in an arbutus bed.

Moose season was over a month away, though that wouldn't prevent a bold poacher from filling his freezer illegally. She had made a mental note of the Ontario "Yours to Enjoy" license plate: AHCK 245. AW HECK, bring a 2-4 at 5. If she heard shots or saw fresh signs of ad-hoc butchering, reporting the plate would be a pleasure. The Ministry of Natural Resources had the right to search and seize vehicles and even check a residence for contraband meat.

Stopping on the forest path a kilometre later, she spied broken ferns and crushed bracken where the macho machine had left the trail, then looped back. Too lazy to hike into one of the interior swamp lakes and perch in a tree stand? Over the years, hunters had erected three or four in the vicinity. Then around the next blind turn beside a grandfather yellow birch came a rider wearing work pants and a ubiquitous red plaid flannel shirt. The green monster Yamaha Grizzly 660 quad had a large wooden box attached to the rear carrier, and a water bottle dangled from the handlebars.

On a whistle, Freya moved to Belle's side, and she placed a gentle hand over the chain collar for safekeeping. Shepherds were extremely wary and very territorial. This was their province, Crown land though it was. Belle could have sworn the old dog narrowed her eyes.

"How are you today, *madame?*" the man asked with a warm smile, cutting the engine. He had no accent, but the last word made him a Francophone, *sans doute.*

"You tell me," she said with a cold expression, folding her arms. "What are you after this time of year? Bear, I suppose. Make sure it's a boar, or don't you care about orphaned cubs?" Curiously, she saw no gun, just a belt knife with a bone handle.

He switched off the engine, his crinkled, butterscotch eyes confused at her hostility. Attractive as Sean Connery in *Robin and Marian,* he could have been anywhere from fifty up, unshaven, but with a healthy head of salt and pepper hair under a very odd pink knit cap with earflaps.

"Why so unfriendly? I'm a licensed trapper," he said with a slight frown and a hurt tone, as if the final word, which would enrage urban PETA members, should be a cachet with bush dwellers. "I have a right to trap here."

"Trap what?" she asked, as a whiff of pong met her nose. Not death, but pungent, foul and laced with hormones.

The man got off the quad and walked to the rear carrier, which he opened to display a large beaver, flat on its back, paws folded over its belly like a medieval bishop atop his marble tomb.

"Male," she said. "Wheew. How do you stand that reek?"

"Don't hardly take notice of it after my beak goes numb.

Not until I get home and the wife gets downwind of me before I hit the shower."

Suspecting the source of the ridiculous hat, Belle relaxed for a moment, waving her hand. "I'm not that fond of beavers." Many waterside poplars and birch had been destroyed by overambitious rodents gnawing down trees too big for their abilities or girdling skyscraper aspens, leaving them to wither. With beaver hats in disfavour since the American Civil War and coats a dangerous fashion statement, the mammals were overbreeding. Obstructive dams often pooled water in the interior, then burst forth into streams, flooding out nearby homeowners.

"What do you get for a pelt these days?" she asked. Fur might be making a comeback, but times had been lean for decades. He didn't finance that ten-thousand-dollar machine on this career.

"Hell, no more than twenty bucks at the North Bay fur auction," he replied. "This is just a sideline since I retired from Mother INCO."

Sudbury's International Nickel Company together with little brother Falconbridge had employed over twenty thousand people in their Seventies heyday. Now only six thousand remained on the payrolls, but thanks to modern technology, still produced the ore for one-fifth of the world's metal. Until recently, increasing numbers of retirees barely maintained a shrinking population as the young left for greener urban pastures down south or out west. Since miners often started work at eighteen, the trapper could have retired before fifty, a just reward for half a life underground.

"Word was passed on to me from a survey team on the Nickel Rim South Project about a nuisance pair back there at the swamp lake. They're putting in a tailings pond, and you know how these watercourses all connect up," he explained.

The new mine. Flags from surveyors had started showing up everywhere, paths chopped into the forest. How she resented intruders with heavy lug tires despoiling the trails she ambled. Boys and their toys. "So that's it for you in here, then?" she asked in a brusque tone, still cautious as she remembered the strange deviations into the bracken. Beware of men bearing dead beavers.

He rummaged in a canvas pack, handing her a wooden apparatus the size of a shoe box. "I'm scouting places to put up a few of these."

"What are they?"

"Marten traps."

Belle clamped her jaw in recollection of the rare sight of the dry-land counterpart of the familiar mink, a boreal forest inhabitant. Weighing in at only a few pounds, the weasel family members were fond of blueberries, a signal feature in their small scat, usually on a prominent rock in the middle of the trail. Wild animals had a sense of humour. She was unfamiliar with the finer points of trapping, but alarms were ringing. "Where do you put them?"

He pointed down the trail. "You might have seen that fir grove near where I drove off. Martens make their dens in conifers. So I nail these on."

She peered into the trap, a coffin with a cruel spring vice inside. "What's the bait?"

He waved his gnarled hand, red with toil. "Hamburger. Porkie strips if I catch one. Martens are fierce little creatures. Take your finger off."

Belle's stomach churned in disgust. Martens were rare and shy. She'd seen only a few in her lifetime, these cousins of Herman the Ermine, who lived under her boathouse and kept mice at bay. "And what do you get for *their* skins?"

"Around sixty bucks. Enough to add a bit of Christmas cheer."

She flipped back the trap. "Make sure you don't catch any dogs in the process of accumulating that cheer. My friend's mini-poodle could crawl into this." She turned away and stalked back down the trail, calling over her shoulder. "Too much trouble to go to the real wilderness? Why not use the bus and trap downtown in Bell Park?"

Before he could reply, she was gone around a turn, walking as fast as her mid-forties legs could carry her. Though Freya bounded ahead, the walk was spoiled. She felt her blood pressure simmering. Hunters, quadders, snowmobilers. Now trappers. Was she living in a *North of 60* rerun? Her once-peaceful road with barely a dozen full-timers now had over forty. What next? An Indy 500? A Wal-Mart?

Stopping to catch her breath and savour one last moment, she admired a sleek apricot mass on a maple tree. One-inch-by-two, it encased the Hebrew moth's eggs. She had wondered, weeks ago, why the sand-brown creature with dark script-like markings was biding quietly. Stopping the next day, she had perceived the patient laying, a velvety covering protecting the hatch from winter's savage assault. Gently she stroked the case like a present to open in spring.

Taking a deep breath, she headed back to the trailhead and along Edgewater Road. As she came to the "An Old Crow and a Cute Chick Live Here" sign with gaily painted cartoon birds, she turned into the driveway of her retired friends, the DesRosiers. Ed was tinkering in the open garage with his snowmobile, a snazzy Phaser, too rich for her blood, and as a pensioner nearing seventy, too fast for his. The Northern version of a sports car convertible.

He gave a wave, and their chocolate-red mutt Rusty ran up for a pat, grovelling on the ground in submission. Freya was her elder, so she respected her status. "Come on in for a coffee. Catch up on the news about these damn murders," Ed said, wiping his hands on a rag.

She groaned, wrenched back to civilization with its own terrors in the night. "It's the lead story for all the media. I'm glad I live out here, or am I?" She told him about meeting the trapper.

"Ford 100, eh? Had one myself. Three hundred thousand K and had to beat it to death. Don't see many of those old guys. I'll keep an eye open." Ed had forged his own paths far into the woods decades ago and had a healthy suspicion of strangers. A recent hip operation had cancelled bush hikes, and even he drove a quad down the road occasionally to give neighbours a hand with their plumbing, his former profession. If cake was served, it wasn't his fault.

Passing a small oak festooned with plastic juice jugs of seeds, she noticed the rose and grey splashes of a pack of pine grosbeaks chattering in the branches.

Inside, around the corner in the kitchen, Hélène was rolling out pastry. "Decaf's fresh. It's all we drink now that Father has angina."

Ed grunted as he propped up his fancy carved cane in the corner. "I'm not your father, woman. Or I'd take you over my knee."

"Baby those knees. The health care system's not your personal orthopedic clinic."

A Swedish enamel woodstove in the large living room maintained an even temperature in the cooling afternoons, though their floor-to-ceiling windows in the cedar bungalow led to bitter complaints about hydro bills. Belle took off her jacket and pulled up a chair at the combination kitchen and dining room table. Dusting off her hands, Hélène poured coffee and presented a heaping plate of Nanaimo bars. "Low-cal. Made them with sweetener." She plopped down a bottle of French Vanilla Coffeemate. "This has no fat at all. Or do you want two per cent milk?"

"Milk's fine." Paint had no fat either, but she wouldn't drink it. Belle tested the confection. Nuts, cocoa, butter. Hélène took no shortcuts. With curling grey hair and an urge to feed the world, she filled the role of an older sister or perhaps a younger mother. Ed's belly scooched over his belt like a bag of flour. His slim wife, with energy to burn, never glanced at a scale.

A copy of the *Sudbury Star* lay on the table. Belle gave it a scan. "No arrests yet. Not even a person of interest, or whatever they call it."

Ed cocked his head toward a .22 mounted on the wall. "A lady's best friend. City folks ought to keep one handy."

"My shotgun's wrapped in a garbage bag in the basement rafters. Safe from thieves but hardly handy," Belle said. "And no, it's not registered."

"'Peace and good government' is our country's motto. Not 'Life, liberty and a handgun in every drawer.'" Hélène paused thoughtfully. "I worry about my girlfriends in town who live alone."

Belle nodded, taking another bar. It was only three o'clock, not that close to dinner. "Radio said that a task force is already on the job. Maybe there will be a break this week."

"Everyone's talking. Even my cousin Bea is concerned for her female workers."

Bumble Bea Bakeries. The venerable family business downtown had been a legendary source of luscious breads and pastries. Hélène had said that Bea's grandfather named it for her.

"I have some news about her that might concern you," Hélène said with a mischievous grin that brought out her dimples.

For Belle, good news came in colourful pieces of paper bearing the pictures of prime ministers. Fall was a slack time for realtors, especially in cottage country. Such a cheat to enjoy the property during the fleeting summer then opt to sell in the fall, except what buyer wanted to freeze in an uninsulated camp with no water until the following May? Didn't Bea live in her grandfather's home on John Street overlooking Lake Ramsey? The city's first luxury homes had been erected there early in the last century by upper management at the mines. Now it was an enclave of doctors, lawyers and other professionals with six-figure incomes. "Am I going to owe you? I'm five dinners behind."

Hélène stirred her coffee with leisure, pulling out the moment like saltwater taffy, gauging Belle's cash-register eyes. "Bea wants to sell the property and move to a smaller home, maybe in the Kingsmount area."

Sell. The musical ride. She took a sharp breath. "That deal could be worth a million or more, depending on the lakefront. A thousand a foot on serviced lots."

Hélène shrugged. "They used to own acres, but her father tore down the old coach house and sold parcels on either side in the Sixties to finance the bakery's expansion."

One dismaying thought entered Belle's mind. "How old is the place?"

"Cayuga House dates from the twenties, eh?" Ed said as Hélène nodded. "Brass plate by the door like it was owned by some English lord."

Belle was already calculating her commission. Every sale counted for the smallest realty in town. "If the house is that old, a new owner might demolish it. Time, roofing and plumbing march on. I'll bet that the heating system needs an overhaul, too. There's a dinner at Verdicchio's in your future if I ace this." She named the most expensive restaurant in town. The bill could qualify as a tax deduction.

"I don't think you've ever met her. Bea is such a dear, and what she's gone through." Hélène's face lost its customary sunshine and turned sombre.

"Health problems? Or please don't tell me the bakery's going belly up. Their sweet rolls are better than yours, and you wouldn't deny it."

"I gave Bea the recipe." Hélène recounted how seven years ago, her much younger cousin had lost her husband Michael Bustamante and six-year-old daughter in an accident on Lake Ramsey. "Bea saw it all from her garden. July 1st holiday, it was. Mike was canoeing with the girl, life jackets of course, when a drunk driving a speedboat blasted into them. Mike died instantly of head injuries. Dear little Molly..." She stopped, gulping back a sob.

Ed patted her back with his walrus paws and turned to Belle. "Couldn't get her to stop crying for a week."

"The propeller. Her injuries were traumatic." Reaching for a tissue, Hélène continued. Left to raise her five-year-old son, Michael Junior, Bea had married Dave Malanuk a year ago, a fundraiser for local charities. He'd adopted the boy, but left him his birth father's name.

Belle hardly knew what to say except to make compassionate female noises. Some families were magnets for tragedy; others skated free and complained about hangnails.

"Malanuk. I know that name. Didn't he organize the Run

for the Cure?" With a memory of her co-worker Miriam's breast-cancer scare, Belle had jogged five miles and collected two hundred dollars from her neighbours.

Hélène nodded, wiping her soft grey eyes. "He's a wonderful guy. Just what she needed to restart her life."

"Sounds like a solid man." Belle couldn't imagine the challenges of a single parent. "Kids need a father."

"It's been bumpy. Micro loved—"

"Micro?" Belle leaned forward as if she'd misheard.

Hélène blew her nose and managed a smile. "Michael Junior. Kids and their nicknames. Computers or something. Anyway, he loved his father and won't accept a replacement. Problems spilled over his last year in elementary school. A bullying situation."

Engrossed in the sports section of the paper since Hélène had calmed down, Ed finally joined in. "Some rotten kid stole his lunch. Micro was just standing up for himself. Nothing wrong with a good shove."

Ed reached for a fifth bar and received a tap on the hand from his vigilant wife. "I remember our sons at twelve, don't you, Ed? Always testing limits." He grunted, and she continued. "And shamefully enough, for some ignorant people, there is his ethnic origin." Belle guessed from the context that she used "ignorant" in the sense of "rude," a Northern trademark.

"Bustamante? Sounds Italian, like your side of the family, or is it Hispanic?"

Hélène gave a bittersweet sigh. "No one ever said Bea didn't know her own mind. When she was thirty, still unmarried, pouring her life into the business, she took a singles' cruise and met Mike in Kingston, Jamaica. Love conquered all. It was a fairy-tale marriage. He was a fine doctor. Once he'd qualified in Ontario, he set up an office in Onaping, where they'd been without a general practitioner for years."

"She must have been a brave woman." In large metropolitan areas, interracial marriages were common, but not in the North, where people of African or Caribbean descent had been as rare as roses in May. Hélène had spoken of the benighted days in which a mixed marriage involved a Catholic and a Protestant.

"Bea was an only child, so she had her father wrapped around her pinkie, and his word was law with the relatives." She began to chuckle, poking Ed. "Except for Great-Great-Aunt Mafalda. Eighty-eight. Five feet of firecrackers. Pounded up to the main table at the wedding. 'Have to see this darkie for myself,' she said, waving her cane. Mike just gave a bow and tamed her like an old pussycat."

"A darkie. You have to be joking. Shades of Stephen Foster," Belle said, wiping tears of laughter from her eyes.

Ed added, "We had the family over for fishing this summer. Dave pulled out all the stops. Took Micro to Ramakko's for new tackle and gear. Didn't he land a big pike off the rock wall. He's a quiet lad, but a good boy. Give them time. They'll get over this."

TWO

September 1st struck the coup de grâce for Northern gardeners, a dust of frost at -2°C that morning. Carrying a steaming coffee and dressed in her long green terrycloth robe, Belle walked out onto the huge deck which wrapped the front and side of her storey-and-a-half cedar home. She stared down over her garden, site of the old cottage. The carrots and beets were snug and the broccoli impervious, but this was game over for the tomatoes. She'd pulled in several pounds on the vine last night to ripen in the cool of the basement utility room.

Across the eight-miles-by-eight meteor-crater lake, a shallow fog kissed the far shore, rolling down the North River like a phantasmagorical glacier, another sign of fall in this cinemascopic window on the four seasons. Facing north by northwest, her property bore the brunt of the fiercest winds instead of snuggling in a safe bay. Along the boathouse, a cement walkway led to a dock, which connected to a wooden crib with a concrete pad bearing her huge satellite dish, an historical artifact now used as planters by inventive owners. From there, a double telephone-pole bridge led ten feet to the protective rockwall.

Before leaving for work, remembering the trapper and his evil boxes, she logged onto the Ontario Fur Managers' site. "Managers" of a business governing the heartbeat of a soul. There she learned that in the early 1900s, over sixty thousand marten pelts were sold in Canada, driving the animal to near extinction and entirely out of Prince Edward Island. With a keen sense of smell, martens were easily baited in their ranges from two to three square kilometres. One sickening fact hit home. Trappers often left beaver carcasses near marten grounds in order to provide food and increase the carrying capacity of the habitat. Whether or not he'd been sent after a nuisance animal, he probably had availed himself of this trick after he'd stripped the pelt. It reminded her of the witch fattening Hansel. She'd have to return soon and find his site.

On the way to her all-wheel-drive Toyota Sienna van, Belle peered at squiggly bike tracks in the yard. Too cheap to subscribe, she got no paper delivery, knowing that Miriam usually brought hers to work to check their ads. Had someone selling school candy come by? Then she saw a paper slipped under the wiper, which was bent at an awkward angle. From a scratch pad, it bore the official logo of CRIME STOPPERS. A crabbed, childish scrawl read: "Your place in the woods has been puled down. Don't try it again." What the hell? Belle hadn't as much as set a nail in the bush, used it only to stroll and admire the sights. Was this about the bear and moose stands? She'd knocked a few boards from them herself out of sheer spite. On Crown land, the stands weren't illegal, so what was Crime Stoppers griping about? After crumpling the note, she tore a cuticle trying to straighten the blade.

Fifteen minutes later, leaving Edgewater Road to turn right onto the airport highway, she passed a dozen cars angled into the bush, collectors of the season's last blueberries, a local industry. Finally she could tune in the CBC local news. In an effort to comply with the 911 system, nine hundred streets in the region would have to be renamed. There were eleven Pines, eight Maples and eight Firsts, nine Birches, seven

Alberts, and so on down. This challenge could take five years with unimaginable costs. Think of the stationery, maps, and street signs. She blew a sigh of relief. Her business was located on Disraeli Court, one of a kind. Punching more buttons, she found a strong signal at 105.3. "Gimme the beat, boys, and free my soul" drummed from the speaker. A good song, but every half an hour? She grabbed an Enya CD and let "Marble Halls" smooth her journey past the airport, where she watched the plume of INCO's 1250-foot Superstack rise over the distant hills, symbol of industry. West wind as usual, blowing what remained of the scrubbed smelter air to North Bay.

Navigating the busy Kingsway and swivelling around Lloyd Street, she noticed that a large cement wall had been spray-painted with a bulbous, cartoonish "Nix" tag in red and white. It was rather artistic, but she didn't suppose the owners appreciated the effort. On one of the few residential streets downtown, she pulled into the parking area of a mock-Victorian house which made a convenient business address for Palmer Realty, founded by her late Uncle Harold. When she'd left Toronto behind twenty years before, kissing off a stressful high-school teaching job without a second thought, he'd paid for her realty courses, then made her his partner. The upstairs rented to a quiet and reliable snowbird couple. She gazed up at the mighty cottonwoods, the few large trees spared from the core ecological damage of the last century. The day had warmed up, so she hung her plaid jacket in the van, leaving her in designer jeans and a red silk blouse.

"Life is just a bowl of blueberries," she said to her only employee, Miriam MacDonald, her elder by ten years and a hundred grey hairs, whose baba's bunion legacy enjoyed a daily massage from a wooden foot roller beneath her desk. "And to mix a metaphor or two, if my new lead pans out on Lake

Ramsey, we're in the proverbial clover, four leaves every one."

Miriam munched at a cheese croissant, wiping crumbs from her mouth and pointing at a brown bag. "You mean Bea Malanuk? She dropped in this morning looking for you. Brought a half-dozen of these. Don't you love their dark rye? It's more sinful than an Aero bar."

Belle struggled to maintain a cautious optimism about the dream sale. Cottage properties were her cornerstone, so six per cent of a possible mid-six-figure range nearly made her drool like a St. Bernard, especially when the average price for a home was a piddling $115,000. In a region with forty other realty companies and home sales last year of only 2167, the pie was getting smaller, even if prices were gradually rising. She needed to average four or five closings a month to make a slim profit, buy kibble, and keep Miriam in foot rollers. "What's she like?"

"Tall, broad shoulders, strong arms. Probably comes with the baking territory, all that kneading. Nice, though. She reminds me of someone from those classic film tapes you give me. Can't place the name and face. A formidable woman with a great comic talent."

"Marjorie Main?"

"Ma Kettle? Don't think so."

"You have me intrigued." After grabbing a croissant en route to her nearby desk in the compact office, Belle saw the note with Bea's number at the bakery.

The busy clatter of a business set a background for the woman's upbeat, mellifluous voice. "Hélène's told me so much about you, Belle. I'm surprised we've never met."

"Thanks for thinking of me. Business is slow in the fall." And winter and spring. Slower than maple syrup poured onto the snow for an instant candy treat. Except for Cynthia

Cryderman, the biggest realtor in town, with San Antonio-size hair and a pink stretch limo to accommodate it. Her advertising bill alone doubled Belle's salary, even if the mindless radio jingle set teeth on edge. Sometimes she woke at midnight hearing its annoying words bouncing off the corners of her mind like billiard balls. But media coverage worked. That was the galling part. Cynthia sold nearly three hundred houses per year.

They set a date for three thirty that afternoon. In the meantime, Belle logged up her morning's calls and browsed a real estate tabloid. "Listen to this headline. 'Unshamed quality'. Do they mean 'unashamed'? And 'enter the lovely foray'." Miriam clucked disdain as she stuffed envelopes.

Belle turned to the rough copy of some ads her cohort had composed. "I can always count on you for correct punctuation. Don't you hate it when you see 'Five bedroom's'? Then she froze, making a gasping sound. "What's this? 'Affordable lakefront ten minutes north of New Sudbury'? That's impossible."

Miriam rose, walked confidently to the regional map on a bulletin board and traced a route with her ever sharp pencil. "Straight to Whitsun Lake."

"Get serious. You're pointing to a snowmobile trail."

The wily ex-bookkeeper, who had once sliced, diced and sauteed accounts for several marginal businesses in the Valley before joining Belle's company, folded her arms coolly over a beige linen pantsuit with a floral-print blouse. "Not exactly a lie, though."

"I want to be competitive, but not at the expense of the truth. Let's compromise at twenty minutes, speeding tickets aside, or you'll never make partner in the firm." Realizing that she had overextended herself, she added, "Not that there's enough room in this pond for more than one lily pad."

Miriam barked out a laugh and added a dollop of Frenglish. *"Hostie.* Splitting the profits. Now that would be the day...of judgement."

"Did I say 'splitting'?" Belle turned with a frown and began balancing the chequebook, a high-wire act.

At lunchtime, she headed for the nearby Tim Hortons. The venerable doughnut chain, now American-owned, had a history of nearly half a century based on the joys of bubbling fat, popping franchises across the country on every strategic street corner, promising a sweet, warm antidote for the never-ending Canadian winter. Iced tea and cappuccino in the summer, but no latte...yet. Other chains folded tent, and lately Tim's had aimed its sights at another border crosser, Krispy Kreme.

Collecting two Meal Deals, which included a sandwich, coffee and doughnut for mere pocket change, she saw Steve Davis coming through the door. As a detective, he wore a light-grey suit and carried a raincoat like any businessman. His six-six frame would look good in a burnoose, but she missed the handsome uniform from his younger days when he'd done off-duty security work for her Uncle Harold.

"I haven't seen you for weeks," she said, opening her coffee and pushing Miriam's towards him as they found a booth. "With those terrible murders, you must be in triple overtime."

He winced, sipping the brew. Ojibwa with a Scottish grandfather, Steve had been raised on a reserve in remote northwestern Ontario. His coal-black hair, thick and lustrous, shaded to silver at the temples. Her junior by a few years, he nevertheless felt a solemn obligation to play big brother, law vs. justice their favourite debate. "It's a nightmare. I was called to the second homicide. The mayor's courting a coronary. We're not used to this. Mom-and-pop domestics or bar brawls head up the usual list."

Belle leaned forward to hear his lowered voice. The police were not flavour of the month these days. Every pensioner in town punched in at coffee shops to heap abuse at the boys and girls in blue, usually in comparison with American television dramas where homicides were solved in an hour when dog DNA from a scrap of a cigarette filter of a suspect whose dachshund liked chewing paper turned up at the crime scene. "The methods seem similar, the victims, too. Are we talking serial killer?"

"Getting close." He frowned, dark clouds gathering in his eyes, as serious as Belle was comedic. "The magic number is three for that definition. You know I can't tell you much more than the papers. Strangling's the hardest kind of murder to solve. No blood, no mess, no fuss. If you have the cold determination to kill another human being and the muscles to carry it out, you may beat the odds."

"I see what you mean. Up close and personal." Remembering arcane details from the Kathy Reichs novels she often read before bed, she added, "Hyoid fracture. Thyroid cartilage. Petach...petrach... Help me out here, expert."

He rolled a tongue around his cheek in mockery. "A kindergartner knows the drill. Except that sometimes petechial hemorrhages appear for other reasons."

"No prints, though. Right?"

"Fingerprints can show up on skin with hi-tech fuming devices, but you have to get them fast. With whisper-thin latex gloves, it can be marginally possible to retrieve prints, too."

"Latex? Then rule out everyone with an allergy."

"Very funny. You might get hired as our departmental joker."

She was on a roll. "Trace evidence turned up by your forensics folk in white spacesuits? That theory that you take something and leave something—"

"Actually, the suits are black. You're talking about Locard's Principle of Exchange. If it were one hundred per cent true, few murders would go unsolved."

"I haven't heard anything about rape. Are you holding that back?"

"No more leaks." He stroked his jaw, the noon shadow beginning to shade his bronze face. "I should get out of this sorry business, except that I don't seem to have any other talents. The price of life's so cheap. A few thousand in portable property."

"You told me drugs were behind most crimes. Supporting a habit. Look how many times the Dairy Queen gets hit. What about the Hock Shop? Have you—"

They were interrupted by the loud guffaws and table slapping at the next booth, one coneheaded bald man with a pyramid of maple cream doughnuts, the other with a Godzilla hunk of coffee cake. Both wore hearing aids. "Friggin' idjits. Whatta we pay them for, anyways? Couldn't find their arsehole with their own thumb. There's a squad car at every Tim's."

Steve winced. "Glad I walked. I'd better hustle back to the station. We have another task force meeting this afternoon. Some hot shot profiler flew up from the Big Smoke."

"Let me guess the result. Male. Loner. Twenty to thirty-five. Hated Mommy Dearest. Works at a min-wage job." She looked around at the staff, mostly earnest women, but what about the kitchen help? "Maybe twenty feet away operating a deep-fat fryer."

"Not any more. The doughnuts come pre-cooked." Finally he smiled, tapping her cheap watch, well-worn with a cracked crystal. "I'll pass on your theory to the chief. But don't buy a Rolex on the expectations."

"One other thing. I had a nasty note from some Junior Crime Stopper. I suppose those in charge will give me some privacy baloney if I complain. Can you ask around and see if they have an overambitious kid on the roster in my area, maybe in Skead? A bike could do it in less than an hour." She explained the wiper incident.

"Everything is routed through Toronto, but I know our liaison sergeant, Rick Cooper." He pointed across the street to the Ukrainian Seniors' Centre next to Ray Hnatyshyn Park. "Crime Stoppers could have used more eyes over there in June. Kids painted swastikas on the back wall near the garden. Makes me sick."

"That's low. I saw some graffiti on my way in, but it was rather artistic."

"Graffiti's no trivial issue." He let out a slow breath in mute comment at her naïveté. "There was a dramatic increase over the summer. Over eleven thousand dollars in removal costs around the city. Besides that, it creates an environment that appears unsafe."

"True enough. Reminds me of L.A. streets in that movie *Colors*. It'll taper off soon. Spray paint doesn't work at -30°C," she said, coaxing a smile from his classic, chiselled lips.

As they parted company outside, she watched him stop momentarily to eyeball the stragglers in a crossover area between Tim's and the LCBO. Booze it up and then sober up. This volatile combination with the nearby bus station attracted drifters. He fished in his pocket for loose change and passed it to a tall, thin man who gave a theatrical bow, sweeping his Peter Pan hat to the ground, a rare character in the staid mining town.

Later that afternoon, she pointed the van down Paris and turned left on John Street, high on a hill, overlooking the jewel of Lake Ramsey. On one side was the venerable St. Joseph

Health Centre with its helipad, beyond that, the snowflake shapes of Science North, then Laurentian, the new megahospital with parking lots far enough from the entrance to weed out the more fragile heart patients. Then came Shield University with its gleaming towers, where the new medical college was breaking ground. At last the doctor-poor North could train its own.

She didn't need to double-check the address. Parked in the circular, bricked drive was a brown, black and yellow Ford Focus, customized to resemble a bee. Its rear was striped, a sharpened, centralized exhaust pipe serving as stinger, with *trompe l'oeil* folded gossamer wings and black legs on the body, protruding from the hood a plastic proboscis and antennae. The bakery logo was stencilled on both doors. Great tax deduction.

Bea's handsome home was constructed of massive grey stone blocks with cream mortar. A pristine slate roof and seamless eavestroughing bore witness to careful upkeep. It had two chimneys, a large wraparound porch with white Doric columns, a turret room and an attached garage, probably a later addition. One absent pleasure after leaving Toronto was the time travel through its varied neighbourhoods as far back as the Georgian period. Gently she touched the cool stone steps, slightly concave from nearly a century of use. Despite its charms, Cayuga House might be replaced by a blocky, cantilevered monstrosity. She hoped it would put up a stubborn fight against the monster backhoe.

Pulling out a small notebook to jot observations, Belle noticed an array of lilac bushes, skeleton pods of their Victoria Day splendour. The ivory hydrangea masses wore a blush of copper frost. Mature maples and ash offered shade and privacy. Caragana hedges were trimmed to perfection. Anyone with sense would kill for the landscaping.

She twirled the quaint bell chime and heard a muted response inside. "Hello."

"It's Belle Palmer."

"Hello, hello," replied the voice, oddly modulated, as if affected by a stroke. Did Bea have an older relative living with her? She tried the handle and found it unlocked. Hesitantly, she moved into the foyer, noting the wide plank floors and Aubusson runners.

"Bea? Where are you?" she called.

"Hello, hello," repeated the voice, sharper now, almost petulant. Belle was reminded of seniors at her father's nursing home who sometimes used double language. Unwilling to maintain the senseless conversation, she decided to look around.

After passing an empty living room, she came to a closed door. From behind it came a piercing shriek. Despite her misgivings, she opened it and found a parrot swinging from a brass stand, its food bowl empty. Beady coal eyes fixed upon her with a strange wisdom, as if it read her thoughts. "Oreo! Oreo!" it croaked, cocking its head and moving back and forth in rhythm. Pinfeathers floated in the air.

A very large woman in her early forties, with a friendly bulldog face, blunt lips, heavy brows and a streak of flour still in her riotous brown hair, slipped up behind her to deposit sunflower seeds into a metal cup. She carried a long, thin marble pastry roller which reminded Belle of the drill cores left in the field in mining operations. Her handshake was supple and strong. The resemblance to an unnamed comedienne which Miriam had flagged bothered her as well, but she couldn't pin down the identity.

"Meet Mackenzie King. He's having a time-out for being a bad boy, spilling his water, aren't you?" She leaned toward him, and he nuzzled her pouted lips. Belle winced. That beak could crack walnuts.

"What kind is he?" Belle would have been surprised to find more than a parakeet in the North, but since the advent of PetSmart, exotic birds selling for as much as two thousand had entered the local market.

"Amazon blue-fronted, which seems strange with that yellow on top. Would you believe he's over sixty years old?"

"They live quite long, I hear."

"A lifetime. Father passed him to me. It's a real commitment." She gave a hearty laugh and stroked its head as it danced, picking up each foot. "Last summer he got loose and went up into the flowering crab. To lure him down, Dave, that's my husband, had to go to Smith's to find the only papaya in five hundred miles. The whole neighbourhood gathered here for the antics."

"Your house is marvellous. I can't wait to see the rest."

Slipping the roller into a capacious apron, Bea clasped her hands together. "All that mahogany wainscotting and the carved staircase with the pineapple newel posts. Plenty of journeymen eager to please for a few dollars a day."

"Is society heading backward? The only woodworker I know delivers twenty bush cords for my stove."

Bea led her into a large living room brightened by towering ficus plants, a large Norfolk pine in a ceramic tub, and on a shaded ledge with stained glass windows, a stunning pink and purple orchid on a leaning stalk. Belle touched the waxy flowers in clear wonderment.

"It is real. Seems to like its home," Bea said with pride.

"Northerners love their Florida rooms, heating bills aside. My grandfather had a greenhouse business on Runnymede Road in Toronto. I guess Canadians thirst for a sign of life over the winter." She glanced down at the honeyed oak floors polished to a gleam, so much more character than laminate. Thick Persian carpets offered warm islands amid plum velour sofas and deep espresso-brown leather chairs. A fieldstone fireplace seemed to anchor the house to the Cambrian Shield.

On the rosewood grand piano were silver-framed pictures of the Bustamantes: Michael senior, a small and vigorous man, towered over by Bea, then Micro and his older sister in their school portraits. There was a wedding photo of Dave and Bea, something shadowy and strained about Dave's face, and a diminutive boy beside them looking at the church steps. In stature, Micro must have taken after his father. In one faded colour snapshot, two men posed on a tropical beach. A young Michael and someone close enough in appearance to be a brother. Belle realized that she was staring, but Bea was straightening a needlepoint on the wall.

Belle admired the tapestry of the Apple Queen. "As once I was, so am I now." The quote came from William Morris's *Pomona*, 1891. A buxom young woman in flowing medieval dress bore apples in her skirts. A complex weave of gold and green entangled trees surrounded her.

"Did you do this? The Pre-Raphaelites are favourites of mine, both their poetry and art. I love the details. And the framing's a great match."

Bea blushed at the compliment. "I like to keep my hands busy after work. If I'm not doing needlepoint, I'm knitting. Micro and Dave have enough sweaters and scarves to last a hundred years."

Jotting notes as they walked, Belle had more second thoughts about the expected demolition when she surveyed the modern kitchen with a Miele range, granite counters, a butcher-block island with copper pans hanging above and legions of German steel knives. She also noted the convenient half bath on the main floor. As they cruised the large dining room with a French Provincial table for ten, Belle stopped to assess a collection of ceramic ladies in a matching china cabinet. If memory served, these were Easter Day, Christmas Morn, and others, all red.

"Royal Doulton," she said. "My mother left me her collection."

Bea's hooded sea-green eyes brightened. "Oh? Which ones?"

"Delphine, Elegance, Vivienne...I sold Paisley Shawl."

"Really? What would you ask for Vivienne? She's discontinued, and red's my favourite, in case you hadn't noticed."

Belle "ka-chinged" a few calculations on her mental cash register. "Two-thirds book value. Three hundred?" Chasing the elusive loonie again. Would her mother haunt her tonight?

Bea pressed Belle in a giant's embrace, a wisp of lemon, vanilla and cloves in her wake. "It's a deal. Bring her with the first interested parties. I'll leave a cheque on the mantel."

Upstairs were five bedrooms, another full bath and a master suite. One bedroom was a sewing room, another an office for Dave, one appointed with the pink colours, chintz curtains and a flouncy bedspread that young girls would like, yet no toys or personal items. Sadly, Belle recalled the dead child and understood why these poignant vestiges of a short life remained to honour her memory.

The charming turret room had windows of rounded glass and a distinctive green, yellow and black flag hanging from the ceiling. "Keep out! This means you!" read a sign taped to the open door. Bea gestured to the skateboard, Gameboy and Superhero comic books. One wall displayed *Lord of the Rings* posters and a picture of Bob Marley, Rastafarian dreadlocks flying. A state-of-the-art PC with twenty-inch flat screen sat on an L-shaped desk. On a shelf above was a Harry Potter

collection in addition to the book *Son of Web Pages That Suck.*
Mine sure does, Belle said to herself, having constructed it
amateur-style using FrontPage Express.

"Don't they like their privacy? And my son hasn't even
entered his teens."

"What an unusual flag. I don't recognize it."

"Jamaica's. My late husband Michael wanted Micro to
appreciate his heritage." She picked up a hardcover book,
Heroes of Jamaica. "His distant relative was Alexander
Bustamante, the island's first Prime Minister in 1962."

"I have to confess that I know nothing about that lovely
country, except that its climate is heaven next to ours."

Bea smiled softly. "You're not alone. Many people think
only of gang wars or deportations. Jamaica had a proud
history of fighting oppression, British, of course. Many of its
people had been brought over as slaves."

"But there is the reggae music," Belle added.

"Michael loved the old folk songs. He used to sing Micro
to sleep with 'Clap Hands Til Papa Comes Home'." She
hummed a few bars and swayed with a gentle rhythm.

Belle noted the Snickers wrappers in the wastebasket and
the pile of textbooks. "I used to teach high school. Bailed out
after a few months. English was not foremost on their minds."

"Sounds like a sudden decision."

"Certainly was." The incident was as fresh in her mind as
this morning. "Why you always say I'm acting like a fool?" one
tenth-grader had demanded, and she hadn't been able to resist.
"Brian, you don't have to *act* like a fool." "Kiss my ass." Off to
the principal. Parents' conference. Everyone crying except her.
And a Greyhound bus ticket that weekend.

"They don't miss much." Bea's chuckle spread over her
face, an invitation to mirth. "Every year is a whole new world

with kids. Thirteen's coming up, and my friends tell me to fasten my seatbelt."

The master suite was immense, with walk-in closets and a Jacuzzi in the custom-tiled bathroom. The Mexicana furnishings, warm, weathered pine with copper fittings, were a surprise, a king-sized bed, drawer chests and nightstands, a splendid armoire, and in the corner, a box table. As always, in the more intimate parts of a house, she felt strangely voyeuristic. In the corner was a cherrywood antique prie-dieu.

Bea ran loving fingers over the fine petit point on the kneeler. "Great-Great-Aunt Mafalda's. For show rather than usage now. It's a bit creaky with age."

"I know the feeling."

While Bea fixed tea downstairs, Belle relaxed in a sunny breakfast nook, enjoying the antics of chickadees around the feeders. She looked past the deck to the choppy diamond waves of Lake Ramsey, where Bea's husband and daughter had died. From her Canlit class, she recalled a sinister poem by Margaret Atwood: "This is a Photograph of Me." The speaker addressed the reader like a friend deciphering a blurred black and white picture, so casual, lulling him into a reverie with "a gentle slope," "a small house," "some low hills," then adding, "The photograph was taken/ the day after I drowned./ I am in the lake....if you look long enough,/ eventually/ you will be able to see me." What a mistress of understatement Canada's icon was.

Bea's pastries proved that her talents ran in the genes. Rum-butter squares. Apricot clusters with pecans. "My grandfather bought Cayuga House in a distress sale during the Depression. The owner had invested heavily in Cobalt silver mines and lost everything. When you're an only child, it's hard to sell your family home, but it's simply too big." She gave a small sigh. "Has been for years."

Belle nibbled at a coconut square, piquant with lemon rind, its sweetness opposed to the bitter personal loss left unspoken. "As a realtor, I wear two hats, Bea, one for the buyer and one for the owner. I had imagined that Cayuga House might be demolished. People want modern homes." She tried to couch the observations in language that wouldn't insult the woman.

"I suppose so." Bea's large mouth sagged at the corners.

As the winey taste of Earl Grey cleared her palate, Belle added, "Now that I've seen everything, I'm not at all sure that will happen."

"The heating bills are plain murder, even though I love the old hot-water system." She put down her cup and patted a radiator near her shoulder. "A convenient place to dry mittens and toques."

"It's a stellar property. I'll get a lockbox set up for the front door tomorrow and take out a large ad in the paper for the weekend. MLS will reach outside the city. We'll keep our fingers crossed." She gave Bea a reassuring smile and opened the attaché case for the paperwork. "Hélène said that you liked the Kingsmount area. 'Historical' is the latest catchword for that part of town. I have a classic little place on Roxborough Drive. Mullioned windows. Fretwork. Steep gables. Private gardens out back." She paused for effect. "And a spanking new gas furnace."

On a tour of the property, Belle noticed a cozy doghouse in the backyard. A large grey and white sheepdog ambled out and shook itself. "Buffalo. Dave said a kid should always have a dog."

"I agree," Belle said, kneeling to embrace the massive shaggy head. "Mine's a German shepherd. Not as laid-back as this guy." She noticed that the left incisor was broken. Probably a stone chaser like Freya.

Bea pointed to a caragana hedge at the rear, beyond it a tiny cottage barely visible through the maples. "He can be a noisy one. Kids running through on their way home from school get him barking. Jean McBride over there calls me every now and then when he bites his rope and gets into her yard. Buffy's only outside a few hours a day in good weather. He sleeps on Micro's bed."

They strolled for a few minutes, remnants of the old estate adding charming touches. Bea's "secret garden" had a verdigrised sundial, a gazebo, and rock terraces to hold the soil against erosion on the steep slope. In the distance, a cigarette boat streaked across Lake Ramsey, two minutes across, then a turnabout, throwing up spray as its engines roared like 747s. A kayak struggled to position itself against swamping waves.

"You don't want to know my opinion of jet skis. And the snowmobiles are even worse," said Bea. "Here we are in the middle of town and have to put up with this."

"Perils of lakefront, I guess. But it adds one heck of a punch to the property values."

As Belle prepared to leave, Bea stood under a huge sugar maple by the front steps. One hand touched the rugged grey bark. Leading upward was a trail of nailed boards. In a spreading crotch twenty feet up, Belle glimpsed a structure. Bea's grin lit up her face. "My treehouse. Mother nearly had a heart attack passing up the heavy boards. Micro loves to camp out up there. And don't I provide the catering."

THREE

After breakfast, Belle ripped a page from her Tough Dames calendar, with its daily quote. "You gotta get up early in the morning to catch a fox and stay up late at night to get a mink." Mae West wore the minks, but Belle was determined to save their relatives.

Rousing a snoring Freya from her overstuffed easy chair in the computer room, she set off behind her house, taking a secret cut to the Bay Trail. She headed for the area where the trapper had verged into the bush. The dog lagged behind, flaring her nostrils at a mustard-yellow mound of grouse poupon under a branch.

"Leave it, girl. We're on dawn patrol."

Brushing aside drooping alders, she marched up the peaty path, narrowing her eyes and scowling at black tips of delicate earth-tongue fungi and a brilliant fly agaric dislodged by the quad. She imagined serving him the poisonous reddish mushroom on a silver platter. Rounding a turn at the Paper Tree, a birch divesting itself of bark like the dance of the seven veils, she spied his tracks trampling a lovely grove of interrupted fern as the quad verged from the trail. The four-foot plant boasted fragile brown seed pods dripping like caviar from its fronds. Freya started going wild with scent, plowing into the bushes, raising her ruff. "Come here!" Belle commanded, but the dog ignored her. Something reeked. All she needed was for the dog to start rubbing herself over a carcass or even eating it.

As she ran, she pulled the leash from around her neck. Rarely did Freya disobey, but this temptation even her excellent Schutzhund lineage couldn't ignore. Belle's yells distracted the dog and slowed her pace as she neared a low mound buzzing with flies. Leaping over a cedar stump, Belle lunged for the chain collar. "What's the matter with you?" she asked in a firm, low voice. Never yell into a dog's face. They had a clear sense of rudeness.

She looped the leash around a small oak, then clipped it to Freya's collar, giving her hand signals to reinforce the verbal commands. Sobered by the rare physical message of a leash, Freya sat and began a small whine, swivelling her plumed tail in agitation. With caution, Belle approached the shapeless mass. It was the flayed carcass of a beaver, gnawed by a series of flesh eaters in the usual food chain. Foxes had been on the scene, judging from the appearance of the entrails. She looked around with concern, aware that a wolf pack had territory less than a mile away. One December she'd seen their tracks on the ice of Surprise Lake and noticed a young moose drinking in the broken shallows below the beaver dam, a deep gash raking its flank. With this wholesale baiting, the trapper could be inviting guests very unwelcome to hikers, perhaps even an opportunistic, omnivorous bear. Feast on, fellow carnivores red in tooth and claw. The late Mr. Castor would be bones before a few more sundowns. Until then, she'd stay off the trail.

Scrabbling through the underbrush toward the fir grove, she located several marten traps, all nailed a good six feet up the trunks. At least he was keeping his promise about placement. Grabbing a sturdy grey stick, she broke off the side branches, squinted up into one trap and began to poke. Snap!

The cruel spring gave way. A wad of ground beef, greasy and grey, splatted onto the leaf mould. Snickering, she followed suit with the rest. It wasn't as if the man was making a living from the sales, but so many people used the bush as a supermarket or woodlot.

Finally she released Freya, giving her a warning wave, and they headed back down the trail. A few minutes later, she relaxed at a job well done, checking a rare patch of Indian cucumber root in a shaded maple grove. A single purple berry rose from leaf whorls blood-streaked in the centre. Suddenly she was aware that the dog was absent. "Not again!"

Seconds passed, and a brown form came barrelling through the undergrowth. Belle looked down in horror to see quills protruding from the dog's muzzle. "Jesus. You're a handful today." Making her sit under the wrath of Mom, she yanked each one quickly, and the dog made no moan. She ran her eyes over the rest of the body, satisfying herself that Freya had been either smart or lucky. Some dogs ran wild with pain, driving quills into their pads and even blinding themselves.

*   *   *

After a long day at the office, she arrived home at six and opted to go vegetarian, making a potato curry with a can of Madras sauce. Diced zucchini, green onions and a sprinkle of mustard seeds completed the medley. Soon, nutty aromas of basmati rice floated from the microwave. For some reason the dog wasn't eating her chow, but slopping her chops as if something was bothering her. Belle tipped Freya's head back, parted the giant jaws, and nearly cancelled dinner. A porcupine quill was lodged deep in the ribbed roof of the animal's mouth. She closed her eyes, unable to imagine the discomfort. Then shaking herself into action, she took pliers from the utility drawer and pulled it free. Without delay, Freya began steamshovelling her kibble.

After assembling her meal, Belle relaxed on one of the pasha chairs with ottomans in the television room and beamed up to TCM. The Television Police, aka the CRTC, limited Canadians to Bell ExpressVu and Star Choice. Neither offered Ted Turner's Classic Movies Network. Many neighbours had pirated systems, but she dutifully paid her fifteen dollar yearly subscription to a grey-market address in Southern Ontario. She sipped a mild New Zealand beer, an antidote for the flaming curry, and tuned in.

Silent films night. Marie Dressler in *Tillie's Punctured Romance*. The Cobourg, Ontario, native had left a music-hall and stage career which climaxed with her smash hit as Tillie Blobbs singing, "Heaven Will Protect the Working Girl." The Rosie O'Donnell of her day, she'd broken into pictures in 1914 with Charlie Chaplin. As the movie unfolded, Belle noticed why Bea had looked strangely familiar. Belle was used to Marie at nearly sixty in Garbo's *Anna Christie*, which had rejuvenated her flagging career. And yet there she was at Bea's age, flaunting comic talents as big as her size, a huge, hatchet-faced woman in love. Belle found herself laughing as hapless Charlie manouevered the woman on a dance floor like steering an elephant dressed in tulle, Marie's wild hair flying loose, except for a curl pasted around each ear. One leg bent back as Chaplin moved forward.

Later, upstairs in the master suite in her snug waterbed, she tamped a cigarette into Adolphe Menjou's jewelled holder, which her father had bought her at Universal Studios in Florida on their last visit before his collapse. In typical Canadian fashion, the pack of Number 7s, a cheaper brand, bore a warning: "Each year, the equivalent of a small city dies from tobacco use." A horizontal bar chart tagged car accidents at 2900 and tobacco-related deaths at a whopping 45,000. Homicides were the smallest category. Only 510, probably the same as Detroit. Belle hoped that the two latest deaths would be the last, an early Christmas present, but logic implied what the police hesitated to mention, that often another killing had to occur if only to provide the vital clue. A few tots of bargain-basement scotch smoothed her evening as she savoured Nevada Barr's *Blind Descent*. What a coup the former park ranger had achieved by making the landscape hundreds of feet below in Carlsbad Caverns as vibrant and alive as the desert surface.

What would the trapper do when he found all four snares sprung? The Fur Managers' website said that the traps had to be checked daily. Who monitored that? Getting up to gaze through the patio doors over the tiny balcony, she watched the moon gleam through the scudding pewter clouds, the waves pounding her rockwall. The lake was perilously high for September. The elusive and all-powerful Hydro One Keeper of the Keys hadn't opened the dam at Outlet Bay yet, leaving the levels for better boat access, especially at Rocky's, the restaurant and marina at the Wapiti First Nations Reserve.

The next morning she let Freya out, and busy getting ready for work, didn't notice that the animal was AWOL again. Rarely did she go to the road, unless a passing dog challenged her. After that porkie attack, what next? A skunk? No tomato juice in the cupboard, nor enough toothpaste, an apparent miracle worker when diluted.

Belle went to the side deck, scanning the yard. The wretch stood at the corner of the septic bed grass, her muzzle working at something which had to be food. "You sneak!"

She ran down the stairs to the parking lot, motoring towards the dog, who ducked her head in shame and backed away from a familiar green plastic LCBO bag. Out of the container spilled the remains of pale ground meat. Freya was still licking her black lips as Belle's heart did cartwheels in shock. "What have you done now?"

FOUR

Frozen in time as the horror sank in, Belle looked at the road, only twenty feet away up a grassy bank. Someone had tossed this bag down, knowing curious dog behaviour. A poisoner was the lowest life form. Now she regretted bearding the trapper in his den. This kind of payback, likely done in the dark from typical cowardice, would be impossible to prove. A police department mired in unsolved murders would be ill-inclined to be testing for prints and summoning Mr. AW HECK to the station.

The dog wasn't frothing at the mouth or trembling, but who knew what she had ingested? The average medicine cabinet or cleaning supply shelf had enough toxic chemicals to fell a moose. Hauling Freya to the van and shoving her in, Belle dialled the vet on her cellphone. A familiar perky young assistant listened while she related the emergency. "Shana's away on a conference, but Dr. Uyi is acting as standby. I'll slot you in, no problem."

As she drove, Belle glared in the mirror at the reclining dog, one paw over the other, probably expecting a leisurely walk on the trails behind Skead. Was today a holiday? "I'd gag you myself, but I'm not into slobber," she said with a vengeance.

She made record time to Petville, rushing in with Freya on leash. A bow-backed man with a yippy Pomeranian backed away instinctively at the large shepherd, its vicious reputation as undeserved as the doberman's. The vet tech ushered them into an examination room, and just as swiftly, Dr. Uyi came through the door. He was a handsome Polynesian with a boyish face and smooth coffee skin, laugh lines at his eyes revealing two more decades.

"I was told that she ate something. Do you have a sample?"

Belle handed him the LCBO bag containing a few ounces of meat. "Ground beef, seems fresh or just-thawed. Someone tossed it into my yard."

Slipping on latex gloves, Uyi moved to a sink and began inspecting the contents. "Doesn't seem like anything's been added," he said.

Belle shuddered, observing Freya for imminent convulsions, bloody vomit, paralysis. Five dogs had been poisoned in a Toronto park that week. "What were you looking for?"

He bent to examine the animal's mouth and gums. "Antifreeze is green. Or ground glass. Both are quite fatal, and the end isn't pretty."

Belle felt her legs turn to linguine and sat down on the wooden bench. "My God!"

His tone was reassuring as he ran slender fingers over Freya's body, probing her stomach area. "It's a ninety-nine per cent bet that she's fine."

"Not good enough. What would you suggest? An emetic?"

"Err on the side of caution, then. To treat her at home, a few ounces of hydrogen peroxide would do the job." He rose and reached under the sink for a plastic pail, then opened a drawer and took out a small paper packet, ripping it open. "Don't fancy swallowing that stuff myself. This is a bit gentler. Apomorphine disc. Goes in the corner of the eye. Within a few minutes...stand back."

An hour later at the office, Miriam checked the wall clock

and said, "I was afraid you'd miss your showing at Bea's."

Nose in the air, Freya trotted over for a piece of bagel with cream cheese. "Hi, sweetie. Come to keep me company? By the way, Strudel didn't take kindly to that Far Side book you gave me. *Poodles, the Other White Meat*." Miriam's fierce little dog had once made Freya's life sheer hell by ravaging her tail on an hourly basis.

Belle put her hand over her mouth as the dog disappeared into the back room, where they had a small lounge for lunch and an occasional nap. "Don't mention food." She explained what had happened.

Miriam gave a low growl. "Sometimes ex-husbands come in handy. Jack would have pummelled that scumbag. But she seems fine. It sounds like you acted quickly."

Belle checked her watch and headed for the Mr. Coffee, transfusion for all seasons. "Soldier's breakfast minus cigarette for me. The Nortons will be here in ten minutes."

She saw a car pull into the lot. "Minus coffee, too," she added with a mock sniff, rebuttoning her coat on the way out.

A couple in their early forties, the Nortons had relocated from Ottawa to open a joint practice: urology and dermatology. They were renting a luxury apartment at 2200 Regent but wanted to settle into the community and entertain on a larger scale.

"It sounds perfect. So close to our office at the Four Corners," Dan said, wearing an aubergine overcoat matching his wife's. His razored blond hair gave him the appearance of an albino porcupine. They were seated in the spacious rear of Belle's van, where he baptized the ashtray with a flick from his gold lighter. "Location is the most important thing. If this older house doesn't suit, we'll have all winter to finalize building plans. Do you know a good man?"

Bristling at the sexism, Belle thought about her own home,

constructed as finances allowed beside the cottage on the property. She'd done all the painting and tried to drywall before giving up when the dust made her sneeze and the closet angles under the stairs caused tears of frustration. "Bruno Bravo has a reputation for quality work."

His wife Dilshad, an East African woman with long, lustrous raven hair and pearl studs in her tiny ears, added a sweet soprano chime to his firm baritone. "The kitchen is the heart of a house. Gourmet cooking is my hobby. So different from Ottawa here. They are carrying tilapia and yams at the A&P, but oh, the trouble I am having buying palm oil."

"Try Café Korea in the Montrose Mall. They stock Far Eastern groceries," Belle said.

The night before, Bea had mentioned that she would be at work, and Micro would be taking the noisy parrot to school for show-and-tell day. Her husband Dave had been out of town all week. Belle preferred a home furnished but free of fulsome owners hovering at clients' shoulders like unwelcome ghosts, spotlighting bordello-style flocked red wallpaper, sparkled stucco ceilings, mirrors over the bed, and grotesque hockey-themed rec rooms.

At ten thirty she drove into the yard and pulled up beside Bea's trademark Ford Focus. Had the woman gotten a ride to work? Become ill and stayed at home? She inspected her cellphone. Fully charged. Miriam hadn't sent a last-minute message. She tried to project a professional confidence as she passed a small box attached near the front door.

"The key's in the lock box, but since her car's here, I'll ring anyway," she said. From the backyard, she could hear Buffalo barking and added, "Belongs to the family. Only dog on the block." Could be true as far as she knew.

The door chime sounded once, twice, then three times.

Belle was growing uneasy. On instinct, she pressed the lever on the massive brass handle and found the door unlatched. While she left her house open with Freya on guard, few townies risked that option. Managing a weak smile, she went inside and held the door for the Nortons. They were still chatting about the glorious view across Lake Ramsey.

"Hellloooo," she called with no response. Spotting a purse on a table by the door, she turned to them with embarrassment. "The owner may be home. Why don't you look around the main floor, and I'll go upstairs? Shouldn't take a minute."

Belle took the stairs two at a time and craned her head into the rooms. "Bea, Bea," she called softly. In the master bedroom at the end of the hall, a Chinese silk dressing gown lay on the neatly made bed. The door to the ensuite bathroom was open, but she could see that the room was dimmed, the vertical blinds shut. At least the place was tidy. A home needed to look lived in, but not by a band of Visigoths. After a deep breath, she paged through her notebook to refresh her mind about the highlights.

Downstairs again, she showed the Nortons through the house. As soon as they saw the modern kitchen, the expansive living room and dining room, his smiling wife clapped her deft brown hands, shiny chestnut eyes sparkling. Belle rolled with the flow, prepared to offer reasons against building anew, which might increase her commission since the home would retain its value. "Here's the best of both worlds. A classic house with refits. But I must be honest." She paused as Uncle Harold had advised her after using this phrase, an element of theatre in the realty business. They turned to her with wary looks. "The furnace should be replaced. Still, saving the cost of demolition would buy the best on the market. A natural gas line just came down the street, too."

"Very tempting," Dilshad said. "If the upstairs is as

wonderful…" She gave Dan a sweet smile, her tiny wrenish face lit with excitement.

"Anything you want, my dear." His brows contracted, and he shuffled his feet as he checked his watch. An appointment?

When they passed the mantel in the living room on their way to the winding stairs, Belle saw the cheque for the Doulton figurine. She had left Adrienne in the van. A little personal pocket money. All this and heaven, too, Monsieur Boyer?

The Nortons looked out the windows of each bedroom, pointing and gesturing, entranced by Micro's retreat. Belle hoped that a train wouldn't roar by across the road, though rail traffic was minimal with CN downsizing and their acquisition of U.S. routes.

Saving the best for last, she led them down the hall to the master suite. Dan cleared his throat, then asked, "Do you mind if I use the washroom?"

"Of course," she said. "Over there. The tub is a top-of-the-line Jacuzzi." He lingered for a moment as his wife pointed out the Superstack in the distance.

Belle chuckled to herself, admiring a thriving Persian violet on a bay window. That bathroom was the final selling point. Bea had said that they'd combed Toronto for the art-deco fittings, complete with bidet. When the sale went through, she'd take Miriam on a trip to Costa Rica as soon as the prices dropped after the peak season. There they'd be, basking in the cloud canopy instead of shovelling snow. What about mosquitos? In the movies, no one seemed to be bothered by insects, except in *The African Queen*. She could still see unshaven Bogie slogging along…

A yell came from somewhere. "Jesus Christ!"

FIVE

Belle rushed into the bathroom to discover Dan leaning over the triangular ice-blue tub. Bea lay naked on her back, a trickle of blood seeping from one ear, deep-purple bruises circling her neck. Her pendulous breasts, the size of melons, were capped with glistening, dark aureoles. Large sea-green eyes stared at the ceiling as if divining a way to heaven.

"Quite dead, poor woman," Dan said, as he stood and studied his hand with a grimace as if despairing of where to wash it. Everyone who watched television was familiar with death-scene protocol. "No pulse at the carotid artery."

Turning with protective gestures to block Dilshad from entering, he left the room. Though she could hear voices behind her, Belle remained rigid, her mental camera capturing in grim fascination an assortment of details: the lower body blurred by soap scum on the still surface, a pink bottle of bubble bath on the Italian ceramic tile rim, fruity shampoos, a fresh bar of peppermint-scented soap, an oval pumice stone. The shell colour of the tile echoed Bea's buffed natural nails. She trailed a finger in the water. Cold. If the woman had drawn the bath herself, hours had passed. The other possibility was even more chilling.

A discreet cough fractured her thoughts. "Miss Palmer. I called 911 on my cell. We're to go directly outside and wait." He seemed cool and clinical, like many specialists.

On the sheltered porch, she and Dilshad found awkward seats in Muskoka chairs, silent as mannequins. Dan excused himself and disappeared behind a cedar hedge. "Weak bladder," Dilshad explained with an eyeroll.

Within minutes came the sound of an ambulance, a squad car siren wailing close behind. Being near a hospital had clear merits. Belle remembered a competitor's ad for a home on York Street: "St. Joe's area. Good for newlyweds or retirees." Pediatric or geriatric care in a thousand feet, cradle to the grave.

The officer, fresh out of Police College, popping mint gum with abandon, complimented them on preserving the crime scene after he'd asked a few questions and scribbled in a palm-sized notebook. "You got no idea what people do. Grab a brew from the fridge. Make a friggin' sandwich. Even take a dump in the toilet." Belle flashed him an evil look, and Dilshad gave a laboured sigh. On this Indian summer morning, fast warming up, they sat protected from wind, but Belle shivered more from the dissolution of an adrenal rush. Buffalo was ready to collect a trophy for consecutive barks.

A mere matter of course, the ambulance was dismissed, and everyone waited for a team of detectives to arrive.

"How long will we have to stay? I have appointments I can't cancel," Dan asked, mopping sweat from his freckled brow. His wife had taken out a PDA and seemed to be checking her email.

Belle shrugged and shook her head. In a perverse way, she felt responsible for this disaster, and the sale was certainly as dead as...the talented and sensitive woman who lay upstairs. A jolly baker en route to a cold tray at the morgue. Was this a third serial killing?

Disappointed that Steve hadn't caught the case, but not surprised, since the department had over a dozen ranking operatives, she and the Nortons gave their statements to

Detective Milt Burns. A bean pole with a shock of taffy hair, in his late thirties, thorough and professional, he seemed especially interested in the time frame. As they were leaving, a coppertone SUV pulled into the yard, and in her mirror she saw an athletic man jump out and sprint towards the house. Probably Dave Malanuk. What would it be like to return from a trip to find your wife dead from a violent attack, perhaps including a rape?

On the solemn procession back to the office, Dan's chain-smoking led Belle to hit the climate-control feature. The lump in her throat didn't prevent her from remembering her primary mission when they pulled into the lot. "Long Lake isn't far from the Four Corners. I have a colonial listed on—" she began as they climbed into their Mercedes, but they shut their solid German doors decisively. Even with this fiasco, she hoped they hadn't changed their minds about relocating. Thirty per cent of the population had no general practitioner, and specialists were rare as a January thaw.

When she entered the office, Miriam leaped up in congratulations, then did a double take at her stony face and drooping shoulders. "You're a real sunshine pump. What happened? They seemed perfect."

Belle sank into a chair as Freya came up for a pat, stretching and yawning. "I found Bea dead." The details arrived with no holds barred. Miriam was a tough bird.

Her friend took off her bifocals and rubbed the bridge of her Roman nose. "How are you going to tell Hélène and Ed?"

No phone call could substitute for human contact when bad news was concerned. Perhaps Dave had already relayed the news. Even so, she owed her best friends an appearance. On the way home, Belle thought of everything but her sad duty. She passed through the small suburb of Garson, ordering a large coffee to go at the Tim's drive-through, then casting an eye down a side street to the windows of Rainbow Country Nursing Home, where her father lived. The way the day had gone, she half-expected an ambulance to be pulling away, carrying him to his last game show. Tomorrow was Tuesday, their lunch date, and while she often made extra stops to deliver an ice cream sundae or walk him down the hall, this wasn't the time.

As she drove towards Radar Road, she passed the steaming exhaust blower which ventilated one of countless shafts reaching deep into the bedrock. Occasional dynamite blasts reminded civilians that if all the drifts which honeycombed the region were laid in a straight line, a person could drive from Sudbury to Vancouver. Cutting-edge technology continued to extract more and more ore from the generous meteor that had formed the enormous seventeen-by-thirty-seven-mile elliptical basin nearly two billion years ago.

Half an hour later, as the sun weakened in the western sky, casting glints through the poplars, maples and birch overhanging her road, the first pure crimson leaf in the canopy of green struck her like a gunshot. This blow signalled the beginning of autumn, which normally she greeted with expectation. September, free of bugs and full of show, was the most beautiful month of the year. Now it was a metaphor for Bea's death, and the difference was that the cherished mother and wife would not return like Persephone in the spring. She parked at the DesRosiers', leaving Freya in the van. A reluctant messenger, she needed to steel herself. As minutes passed, all the vacuous phrases chattered in her mind like parrots. "Sorry for your loss." "Gone to a better place." Even "only the good die young." She didn't envy Steve his former job ringing doorbells after gruesome traffic accidents.

"Knock, knock," she called, then opened the door in their

casual fashion. Hélène was ensconced in a leather recliner, snug in the Norwegian sweater Belle had given her for Christmas. In the open-concept kitchen, Ed wore an Old-Fart-On-Duty apron over his sweatpants and was peeking into the oven. Savory tomato aromas filled the house. She felt strangely hungry for the first time all day, perhaps a response to the survival instinct...or the absence of breakfast and lunch. That coffee was churning acid in her nether regions. So Dave hadn't paved the way. She could hardly blame him. Micro would be his first concern.

Hélène put down a magazine and snickered. "Ladies' night off. It's only been forty years. I'm finally breaking Ed in. He cannot ruin M&M cabbage rolls. Posilutely not, as my grandson says."

They'd never ask her why she had arrived unannounced shortly before dinner time. With the camaraderie on the road, it might be to borrow dog kibble or ask for a battery boost.

Ed winked and mimed a beer at Belle, who nodded. Opening the fridge, he retrieved a bottle of light beer, twisted the cap, and handed it to her as she took off her jacket.

Hélène cleared her throat. "No glass, Ed? This isn't an ice hut."

Sitting on the sofa, Belle took a deep swallow, wondering if they could hear the drum beating in her chest. "It's fine. I'm a minimalist."

As Ed headed back to the kitchen, Hélène grinned at Belle. "You always said that 'Kept a sparkling house' wasn't what you wanted on your tombstone and that at your place, dog hair was a condiment." She rocked back with laughter, then touched Belle's knee. "You are staying, then? I have some rye from the breadmaker."

Liquid rye would have been her choice. Belle finished her

beer in three nervous gulps and leaned forward, her stomach lurching. How she dreaded casting pain and sorrow across her friend's relaxed and innocent brow. She stared out their wall of windows to the lake, where a sailboat headed for harbour, its white sides lashed with spray as it parted the bruised waves. She bit her lip until it hurt, then turned to Hélène and opened her mouth, but no words came. Suddenly she had the urge to burp and took off for the bathroom, closing the door and turning on the taps before she knelt at the toilet like a college freshman after a binge, its chemically-charged bowl green and deep. Normally she enjoyed the apple pie aroma of the three-wick dish candle on the shelf, but now it increased her nausea.

When she returned, Hélène gave her a curious look but was too polite to comment. She passed Belle a *Chatelaine*. "Take this home. Great article about snowshoeing. You could have written it. Now there's easy money."

Belle held out her hand, but Hélène lowered the magazine. "You're shaking. What's wrong? Low blood sugar? Did you skip lunch?"

Get the words out. Like the headline of an ad. Details to come. "I have bad news. It's about Bea."

Hélène's mouth pursed in disappointment as she picked up a glass of red wine from the side table. "Darn. She decided not to sell? I knew she wouldn't leave that wonderful old house. And that reminds me. It's her birthday Saturday, and I haven't—"

Belle took a deep breath and plunged on. Swift strokes were kinder than a death of a thousand cuts. "Bea's dead. I found her upstairs when I took clients over."

Hélène's glass shattered, its contents pooling like rubies on the creamy tilework Ed had laid on the woodstove platform. "My God. Was it her heart? I gave her that low-cholesterol cookbook last Christmas...oh, why didn't she—"

"It was murder." She sat back on the couch, felt its cushions enfold her. "Like the others, it seems. She didn't live alone. Who would have thought?"

Hélène buried her head in her hands. Belle gently touched her shuddering back. A competent and resourceful woman, suddenly her friend seemed older and more vulnerable.

"Ed," she called, "Hélène needs you."

"What's the matter, girl?" he asked as he came over, searching Belle's face for answers. Then Hélène stood and embraced her husband.

Belle related the news in the briefest possible fashion, omitting the graphic particulars. "Thank God Micro wasn't there," Hélène said, calming as the minutes passed, and the steel in her backbone stiffened. Her eyes were red and puffy, but she turned to the task at hand with no hesitation. "I'm calling Dave first, then everyone else. The shock of it all. He has no other family but us. His parents died years ago, and he was an only child. Like Bea."

While Hélène went to get her address book, with paper towels, Belle cleaned up the spilled wine. One chipped tile, a reminder that nothing is permanent. She cut her finger on a shard of glass and went off to find a bandage in their medicine cabinet. Kid style. With hearts. She wondered if this horror would bond the boy to his stepfather as they grieved together and started a new life.

As Hélène dialled numbers, a box of Kleenex at her side, with no more words for sorrow, Ed passed Belle a Tupperware package of cabbage rolls and a hunk of warm rye bread. She drove slowly down the long dark road, determined to use her friendship with Steve to provide her friends with answers to this tragedy. First thing in the morning, he'd find her message on his answering machine at the department.

SIX

Lunch day with Father found Belle at Bobby's Place, a Garson institution, which changed names as each brave owner tried to scratch a living from a limited custom in the tiny suburb. Their hot-beef-sandwich platters gave the waitresses chronic lumbago, and they made a tasty back-bacon sandwich on a ciabatta bun laced with honey mustard. Since his near-death choking experience, George Palmer was limited to a special order of minced chicken with mashed potatoes, gravy and peas. "No charge this time," said the young owner, a muscular blond with a huge, gleaming set of teeth as pearly as his apron. "I like the way you take care of your dad." She had a hard time believing the local gossip that Bobby had a rape charge pending, except that his front window kept getting smashed. Bobby was the nicest guy, and not all women were trustworthy. Perhaps some spurned girlfriend had decided to take revenge.

After picking up the meal, she drove the few blocks to Rainbow Country Nursing Home, its former bachelor apartments converted for an aging population. Class-conscious perfectionists found it worn at the edges, but unlike the institutional high rises that catered to townfolk warehousing Oma and Opa, the compact facility had only sixty seniors and matchless personal care. Along with most developed countries, Canada faced a geriatric crisis in the next few decades. With perfect timing, she'd whisked him back from his retirement home in Florida when his cognitive abilities failed a few years ago. He was cruising into his late eighties with the gusto that had served his long-lived ancestors. Cherie greeted her at the nurses' station. Belle knew every staff member, from the kitchen team to the laundry workers and handymen. "Six pieces of toast for him today. Extra marmalade. What an eating machine."

"Every meal my mother ever served him was the 'best ever.'" She presented a box of Laura Secord miniatures to the smiling nurse. Their daily acts of kindness to her father were beyond price.

With a quick stop in the kitchen for bib, serviettes and cutlery, balancing her boxes down the long hall, railings on each side, Belle entered her father's private room, his door decorated with craftwork using gold-painted pasta pieces. She nearly tripped as a plump bichon frisé wove through her legs on his way out. Puffball, the activity director's dog, an irresistible food hound who knew the best places to panhandle.

The new paint and easy-care linoleum provided some cheer, along with the Blue Jays curtains she'd bought. He sat fixated on the blaring television, hands clasped on the lap table of his gerry chair. Up until his breakdown, he'd been a great walker. Three miles with their dachshund Lucky every glorious Florida morning. At Rainbow Country, he'd fallen a few times, the dizziness of age, not Alzheimer's, a future dread. Since seniors ran a risk of broken bones, his chair had become his jailer.

She put down the boxes and turned the TV to normal. "Hello, old man," she said with a grin. "Your usual plus apple pie."

"No cherry like your mother's?"

The man knew what he liked and liked what he knew. "The Berlin air lift was fogged in. Next week for sure."

His broad mouth wreathed a smile. Clean-shaven, baby-pink cheeks, but perhaps not always by noon, though the staff worked like carthorses. As in all health-care areas, the sad truth was that a person needed an advocate who visited regularly. "A la mode?"

"A la everything. Your French is *très bon!*" The first word he'd learned in his new home was *"sables"* from the box of shortbread. They'd shopped for snacks each week when he could still walk, and he picked out apples, bananas and Mars bars, seven of each.

"Your mother was half-French. Remember what my family said when I told them we were getting married?"

She nodded, attaching his bib and opening the boxes. "Everything was hunky-dory because she was Anglican." Toronto, Belle's birthplace, had never been a French enclave. On the other hand, Francophones made the largest ethnic group in Sudbury, the generic "English" in second place, followed by Italians, Germans, Ukrainians, Scandinavians, native peoples and a sprinkling of latecomers from the Middle East, Far East and Africa. No melting pot, but a multicultural mosaic.

The news was broadcasting an update on the murders. A pizza delivery man had been brought in for questioning. As earnest civic faces filled the screen with promises to make the city safe for women, she nibbled at her tender sandwich, taking an occasional swig of chocolate milk. Her father ate at a rapid rate, and she gave him verbal prods to stop and drink water. That choking incident had left him an inch short of joining her mother's ashes in the closet.

"Hey, what's going on here? Another woman dead? I left my sanctuary in Port Charlotte for this and blizzards, too?" His voice rose, but the twinkle in his cornflower blue eyes spelled humour.

With an assurance that any crime perked up his brain cells, she said, "She was my client in a house sale. I found her...body."

He gave his leonine head a shake, the thick white hair parted neatly. "Houses. Harold's business. But didn't you also..." Then he stopped, unsure of his memory. Sometimes D-Day was fresher to him than the morning's menu.

"It's possible that the same person killed all three women."

"A serial killer? Surely not in Canada."

"We're catching up fast. Bernardo and Homolka, now the pig farmer in B.C." As many as seventy prostitutes who had vanished from the Vancouver netherworld over the last twenty years had found ugly graves. Bereaved families were outraged that reports of their missing loved ones had gone into File Zed, merely because they had been street people and not debutantes. She got up to mash the pie and ice cream into mush.

Her father followed her motions and began tapping his watch, his woolly eyebrows contracting, as if he could will the hands to move faster. "Where's that dessert?"

She put the box on the lap table. "It's very sad. A lovely woman. She looked like Marie Dressler in the Sennett comedies." From the time she'd been able to toddle around Toronto, she and her father had spent two evenings a week in a private screening room at Odeon Pictures. As a booker, it was his job to slot each film according to the local preference. The boondocks of Owen Sound didn't have the same tastes as Rosedale.

"What a puss on that one. Last in the Canadian Three-Peat for the Oscar. 1931." He smacked his lips as he savaged the pie.

She sorted her mental files. So many rainy days in her youth she'd sat on the sofa and paged through Daniel Blum's pictorial histories of films. "Marie won for *Min and Bill* with Wallace Beery."

"Mary Pickford was first in 1929 for *Coquette*. Canada's sweetheart. Played a teenager at thirty-seven. She was born where the Hospital for Sick Kids stands. Then Norma Shearer, a Westmount beauty. Your mother always said she had a cast in her eye, whatever that meant."

Belle rocked and rolled into their repartee, striking a vamp pose. "*Divorcee*. Very risqué, since she was trying to hide her pregnancy."

Of the three women, Belle had a special fondness for gruff old Marie with the bulldog face and a body like a bag of fighting Dinky toys. One of the greatest directors of women, George Cukor capitalized on the beauty-and-beast theme in *Dinner at Eight*. Blonde bombshell Jean Harlow was talking about reading "a nutty kind of a book," adding with wide eyes and raised, pencil-thin brows, "The guy said that machines are going to take the place of every profession." Doing a stage-trouper double take, Marie scanned Harlow's silvery cling-wrapped body, platinum hair, and shook her jowls, "Oh, my dear, that's something you'll never have to worry about."

"Got a problem." Her father patted his pockets and looked around in annoyance. "Maybe you can find my gol-durn wallet."

She smiled, thought a minute as she scanned the room, then bent and reached into the elastic of his sweat pants for a suspicious bulge over the ankle. "Here you are. We've got to get that pocket sewn up."

He opened it, no credit cards, no identification or money, only a picture of her with her mother. Poignant proof of time, the identity thief. "Miracle Worker!"

She mock-punched his arm. "Patty Duke and Anne Bancroft."

As she turned to leave, an old ebony man with a walker

shuffled into the room. His short hair was curly white, and his dapper moustache reminded her of Cab Calloway. He wore suit pants, a white shirt, tie and a vest. "George," he said, "come on down and join our rummy game." He introduced himself as Henry Morgan, a retired miner.

Belle knew that her father didn't like to leave his room, but this might be a chance for a short stroll and healthy socialization. "We'll walk, and Henry can get a wheelchair for your return. Okay? Bet you win the pot. Think of the chocolate bars." She knew he'd never cooperate with anyone else.

Always eager to please her, his greatest asset, George agreed, and she took the tray off his chair, made certain of his slippers, and hoisted him, one arm around his shoulders, once so strong and muscular. The effort was costing him, his breathing heavy, but he rattled on. "Told Henry here that my grandfather went down and fought to free his people in the Civil War."

Henry nodded as if he had heard the story 1002 times, and Belle sent apologies through her eyes. She'd seen the tombstone in Prospect Cemetery in Toronto and had always wondered what prompted Reuben Palmer to join the 22nd New York Cavalry. Wounded in the heel, spawning a family joke about his direction, eventually he predeceased his wife, leaving her with a U.S. service pension.

Driving home from work later, she realized that she'd managed to forget about Bea for a moment. What about this delivery man? No leads all this time, and then suddenly... She supposed that the police worked methodically, careful not to rush to judgement and jeopardize the case, bringing charges only when a conviction was likely. The law was like a tapestry, messy behind, but when everything worked, sheer artistry on the other side. Certainly Micro and Dave deserved to have this tragedy put to rest as fast as possible. She pulled out to pass a double slurry truck and winced as a piece of gravel bounced off her windshield. Auto-glass companies did big business in the Nickel Capital.

Turning into her drive at last at the Parliament of Owls sign with her totems, the furious brown Horny and the mild white Corny with their marble eyes, she noticed the long grass on the septic bed. Once more into the lawnmower breach, fall or no fall. As she exited the car too quickly, she felt a slight twinge of back pain. Since wrenching it last year, she'd been more judicious about overextending herself.

On her answering machine, she found a dinner invitation from Hélène and put the box of Kraft Dinner back into her former Millennium supply closet, now used for hydro outages. In full recovery mode, her friend sounded cheerful and animated. Ed didn't wear his emotions on his sleeve, but the old bear was as solid as her rockwall.

She changed into jeans and a light blue denim shirt, collected Freya and hiked down the road for long-overdue exercise. The fall wildflowers were staging a brave show. Pale lilac asters nodded acquaintance, and downy fluffs of fireweed lifted into the wind, triggering Freya's prey drive. Two kinds of goldenrod captured Belle's eye, one with a simple plume and one elm-branched. Over thirty varieties, according to her Peterson guide. She was tempted to pick a few pearly everlastings to make a dried bunch, but stopped as the season's final tent caterpillar, Born-too-Late, inched across the road. "Gotcha!" She mashed it without remorse, as did most people. The birches, aspens and poplars had barely recovered from the last infestation.

At their gate, she saw Rusty barking and running in the yard as a small boy tossed a tennis ball for the eager dog. Primed for a game, Freya streaked in to snatch the throw from

Rusty's chubby efforts. The boy stepped back, raising his hands, assessing the eighty-pound shepherd. Then he knelt and let Freya lick his face while he scratched her ears. His café au lait face, with fine features and long lashes, was serious, but his eye contact with the dog was as sweet as the ice wine Belle reserved for special guests.

"Hi," Belle said, giving Rusty a pat so that she didn't feel left out. "Are you Mich—"

"Micro," he said as he rose, head proud and spine straight, a defensive cast to his jaw. She could swear he stood on tiptoe in his red basketball shoes. He wore baggy jeans with carpenter's loops and a Sudbury Wolves sweatshirt. The jeans sagged so much that in another inch his bum top would appear. Kids and clothes. Pass the Xanax. Make that a double.

She introduced herself and was pleased that he shook her hand firmly. Climbing to the porch, she noticed an upscale Santa Cruz mountain bike with sleek lines and a hi-tech alloy frame leaning against the steps. Inside the foyer, she slipped off her shoes, precise Canadian behaviour that would make a good clue in a murder case. Was that all she could think about? But seeing Micro, with his mother's wide green eyes, made the poignant connection. She remembered the picture of his father with the same diminutive build.

Belle helped Hélène set the table. "He's cute. Polite, too," she said, pointing outside. "How's he taking his mom's loss?"

Hélène made a gesture of disbelief with her hands. "I've never seen him cry. It's as if he's acting in a play, like it's not real. First his father and sister. Now this. Too much for one boy."

"Is he staying with you?"

"Dave and I thought it was a good idea, so he dropped off Micro yesterday. Dave will be travelling in the Maritimes for the next few weeks. Commitments he couldn't cancel. The boy needs a woman's touch, he said." Her lip trembled, but she firmed her mouth and turned to reach for a pot bubbling on the stove. "Staying around that place with a housekeeper might give him nightmares. He brought his school books, clothes and some computer games."

"Getting along okay, then...all things considered?"

"Too soon to say, but he'll probably get pretty bored. No young people down this end of the road. There's a computer in the spare room where he bunks. He likes some kind of Internet role-playing game." She smiled softly. "It's different raising a child these days. I keep telling him to pull up those pants. Honestly."

"I've got a few computer games he could play, and on my hikes, he's welcome. If you need a break, give me a call."

As the boy came in, Hélène asked him to wash his hands, and with a muttered "Sheesh," he ambled down the hall. His aunt lowered her voice. "He resented Dave from the get-go, though the poor man tried his best. The computer he bought Micro cost the earth, not to mention the bike. Six years alone with Bea had made him the man of the house."

"Sounds normal. Dave and Bea were married for only..."

"Less than a year. But by now you'd think..." She broke off her conversation to remind a returning Micro to pour himself a milk.

They sat down to Hélène's redoubtable pot roast, simmered in Chianti. Bowls of garlic mashed potatoes, then a succulent mixture of roasted root vegetables from the garden, including a sweet parsnip, arrived from the grill outside. Belle noticed that Micro helped himself to large portions of everything but meat, even the rutabaga, a preposterous but nourishing turnip which had likely been the mainstay of her forebears in 1845 Bowmanville.

After assuring herself that everyone had mounded plates, Hélène said grace. Then she cleared her throat. "Micro's a ...what is it, dear?"

He forked up the potatoes. "A vegan, Aunt Hélène."

Another side to this intriguing boy. Belle asked, "Lacto, ovo, what kind?"

"I'm breaking myself in, but fish, eggs and milk products are okay." His intelligent eyes fixed on her. "Kids need calcium. But as for meat, have you read *Fast Food Nation?* Do you realize that..."

As her throat constricted, he named perils of undercooked or suspect flesh, including CJD, cancer in chickens and e-coli. Finally Ed tapped the boy's plate with his knife and grunted. "You're putting me off my meal, sonnie, and that's a no-no in this house. At my age, I don't have many pleasures as reliable as my wife's fine cooking."

Hélène frowned at the mixed message, but Belle found herself warming to the boy as talk turned to the Jays' resigning of a twenty-two-game winner, the only bright spot in a .500 season. "They won the Series? Unreal," Micro said. "Gotta be before I was born. Bet my *Dad* saw it, though." No question who Dad was.

An awkward silence seemed to hang in the air until Hélène added, "Micro designs websites for his friends, but he can't do that from here. Our computer is Stone Age."

Belle flashed him an inviting smile. "If you're going to be around this weekend, would you like to earn some bucks? I could use a hand mowing the lawn."

He cocked his head. "Min wage?"

"I vote NDP. Much more generous to labour. Ten an hour sound good?" She extended a hand to seal the bargain.

The following afternoon, though she had met Bea only

once, as a courtesy, Belle felt compelled to attend the viewing. Civilities weren't bad for business either. No telling whom she'd meet. A pale grey pantsuit with a cobalt open-necked shirt and low-cut black boots seemed formal enough. With a rare nod to jewellery, she added a silver bracelet and matching leaf pin.

One of the flagship Sudbury parlours, burying miners and their kin for over a hundred years, Johnson and Poniard was often dubbed Johnson's Boneyard. It had been taken over by the Halverson chain, but the new owners had kept the original name. Tradition was important in a town with a short history.

The yellow-brick complex sat in an older section of town off Regent Street, where many marginal businesses such as small-appliance and shoe-repair shops clung to life. Other stores with newspapered windows testified to the dominance of suburban malls. The brilliant late chrysanthemums in the flower beds around the parking lot weathered the light frosts but reminded Belle that fall would soon freeze the ground and prevent bulb planting. Micro's help would arrive none too soon.

She'd chosen four o'clock, with the idea of disappearing for home soon after. As she left the van, she saw a tall woman with dark red curly hair leaning against a late-model Oldsmobile, a large white poodle in the front seat, its handsome head peering through the open window. She wore a faux-fur ocelot coat with a bright silk scarf. Her shoulders shook in great sobs, and her purse fell to the asphalt. "Are you all right?" Belle asked, stooping to hand her the bag.

The woman dabbed a tissue at her eyes, smearing the running mascara. She had a heart-shaped face, olive complexion and a long noble nose, which Belle appreciated. With genetic planning and cosmetic surgery, soon everyone would look like

Britney Spears or Christina Aguilera. "I will be, I guess. Once I get through this. I hate viewings and funerals. Call me in denial, but I'd rather remember people alive."

"I know what you mean. These rituals aren't for the loved one, are they?"

"Bea was so young. I can't believe what happened. In her own house. Tomorrow I'll walk into that bakery, and she won't…" Her voice trailed off, and she gripped her arms in an effort at composure.

"I'm here for her viewing, too." Belle introduced herself and found that she was talking to Leonora Bruce, Bea's business partner. "What's your dog's name?"

"Windsor. Even as a puppy he had such a regal look."

Belle stroked the expressive, aquiline nose as the poodle batted its eyes at her. Was it true that people came to resemble their pets? "My friend has a mini. A hyper squirrel. Cute doesn't cut it with me. I much prefer this serious standard poodle."

"They're even used as guide dogs, so that's a real testimony." Her spine straightened, and she managed a feeble smile as she reached into the car for two bakery boxes. "It's *crostoli* and *frotoli*. I made them special. A touch of brandy. They were her favourites."

They walked in together, but Leonora went to the ladies' room to refresh her makeup. Leaving her coat with an attendant, Belle looked at the options board, like selecting a movie. Beatrice Malanuk: Continental Room. Almost like a Vegas show.

Down the thickly carpeted hall she proceeded, following discreet brass signs and listening to faint strains of Delius's *Florida Suite*, an inoffensive, almost spritely choice. Did funeral directors take a music course? Hard-rock miner Jack

MacDonald, Miriam's ex, would have requested "Prop Me Up Beside the Jukebox When I Die."

Two women in their thirties, both wearing dark blue dresses, passed her coming out, and she heard one say, "That *panettone* of hers was a miracle. I hope the next owner maintains the standards." Who would take over the bakery? Would Dave step in?

Belle reached the Continental Room with her heart beating double time. No matter how often she experienced these rites of passage, she couldn't grow a protective shell. Fortunately, Myron Halverson and his siblings had found their groove in meeting the needs of sorrowing families. Like selling a house on Landsend Street overlooking the mountainous slag pours, someone had to do it. She'd heard Myron speak on the CBC about the psychology of bereavement. His was a sincere and professional calling.

She stood for a moment at the entrance, picking up a memorial card from a table. The front pictured an angel with hands clasped: "Sadly Missed and Always Remembered." Inside was a picture of Bea's smiling face, perhaps cropped from a family photo. Belle thought about the gruesome duty of choosing the image. Uncle Bert at eighty-five had been replaced by his army picture in the Princess Pat's Regiment. Bea's family history was recorded on the facing page, all those predeceased names like a welcoming committee, parents, grandparents, husband and daughter.

She signed the guestbook, leafing through the gilded pages, amazed to note more than two hundred names. Bea was a fixture in the community, and with his high profile, Dave had many friends who would wish to offer their sympathies. Thirty people milled around, chatting quietly in small groups. On one side of the room, a huge buffet table held silver dishes pyramided with an array of pastries and a beverage selection, wine included. Trust the Italians to bend the rules. Her gaze moving forward a step at a time, Belle was wrapped in a cloud of roses. Long-stemmed and gorgeous, they sat in crystal vases on French provincial side tables and in four-foot sprays on racks. Pink, red and white. No yellow. Wasn't that for infidelity in the quaint language of flowers? She saw Leonora, apparently recovered, embrace a man, whose broad back was turned. They seemed to cling to each other for a moment more than necessary. He went on to shake hands with a young couple, both in jeans and jackets. Perhaps workers from the bakery.

Micro wasn't there. Perhaps he had come at the beginning for appearances, but she appreciated Dave's forbearance against letting a young boy endure hours of heartbreaking drama. At one side of the long room, seated in Jacobean armchairs, two men with short hair and dark, nondescript suits talked briefly, and one of them slipped a notebook from his pocket, glancing around for a second as he wrote. Both looked like detectives that she'd met through Steve. They'd be at the funeral in case the killer wanted to observe the reaction to his sorry work. Did that ever happen, or was it a television cliché? Then she glimpsed an old German couple who had made tentative noises about selling their camp a few years ago but had decided to hold on to enjoy one more summer, then another and another. The magic age of eighty closed the door. The woman used a walker, and he looked none too starchy, setting his legs awkwardly as if he suffered a pinched nerve in his bowed back.

She headed in their direction when a deep, rich voice claimed her attention. Jack Palance, wearing a charcoal suit and a ruby rose in his lapel, twenty years younger than his Oscar-winning role as Curly in the *City Slickers* films. She pasted on a smile and chastized herself for this silly game.

"I'm Dave Malanuk. Thanks for coming," he said.

So this was the man Bea had loved. Belle accepted his hand, which he squeezed gently, then added his other for an especially sincere touch. The fingers bore keloid scar tissue, and she looked up quickly, feeling gauche about telegraphing her thoughts. "Belle Palmer. I was…" Her syllables stuttered. It wasn't often that you introduced yourself as a corpse finder.

He swallowed heavily and firmed his sharp jaw in an effort to continue. "I heard. How terrible for you. You must have been leaving when I arrived. I saw the police car and thought that we'd had a robbery. That house has been so unlucky for Bea. And now…" He broke off with a cough and lowered his head.

Looking at the spring-green carpet, Belle felt like patting his back or touching his arm, but that seemed too personal for people who had just met, no matter how many intimate details she had learned from the DesRosiers. How amazing that people rose to the occasion with such different coping mechanisms. At her neighbour's funeral, the family had cracked jokes and laughed uproariously as the beer kegs emptied. What else could you do when your mother had dropped dead at forty-five from a wasp sting at a backyard picnic just as she cut her own birthday cake? And as for Belle's mother, not long in Florida and far from friends and relatives, she'd had no funeral. George Palmer had attended a service at the hospital celebrating the lives of those who had died that year. Not very personal but enough closure for him.

In the neighbourhood of fifty, Dave had high cheekbones, a thin mouth with even white teeth, and thick, iron-grey hair. His skin, browned and leathery, seemed stretched too taut across his wide brow, lines etched on his face in irregular fashion. His mica-chip eyes were deep-set and penetrating.

Was this an example of the French term *"joli laid"*? Malanuk, a Polish or Russian background? Jack Palance had been Vladimir Palanuik, mellowed nicely since his early days as Jack the Ripper, Attila the Hun and supporting roles in countless spaghetti westerns.

Suddenly, she noticed the silence. He bent his head to catch her eye. "This must be upsetting for you. How about some water, a coffee? Or a glass of wine?"

She smiled, ashamed that she was supposed to be here to comfort him, not be waited on. "Sorry. Just a bit preoccupied." Fundraising was an odd job for such a virile man. She pictured him on a bold stallion, galloping across the steppes.

"Would you like to see Bea?" he asked, offering his arm as escort as if it were a pleasant invitation to a waltz. Belle had nearly forgotten why she'd come; too many preliminaries before the main event.

"Of course." Walking at a dirge-like pace, at last she reached the far end of the room where on a dias with three velveteen steps, she encountered a coffin as large as PEI. In gleaming red mahogany, it seemed to expand as they walked, a ship of state preparing to weigh anchor and cast off for the Seven Seas. The rose motif continued in arrays of baby pinks and ferns at the base and wreaths on stands behind. The air was thick, almost cloying. Belle sneezed.

"Sorry," she said, and accepted his linen handkerchief, wiping discreetly, wondering whether to return it now or after laundering, her hand wavering. With an easy motion, he settled the matter by retrieving it.

Bea lay enveloped in billowy folds of pink satin, the lower part of the casket dividing her waist like a burnished wooden duvet. Her square face, a pleased smile at the corners, wore light lipstick and discreet complementary eye shadow. Belle blinked twice at the baker's hat which covered most of her light brown hair. Over a silk gown, she wore an apron with a host of buzzing bees. How well Myron's magic had concealed the neck bruises. Clasped in one large, talented hand was a rosary. In the other, a long marble rolling pin. Suddenly, Belle was glad she had come. This vision was what she would prefer to remember when she thought of Bea. Two perfect red roses lay on her chest, with accompanying notes in envelopes, an adult's handwriting to "My darling Bea" and a child's to "Mom." Letters to beyond the grave. She was glad that she had sent hers a few months before her mother died, telling her all the good things she remembered and honouring her with a poem. Some might find the gesture treacly, but her mother had photocopied the letter and sent it to her friends.

Dave placed a palm on the shiny casket, then turned to Belle with wonderment. "Bea was such a comic. She'd been to so many grand Italian funerals. She told me she wanted to enter heaven as a baker, like she'd been all her life."

"Alice blue. I wore that colour at my senior semi-formal." Hardly the time for a fashion statement, but his loving expression didn't change.

"Her favourite colour and her favourite flower. I courted her with roses." He gave a rueful laugh. "Thought I would go broke before she accepted me. I was such a regular at Helvi's that they had the order ready every Saturday at five sharp."

Dave's method of coping seemed to involve time-tripping, revisiting the happy past. Why not, if it worked? Her mother had been so far away when she became ill. After the grueling operation, during the chemo, Belle would call faithfully every Sunday, hearing her grow weaker and weaker. "Do you want me to come down?" she'd ask. Her mother would say no. Had she been saving Belle from sad memories? One day at home, she'd developed a raging infection and was gone in hours.

Time for the obligatory comment, the hardest but merciful final act of the play. "She looks..." Belle thought of the buffet table, her last feast. Good enough to eat? She almost expected the soft, warm eyes to snap open, Bea to climb laughing from her coffin and pass the sweets. "...lovely."

SEVEN

That Saturday at eight, Micro came streaking down the road on his mountain bike, panniers flying, Rusty ten feet behind with her tongue lolling. Belle was glad to see that Hélène had coaxed him into a pair of shorts instead of the baggy jeans. Fine for "hanging" in the mall, but a tripfest waiting to happen.

She led him to the boathouse, where she humped out the lawnmower and a five-gallon red plastic jerry can, spout attached. "It's all ready, but you'll probably have to refill the gas once. Don't spill anything on yourself, and for God's sake, watch the rocks. That blade has as many gravel dings as my van."

He listened alertly, examining the controls with intelligent dexterity. "And the turtle and the rabbit on the side?"

"Choose your speed. It's self-propelled. With a deadman feature." Wincing at another death reference, she demonstrated how the motor disengaged when the handle was released. As she pointed around the yard, she explained the areas which needed cutting and cautioned him against trying to muscle the machine as a weed whipper at the rough edges, a sin of her benighted youth which had contributed to her back problem.

He was barely able to see over the handles, but his strong arms and legs carried him off. Boyz 'n men 'n machines. She headed into the house to read her e-mail.

Three hours later, Belle observed his progress. Micro had

done a super job and earned the right to use her precious carbon-steel secateurs to prune the red osier bushes and maple saplings encroaching her property. She watched him wheelbarrow the debris neatly to the burn pile by the lake. This children deal had advantages. Then she thought about cellphones, cars, college, birth control...an increasingly disturbing order.

Belle spaded up her triangular flower bed by the road and planted sixty bulk tulips from Canadian Tire, a bit of life for the end of May when the last snowpack surrendered. The frozen lake delayed spring just as the warmer waters coaxed fall to linger a few more weeks. She trimmed the hydrangea and cut the monkshood and peonies back to ground level. By the house, tiger lilies with their lush foliage had taken over, so she let them. Freya was enjoying her play date with Rusty, chasing circles around the yard. Above in the cedars, a stunted northern red squirrel scolded them for disturbing his cone harvest.

At high noon, she paid Micro with crisp twenties, which he slipped into a zipped pocket. Hélène had said he was bored. Perhaps she could give him a tour of the bush. "If you don't have plans for this afternoon, how about a picnic in the woods? There's a big swamp I call Surprise Lake. We'll take the dogs." She nodded towards the house. "You can call your aunt."

He shrugged, but she saw a glint of interest in the town boy's neat, sharp eyebrows. A hike might beat watching Hélène cook and listening to Ed snore with a background of the *Blue Hawaii* album on their ancient stereo, but could she compete with computer graphics? "Sounds okay," he said.

Not much later, they were on the trail behind her house, its entrance hidden from quads by drooping willows. How many footfalls had it taken to impress herself into the thin soil which covered the Cambrian rocks like an icing layer? Micro insisted on carrying the daypack with their cheese sandwiches, Smartfood popcorn, water bottles and dog biscuits. Slowly they climbed into the boreal forest, their path levelling out across a ridge. Freya stopped at an object at eye level in a fir tree, and Rusty whined. Micro followed their gaze and jumped back.

"Is that a real head? Creepy. Is it rotten?" His button nose twitched.

"Very old and very dry." Belle laughed. "I call him the Deer Prince."

Micro's eyes widened, and his mouth opened to reveal small white teeth. "Somebody shot it and left it? Gross."

"I found it fifty feet off the path when I was bushwhacking. Must have been lying there for years. Two horns have been sawn off. I think it's required for the Ministry." She gazed in endearment at the Prince, his eyes hollow, his hair thinning, and stroked his white bone nose. "I couldn't leave him dumped and lonely. His spirit belongs in a prominent place."

Micro's voice mellowed, and he took a baby step forward, hand extended as if expecting an electric shock. Then with growing confidence, he rubbed the antlers. "I was scared at first, but now I see what you mean. Wait till I tell my friend Chris."

As they walked, Belle chastized herself. Why did she have to run on at the mouth without thinking? Like Prospero at the end of *The Tempest*, her every third thought seemed to involve a grave or other sepulchral symbol. Micro's last image of his mother had been in her casket, and here she was introducing him to her personal cadaver.

At the next brook, they took a break so that the dogs could slurp the peaty water. "That fellow's at least three hundred years old," she said, gauging the girth of a grandfather yellow birch. "Long before anyone...any settlers came. Of course, there were aboriginals here. On canoe trips I've seen their pictographs, painted symbols, on rocks over by Lake Matagamasi."

He picked at the balsam pitch leaking from a fir tree. "Awesome. I saw a big tepee at Shield University. Some guys were drumming and everything."

She laughed and picked up a heavy sheet of sloughed birch as Freya tossed a smaller round from a rotted log, catching it in her mouth to tempt Rusty. "You're thinking about plains people out west. Tepees aren't practical in our heavy snows, and moose weren't as easy or plentiful to kill for their skins as buffalos were. Around here the Ojibwa made winter dwellings by placing this waterproof material over branch structures. A bit of sticky resin for glue, lashings of willow, and presto, a quick but temporary house."

"Tepees are better." He laughed as Freya speared the round of birch precisely on her nose.

Arriving at the lake, they found a sunny spot on a gentle slope. Something rustled in the brush, and a duelling pair of loons warbled across the shimmering water. The boy picked up the concept and called. "Micro, Micro, Micro" echoed back in the natural amphitheatre.

Belle set their lunch on a level rock and divvied it up. The boy was having fun in the best playground in the world. She couldn't understand why some parents forbid their children to play in the woods, preferring them to ride quads down the road at seventy kmh.

As they ate, she pointed to a wooden blind in a nearby tree. "It's a moose perch. The plywood is camouflaged so the hunter can hide and wait."

"Sit up there and blast away?" Micro asked, flaring his nostrils. "No fair." Not only did he have a love of animals but an inborn sense of justice.

"I don't think so either, but if they get a tag in the fall through the lottery, it's legal. You don't even need one for a calf." She explained how a small herd back in the Crown land was being squeezed between mining interests and a growing population of full-time homeowners.

"Uncle Ed has a .22 for varmints, he calls them. I shot it once. Just at a can in a gravel pit, though."

She recalled the havoc in the boathouse when she'd tried to pull down her snow tires from the high shelves and found them filled with pine cones, a rodent food bank. "Fine for small game, but hunters use higher powered rifles for large animals."

The sun made them sweat, and they welcomed the breeze that riffled down the lake. A splash by the beaver house was followed by the "v" of the irrepressible builder. She passed Micro the popcorn, savouring a mouthful of the white cheddar. He tasted it. "Good," he said, then examined the label. "But I don't think it's so smart. Look at how many calories are in a serving. And you could make it yourself."

Belle felt a tug on her waistband. He was right on both counts. "Dumbfood, I guess."

Micro climbed to the perch, intuiting the use of the birch caller on a nail, and made credible oo-ga sounds. When he returned, she said, "Follow me to something special...if it's showtime." She led him into a shady area where a huge cedar lay crumbling on the ground, transforming into the peat which bore it. "This is a nurse log. Just another cycle in tree life. Now it's a perfect environment for seedlings."

"What's that weird..." he asked, stretching a hand toward a four-inch protrusion vaguely like a dog phallus, pink with a slimy brown tip.

She pulled him back by the collar. "Whoa. Don't touch that. Meet the elegant stinkhorn. Hollow inside, a rare fungi.

Under the right conditions of temperature and humidity, they can spring up in a night, then droop and wither. Look carefully and see if you can spy the 'egg' that starts one."

He walked along the log, peering at every inch. "This what you mean?" He pointed at a small, milky bump like the blind eye of the victim in Poe's "The Tell-Tale Heart". "Will it come out tomorrow?"

"If moisture and temperature are right. This blasted rain we've been having helps the process." She looked at the clouds massing in the sky. "We were lucky to get a window for the mowing and this hike. More's on the way. See the cumulus thunderheads?"

He studied her with a hand on his slim hips. "Did you learn this stuff in school?"

Belle remembered as a child coming up to visit Uncle Harold at his cottage on Lake Penage, entering a new country north of Barrie, where ordered farmlands surrendered to the great bones of the Cambrian Shield. To be at home in the landscape, and to stay safe, she needed to learn its names, she explained. An old woman on her road, Anni Jacobs, had tramped trails into the woods, inviting Belle along. Anni had regarded the bush as a pharmacopoeia, from the use of yarrow for stomach cramps to dogbane for headache. "Curiosity is the best teacher."

"I just thought they were woods. They're like a free store." He nodded as if making new connections, and she could see the wheels turning in his fertile little brain. "Is it okay if I go look around? I won't get lost or anything."

At the wave of her hand, he set off with the dogs to do some exploring as Belle packed up. Craning her neck, she could follow his small form combing the ground with interest. Finishing a few minutes later, she sat under a shady pine near a clearing where yellow lady's slipper had greeted last May's sun. She had taken Anni's place in the scheme of things. Some day, as she grew old, the torch would have to be passed. But to whom? A wee tug at her heart reminded her that her clock had stopped from rust years ago.

"Yoooooo. Belle, come here." Hailing her with waving arms, he directed her through a tangle of scrubby alders, leatherleaf and Labrador tea plants into a boggy section with a small clearing. The level ground was dotted with a few dozen black plastic garbage bags of soil dug into the earth. A wizened plant stem poked out of each one. Leaning against a sheltering white pine was the remainder of a fifty-pound sack of potting soil. "Check this out," he said, a miniature detective.

Belle scratched her head. "What is it?"

"A pot farm, what else?" he said, rubbing a stem and sniffing to his satisfaction. "In the city they call them grow-ops. Like in operations. Kid in my class told me his father got arrested for setting one up in his basement. Sent to jail for a couple of years."

He sounded like a child of the Underworld, but Belle supposed that the language was commonplace. Right in her backyard. This could explain that note on her windshield. The overeager Junior Crime Stopper had seen Belle often on that trail and thought she ran the farm.

Safer than planting in a corn field, where aerial surveillance would find it easily. Random, small and personal, with a convenient water source. Checked perhaps once a week, about the number of times she took this trail. Who could have put it here? A local or a townie? So many new people on the road, yet they would have needed a quad to cart in the soil. Did the trapper have a more lucrative sideline? She monitored the entrance to this path, but perhaps he had a back door connection from the Bay Trail.

Ten years from now, they might not be having this conversation. Not all the armies in the world, nor Nancy Reagan, could stop an idea whose time had come. The Marijuana Party had garnered thousands of votes in the Sudbury area alone in the last election. The Liberal government had legalized medical marijuana and was cultivating it with traditional Canuck caution deep in the abandoned mines of Brandon, Manitoba. Apparently this genetic strain had such feeble buzz next to the muscular B.C. legends that over half the registered users had returned the supply in disgust. They headed for home at a rapid pace. It was nearly five, and Hélène served dinner on the minute. "Suck it up, Buttercup," he said, passing her on a steep section as she paused for breath.

"I'm nearly four times your age and carrying considerable poundage. All those bags of Dumbfood. Be merciful."

As they came down the hill to the trailhead, Freya pointed her muzzle towards the far turn, pricking her rabbity ears. Despite Belle's calls, she refused to come immediately. Impatient to get Micro back for his dinner, Belle jerked her away with a swift command. That dog was always seeing things.

Then an old bike streaked past her, crunching gravel. "Watch it," she called. "Not enough road for you?" The serpent tire track looked all too familiar, but before she could react, a gangly girl, her pipestem legs beating circles, disappeared around the corner.

EIGHT

Two weeks had passed since Bea's death. Belle followed the papers with a sadly personal interest, hoping for a break in the case. According to the news, the pizza-delivery man had been cleared when it was learned that he had been doing his route while babysitting two sisters in his van because their mother was testifying in court against her abusive boyfriend. The ten-year-old twins provided a credible alibi.

Hélène called after dinner. "Come on down. Dave's here. Says he met you at the viewing. He has some ideas about...finding Bea's killer."

Whatever his options were, Belle couldn't imagine, yet the frustration of the aftermath must have been more crushing than the initial anger.

Leaving Freya to guard the house, she walked in the twilight, searching the muted sky as fall's new cast of characters arrived. Vain Cassiopeia, then Perseus, holding the Gorgon's head as he averted his eyes. How priceless to have a front row seat on the constellations with no urban congestion to mask the wonders. Satellite maps of the world at night showed that bright lights were rapidly spreading over the velvet canopy. It irked her that some homeowners on the Molly Maid end of the road had begun installing glaring sodium beams on their property. Couldn't they find their homes without a lighthouse? Then the town had streetlit the mailboxes at the corner. She far preferred the ride with only her headlamps to lead her.

The waves were noisy along the shore, even in the DesRosiers' quiet bay. With alarm, she noted that their dock was nearly underwater. With autumn storms on the way, everyone was in for trouble. Whipped to a frenzy by gale force winds, the water would devour anything in its path. It was like living next to a sleeping dinosaur with a root canal and no dental.

The house was wreathed in woodsmoke, a warm, intimate defiance of the encroaching dark. In the drive was parked Dave's Santa Fe, a living room on wheels that could climb a mountain. All leather and dressed nicely, its metallic copper colour a welcome change from the ubiquitous pewter of every other Sudbury truck. Belle gave it an interested appraisal. According to ads, it beat other SUV prices by ten thousand dollars. She climbed the steps with a shrug. She needed her spacious van with all-wheel-drive to ferry clients and navigate treacherous back roads.

When she was settled on the sofa with a decaf, she had a moment to reassess Dave. After giving her a welcoming smile, he turned with a serious expression to Ed, gesticulating with strong hands. He wore tan slacks and a dark brown flannel shirt with a duck embroidered on the pocket.

Coming in with a plate of sugar cookies, Hélène spoke with excitement. "Tell her about the plan."

Dave took a sip of coffee, then placed the mug on a coaster. Even from a distance, his eyes were bloodshot, reflecting the pressures of the ongoing tragedy. "I'm a patient man, have to be in my profession, but I've really had it with this so-called police investigation."

Belle nodded, her instinct to defend the beleaguered forces tempered in the wake of his grief. If anyone she loved had been so brutally killed, she'd move heaven and earth to balance the scales.

"I've hired a man to search for anything the authorities haven't turned up."

Folding her hands on her knee, Belle smiled. "A private eye? Do we have those in Canada, much less in this town?"

He gave a knowing laugh. "Several, as a matter of fact. Len Hewlitt will think outside the box. His credentials are excellent."

Then what's he doing up here, Belle wondered, barely suppressing a suspicious frown. The North wasn't a hotbed of crime, at least not until this statistical blip. Ed and Hélène were paying rapt attention.

Dave aimed a finger at Belle, cocking his head to examine her face. "I see your skepticism. His life does sound like a cheap thriller, nothing like we're used to. He's from Montreal but spent fifteen years in Israel with the Mossad, sort of a troubleshooter. He was injured in a suicide bomb blast in Jerusalem, nothing serious but disabling enough to force him to settle down. Then since his daughter moved here to work, he decided to relocate, too. Len's a pro."

"Did you find him in the Yellow Pages?" Belle was serious, but she could have phrased the question in more politic terms.

He cast a glance at Hélène, who pressed his hand in her motherly way as Ed looked at the ceiling. "Sorry, I didn't mean to sound flip," Belle said. "PIs remind me of Los Angeles or New York. Guess I read too many mysteries."

Dave cleared his throat and seemed to take a breath. "To be frank, I met him at an AA meeting last fall. No family secrets here. I've been clean and sober for over ten years."

Honest enough, Belle thought, her admiration growing. Admitting an addiction was the hardest part. As a respected part of the community, he'd raced his beast and still was in the lead. Who was she to be smug, with her cigarettes and scotch? "He sounds interesting. I'd love to meet him."

"Your wish is granted." He checked his watch, a Timex sports model. "Len will be here any minute. I told him seven so as not to keep you folks up, but he isn't used to driving this cowpath." Everyone laughed at the stretch of potholes guaranteed to suck a set of struts faster than a kid with a Dairy Queen Blizzard.

Half an hour later, as darkness fell and talk turned to the latest political scandal involving questionable government grants to advertising firms, a car triggered the motion-sensor lights in the DesRosiers' yard. Up to refill her cup, Belle said to Hélène, "I'll get it."

The engine of an ancient Chevette screamed like a young girl and died. The door creaked open, and a fireplug of a man got out and kicked the fender. "You bugger. One more like that and you get recycled into the pop cans you came from," he muttered over his shoulder as he boosted himself to the deck with a slight limp, stopping to pat Rusty's inquiring head. "Hey, buddy."

Belle stood at the threshold, shielding her eyes from the glare of the floodlights. "Welcome, Mr. Hewlitt."

"I had to brake for something dark, hairy and way bigger than my car. Nearly went into a damn swamp. Did I cross the border into Kosovo?"

"You're still in the Region of Crater Sudbury, and I have the inflated tax bills to prove it," Belle said with a smile and an introductory handshake.

Lifting a brown felt fedora, he stared pleasantly at her from behind heavy, square black glasses. As she took his three-quarter-length faded leather coat and hung it on the rack, she saw a greying moustache and spade beard, a weak chin and a deeply receding hairline which lent a gnomish appearance. He was her height, five foot four, but solidly built, a good two-hundred-twenty pounds, harder to knock over than a stuffed cat at a carnival.

Hélène shot a quick look towards the hall to the bedrooms. "Keep it low, and let's move to the kitchen table. We don't want Micro to hear this. His door's closed, but he's got half an hour more at his computer until he goes to bed." A fresh pot and an industrial-sized pickle jar of shortbread made the rounds.

"I've wanted to meet you folks," Len said, pulling out a notebook after everyone had settled down. He also snapped a tape into a mini-recorder. "Dave's told me everything he can. Pardon me for starting off with the nitty-gritty, but I know you want to find Mrs. Malanuk's killer. The machine's so's I don't miss any details. I need your input. Don't be shy."

Ed added, "Damn straight. I'll go first." Leaning toward the recorder, he proceeded to give his history with the family. Hélène took over, and time passed as she related several decades, starting with Bea's first communion.

Ed put down a cookie in mid-bite. "Come on, woman. He doesn't have time for all that stuff."

Len raised a chubby finger in a gesture of acceptance. "No, siree. Everything can be important. God is in the details, or the devil is, never could remember."

Hélène pushed out her lower lip. "I was finished anyway, *Edward.*"

They all turned to Belle, who once again revisited that hideous morning. She fixated on the rose pattern on the tablecloth, avoiding the sorrow in Dave's eyes. Told many times, her story had achieved a sanitary narrative. The gore could be left to the police and coroner reports.

Scribbling notes, when she finished, Len sat for a moment, all eyes on him. He underlined a few words. "Okey dokey. We have liftoff. Now I'll open the floor to questions."

Belle asked the obvious. "Do you think that Bea's death is connected to the other two murders? And why are the police having such a hard time solving them?" With his big-city experience, he'd probably seen dozens of cases.

He finished a fifth cookie and blotted his fleshy mouth demurely, squaring his shoulders. His eyes were pouchy and world-weary. "Answer one: I'm new on the job and don't know jack about the first two women, but I will find out. Answer two: No offense to you kind people, but these folks are purely bush league, pun intended. Bar-room brawl, a lovers' quarrel gone sour, no problemo. Something complicated, where a killer has an IQ no higher than the cost of half a litre of gas, they're over their heads."

Ed nodded, stifling a yawn. "You nailed her all right." His pale silver brows waffled at Belle's glare. "Sorry. Didn't mean your pal, Steve. He's tops."

Belle said to Len, "I have a detective friend on the Sudbury force. Steve Davis."

"Really? Could be helpful." Len tapped a stubborn pen back into action and made a note. "I'm from Montreal, la belle province, and I guess Dave told you about my qualifications. Expect the unusual, but never look for a zebra in a herd of cows. One time in the Gaza Strip when I...."

When Len got talking, he didn't stop for breath except to light a cigarette, despite Hélène's gentle cough. Special training by the FBI at Quantico, Virginia, had given him experience in mingling among "narco-terrorists" as an executive casino host in London, England. He'd also worked as consultant to the Gananoque police in a cigarette-smuggling sting operation and received a special commendation from the mayor. The Sûreté had used him as an agent in their ongoing biker wars. He had been the only Indian-motorcycle owner that the Hell's Angels with their Harleys allowed in their clubhouse.

He slapped his leg, wiggling a worn loafer. Belle noticed that he'd kept his shoes on, unlike the rest of them. "This old guy's not as young as I want to stay. I've been winding down the last years. Some of my old friends in the Association of Former Intelligence Officers became PIs. And I never really got to know my daughter in all my travels. Got her Master's at McGill, and she's settled in at a nice job here. If I can get her married, maybe I'll see grandchildren some day."

Though blanching at the "get her married" quip, Belle lapped up the details. Whatever the truth of his claims, Len was a bona fide investigator, and from his imagination, maybe he could offer fresh ideas. What was Dave paying him? A couple of hundred a day?

The DesRosiers and Belle were usually in bed by ten and drinking coffee by six. As Ed's head snapped up in a snore and they all chuckled, Len said, "Guess we should call her a day. I'll cover every house on John Street and the crossroads. No leads, they say? Bulltwaddle. Someone saw or heard something. Maybe they went on vacation the next day. Persistence and a fertile mind are an investigator's most important tools. Who are your next door neighbours, Dave?"

Dave gave a weary sigh. "Greenbelt on one side. On the other, Miss McBride. Not much goes by her. The north side of John Street is railway land."

"How will you learn more than the police?" Belle asked Len.

"Sometimes authorities can be intimidating. I sit down, enjoy a nice cup of tea, praise the cookies." He winked at Hélène. "And have a long chat. Lots of psychology. Women are my speciality." He used five syllables for the last word and tapped his temple. "And then there's the dog."

They all spoke at once. "Buffalo?"

"Why didn't he raise a ruckus?" He turned to Dave. "Didn't you tell me he was a great watchdog?"

With a grimly set mouth, Dave said, "I thought so. Our part of town gets the occasional break-in. Mostly drug-related. Looking for items to pawn. We've never had as much as a trampled flower bed. His barking can be heard across the lake. Squirrels and coons drive him nuts. Bea leaves him out until she goes to work. But that day, no one heard any barking."

"I heard him when I arrived," Belle said, "but he was tied up. If someone were very quiet and entered from the greenbelt, or came up from the lake..."

"It's pretty steep there," Dave said, rubbing his jaw. He looked half-asleep, running on sheer guts.

Len made another note, flipping a page. "And the door was unlocked when you got there, Belle. And you saw a purse? Do women have more than one?"

Hélène said, "A closet full. I remember two or three of her favourites. A turtle purse I brought her from Florida."

"Bea transfers her things back and forth, leaving the one she's using on the hall table. It was open but nothing was taken, not that she carries much but credit and debit cards. The weekly payroll for the bakery was gone, though. Bea kept it in a leather bag. About five thousand dollars. The police found the bag stuffed in a garbage can a block away. They're withholding that information, I believe." Dave gave a groan that touched Belle's heart. "I know people have been killed for less, but when something like this hits close to home..." His voice trailed off.

"So everyone at the bakery knew she carried the payroll

every Friday. Sounds like a focus." Belle turned to Dave. "Anyone missing at work?"

"The staff's long term, some with twenty years, but Bea does have a few turnovers in the joe jobs. Len's going to talk to her business partner."

The PI removed his glasses to polish them on a serviette. The heavy lens magnified the pattern on the tablecloth. "It's coming together. An inside job, maybe, like the dog knew the intruder."

Belle thought of the one drawback to hiring temporary help. Good old boys get to scope out an isolated lakefront property, marking portable property such as chainsaws, snowmobiles and electronics while checking for an alarm system. "Any handymen at your place recently? Someone you don't know personally?"

Dave searched his memory. "God, that old place always needed a fine tuning. We had the new roof and guttering this year. Furnace man. I've called a yard service when I got too busy to mow. Nick's Plowing, too, for two-foot dumps."

Len was scribbling notes, stuffing out another cigarette in a growing pile of butts. "This lady's got a brain on her, Dave."

Proud to help, trying not to preen, Belle remembered Freya's close call at the vet. "Here's another idea. What about drugs? If someone put a sedative in ground meat, then balled it up and threw it..." She gave a demonstration.

Dave spread out his hands. "But when I got there, Buffalo was fine."

Belle added, "And barking at eleven o'clock, my arrival. But sedatives can wear off fast in a healthy animal."

"Too late now for any toxicology," Dave said, "but I'll suggest it to the detective."

Len said, "I'm spending the day at the bakery tomorrow,

interviewing everyone from soup to nuts. What was that partner's name?"

"Leonora Bruce. Bea sold her forty-five per cent of the business when Dr. Bustamante died. She wanted fewer responsibilities and more time with Micro." After placing a finger at the corner of one moist eye, he shook himself back to firmer ground. "It worked out well. Leonora knows absolutely everything about the staff and the operation. Bumble Bea will run under her direction until the will is probated and the legalities straightened out. My wife left everything to Micro, of course. The business is a family tradition."

Belle asked, "So you're not going to take over?"

He sat back, hands laced behind his head, a faint smile emerging on his face. "Fundraising is my life. A new campaign every month. Not making things, but making things happen for people with needs they can't meet themselves. And in the recent times of government cutbacks, more necessary than ever." He paused and reached into his pocket for his wallet, passing her a card. "You know the phone at home. If anything occurs to you about that morning..."

The card was plain and simple, no embossing, no graphics. David Malanuk, Fundraising Consultant. An office in the old Maley Building. For once, Belle was caught cardless. "I don't have any with me, but of course I'm in the book."

Dave nodded, his eyes catching hers for a moment, but as they all rose, Hélène called him over with a school paper of Micro's which she'd magneted to the fridge. Belle could see a page of math problems and a gold star.

After the two men left, Belle stayed to help Hélène clean up, but more to get answers to a puzzling question. "Dave's wonderful. I can see why Bea loved him." She finished drying a cup, not wanting to sound too crass, but acknowledging the elephant in the corner. "Did he have some...uh, plastic surgery on his face and hands? If you were anyone else, I wouldn't be so rude as to ask."

Hélène attacked the room with a can of air freshener, spreading a berry-scented cloud over the smoky fug. "Such a tragic story. Bea said that when he was a teenager, he rescued a boy at scout camp when a fire from a candle broke out in their tent. Beating out the flames, he suffered first-degree burns on his face, neck and hands. Spent a few months at Sick Kids and had more surgeries over the years. Badges of honour, Bea called them."

NINE

As she snarled at the seventh straight day of rain, Belle lugged her garbage to the coffin-sized box, noticing one over the three-bag limit. Casting an eye down the road, she strolled to the end of her neighbour's driveway and dropped it into their bin. The McNairs wouldn't be coming out until eleven feet of snow threatened the old camp's roof.

She looked along the drainage ditch where she'd planted tamaracks eight years ago as a privacy fence. One of the few deciduous conifers, its golden needles sprinkled a glow across the green landscape of cedars and pines. Already they were threatening the hydro wires. Most ominous, a monster cedar by her house had developed a lean after the last windstorm. Soft-wooded cedars were deceptive. They looked healthy but often were rotten to the core, never falling straight, but twisting like a drooping ballerina in *Swan Lake*.

As she frowned, she wondered whether to ask her handyman Johnny to trim everything. Probably off with hunting buddies getting his moose. Then a familiar rusty white pickup chugged down the road. It stopped beside her, and the driver turned off the motor, rolling down the creaky window. His dark face spoke volumes, a thin cigarillo clenched between his teeth. The lashing of the waves and the croak of a soaring raven, always a curious bird, soundtracked their hostile tableau.

"I know what you did with my traps," he said. "That was a cheap trick."

Cold anger sparked like a welding arc from her teal eyes. "Let's talk about your poisoning job. That's not a cheap trick, it's a felony. What if a kid had gotten into it?"

"What the hell are you talking about?"

"Poisoned meat tossed into my yard. My dog started munching it. You're lucky I got her to the vet in time."

"That's crazy. I have three cocker spaniels, Larry, Curly and Moe, and they sleep on my bed. You had no right to touch those traps. Who the hell are you anyway?"

"If you're so familiar with this territory, why don't you find out? And as for your cruel traps..." She paused for emphasis, then put her hands on her hips gunslinger-style: "Prove it. So what. What are you going to do about it?"

He tapped an ash from his cigarillo. "Take back your woods, madame. I'm heading north to set up my other traplines at Thor Lake. And don't be telling me you hike there, too, unless you like railroad tracks."

Narrowing his eyes, he ground the starter with a flurry of Frenglish curses, and with a chug of black smoke, drove off, his quad bouncing in the back. *"Va te faire foutre,"* he called out the window, adding the traditional digital message. The frost in his deep voice and the way his dark eyes simmered in controlled anger gave Belle mixed feelings and reminded her of Steve. The meat and timing was too coincidental, yet he sounded honest. Who would lie about owning cocker spaniels? They weren't the brightest dogs, so the Three Stooges idea fit. She didn't know his name and presumed he still didn't know hers. In another time and place, they might have been friends. If he'd limited himself to beavers.

"I hope that's the last I see of you." She took off the snick on the latch on her garbage box. Trash collectors were very ergonomic and appreciated one less step. As she turned, she noted more familiar bike tracks in the dirt and paused at a new connection. Was the Junior Crime Stopper another candidate for the meat toss? She remembered a black comedy she'd seen at Miriam's on a girls' night out: *The Young Poisoner's Handbook.*

Ten minutes later, Belle sat in her van by the community mailboxes, having ripped open the new tax assessment with a groan. Closing on five thousand dollars. For what? No sewer, water, sidewalks or streetlights. A whopping increase of eight per cent. Where would she get the extra cash? Propane had gone up thirty per cent, and the hydro rates had risen under the new government.

Then a pink limo with "Call 487-7653, and IT'S-SOLD" pulled up beside her as the fuchsia-tinted window rolled down. Cynthia Cryderman manoeuvered her mammoth burgundy wig through the window. "Belle. Do you still live on this road? I'm out to take pictures of the Givens place. I'm surprised you didn't get the listing. Prices for quality homes on Wapiti are making this the next Lake Ramsey. 465 K. Imagine popping that commission into your bank account." Her large round eyes, accented by veils of mascara, rolled over Belle's van like a judge at a dog show. Not even leather seats. Utilitarian at best.

Belle smiled neutrally and gritted her teeth until her jaw ached. She'd never liked Cheryl Givens, with her patent snobbery and Mercedes SUV. But she wouldn't have turned down a chance to sell that brick monster with 350 feet of frontage, double garage, boathouse with marine railway, sauna and sleep camp.

"Say, the offer to join my firm still stands. Twelve per cent partnership. Run a branch from your office with your own staff. Your cottage connections are pure platinum, and you have the youth to run after them. I'm a city girl." She batted her eyelashes like a coy debutante. "Lord, I can't forget that old brewery at the back of beyond on a logging road southwest of Shining Tree. All my associates came down with the flu, and I had to go up there myself. My driver got us stuck in the muskeg. I broke both heels on my favourite Manolos."

A realtor's curiosity led Belle to continue the unpleasant conversation. "A brewery? Is it feasible? How did it get up there in the first place?"

"There's a natural spring, and they hooked onto a hydro line to the gold mining operations to the east. With a short rail spur to the CN lines and good roads to Timmins and Kirkland Lake, they were in a position to cover the northern market for awhile. Labatt's drove them out in the Sixties. But the infrastructure is there, and with the microbeer hoopla, all natural stuff, who knows? This Allan Ritchie who bought it looks like a drifter, but he must have family money somewhere. Quite the eccentric."

Belle tucked the tax bill into her pocket to gather moss, dust or lint, whichever came first. She watched the limo take off down the hill and bounce perilously over the heaves. Its muffler scraped on the broken asphalt, and one hubcap flew into the bush to join a collection dangling from the poplar branches in a whimsical effort at Found Art. A yellow metal sign read "Rough Road: Chemin Cahoteux." Warnings were cheaper than repairs.

At the office, as Miriam passed her on the way to the bank, she found a call from Steve on her answering machine. "Meet me for lunch at Café Korea. Noon." She tapped her teeth in anticipation and more than mild annoyance. How many messages had she left after Bea's death? Still, a good lunch could make up for nearly anything. And he'd pay. Detectives made more than she did and got regular pay cheques. Like rust, crime never slept.

After driving down LaSalle, she parked at a spot in the Montrose Mall and entered the restaurant at twelve fifteen, her eyes cool with satisfaction. Grow up, lady, she thought as she saw Steve hunched over a small table beneath a framed copy of a *Toronto Star* rave review. He looked up with such a pathetic smile that she melted. His was a brutal profession.

"I'm late." A white lie tickled her throat, but she merely shrugged. He deserved more. When would they graduate from petty arguments? Yet below those scuffles, a solid foundation anchored their friendship, as deep and valuable as the ore load buttressing the city.

"Sorry for not getting back to you," he said. "I was over in Algonquin Bay, our sister city in serial killers. Talked to Detective Cardinal. Remember a couple of years ago?"

She searched her memory, fingering the condiment bottles. Soy, fish and hot sauce. "They got the guy, but he went after teenagers, didn't he? Gory sex stuff. Did you learn anything helpful?" The redolent aromas of stir-fry garlic and ginger root began whispering her name.

He cracked his knuckles. "Our renowned profiler gave us a picture so general it could fit every ne'er-do-well in town. We could sweep down Brewster Street with an industrial vacuum. Then I was tied up helping Janet with her father in the Sault. He had a stroke, and her mother was weighing their options. Hospital needed the bed, but there were no nursing home vacancies."

"How well I know the drill," she replied. "Everything okay now?"

"Holding. Janet will be staying on to organize the home care. Heather's with me, so I'm juggling babysitting arrangements." He looked almost relieved. His fights with his wife, a sunny but brittle character, hadn't lessened since they'd adopted the half-Cree, half-Italian toddler, but merely changed to broils about how to raise the sweet girl, now in Grade Two. Belle remembered meeting Janet's mother once at a birthday party for Heather. The blue-haired former socialite, whose husband had been a VP at Algoma Steel, was a haughty type who always reminded her daughter of her risky marital choice.

She checked the menu specials chalked on a board behind the cash. "So what do you want to try? They have Japanese, Thai, Indian and Vietnamese food, too." Half of the room held shelves with Asian groceries and coolers for frozen items.

He signalled a waiter, who brought two large, steaming bowls of noodles with Korean sauce and vegetables. Steve grinned at his coup. "I know you're busy, so I ordered already. A hottie, like you."

"Maybe fifteen years ago in a tank top. That jargon reminds me of those female teachers with their student lovers."

"Right. You'd rather live in the Thirties in those films you love. If you'd been born then, you'd be my mother now."

"That's a frightening prospect." Tucking into the bowl with chopsticks, she asked the question they'd both been tiptoeing around. "What's going on with Bea's case? Is the detective any good?"

He gave her a warning lip curl but then spread his broad hands in frustration. "Burns made the grade two years ago. He has a law degree from Osgoode Hall, prefers to work the streets instead of the courts. He's been liaising with the guys in charge of the other two cases."

"Guys. Don't you have any female detectives?"

"One of them caught the first murder. Maybe that's why there's been no headway."

"Joking isn't going to bring Bea back. Are there any leads?

You have the time frame. Between Micro leaving for school and my arrival."

"Between seven thirty and eleven. Pretty generous."

"Bea probably got to work by eight. Doesn't that narrow it down?"

He twirled a noodle on his fork. "Yes, I heard that, but there were exceptions."

"Early fits for me. I don't see how she was killed anywhere but in the bathroom. That home was pin neat," Belle added.

"That busy time of the morning, the boy having left, the doors could have been open."

"I'm thinking someone came up from the lakeside or the greenbelt where he wouldn't be seen. Wouldn't set the dog barking." She tossed over the memories of that meeting with Len like coins in her hand. "Did you check out everyone who's worked at the house?"

Steve gave a sigh, but he was weakening. "That might not jibe with a piece of information we're withholding. Near the other two murder sites, we found an empty flower box from the Rosary. No record of any such order in the neighbourhood. It could have been taken from the trash out back of the store. Nothing's turned up yet on John Street, but it's been windy. Could have blown to Mattawa by now."

"Roses were her favourite," she said, recalling the funeral. "Her husband ordered..." She stared at Steve, who was shaking his head.

"First choice in all domestic murders," he said as he worked a stubborn mushroom into his chopsticks. "But Malanuk was in Ottawa all that week, coordinating a telethon to raise money for a Braille library. Jerry Lewis didn't have a higher profile. He left the Lord Elgin Hotel at seven after an early breakfast. At eleven that morning, he was buying gas in North

Bay, still an hour away."

"I'm glad he's in the clear. What a nice man. I met him at the viewing and later at Hélène's."

"You'd make a terrible detective. Those kinds of judgments are fatal."

Ignoring him, she browsed through her dish for a water chestnut. "Micro's a sweetheart, too. He's staying with the DesRosiers for a while. I took him on a hike."

Steve looked around and lowered his voice as two bald motorcyclists in full leathers came in and settled at a nearby table. "Don't get wild on me, but one of the guys today went out on a creepy limb. Kids younger than that have been known to kill their parents."

"What?" Her face flushed with fire hotter than the chilis in the bowl.

"The King brothers in the States. Only nine and twelve. She did have a massive contusion on the back of her head from a blunt instrument. It's easy to strangle someone who's unconscious."

Remembering Micro's small, delicate hands, she leaned forward and said with a hiss that surprised her. "Have you *seen* him?"

"No, I only—"

"Micro is a quarter Bea's size. And then he got on the school bus, carrying a parrot for Show and Tell? Spare me." She tossed him a steely glance. "Oh, and he took the payroll money. Watch out if he buys a car."

Steve crossed his wrists in a mock protection gesture. "The bag turned up in a garbage can down the street. No prints or trace evidence. Relax, I said it wasn't my idea. Are you adopting him or what? This is a new side. I think I like it. Everyone needs to experience the challenge of parenthood. You get off easy with your dog."

"If I adopted anyone, it would be to get help cutting the

lawn, raking leaves and shovelling snow. Freya has refused." She lifted her bowl and finished the rich broth with an "Ay, chihuahua," tears streaming down her face. "What's the buzz on that investigator Dave hired? He seems qualified."

Steve's raven eyes glinted across the table, her silhouette reflected in the darkening pupils. "No lunch would be complete without at least three arguments. It's a waste of money."

"Why? Maybe he'll find some turn unstoned?" She grinned at him.

"Or bugger up the case for us. He's new in town, but his name hasn't set off any blinking lights, not that we've had any time to pursue the matter."

"Your customary excuse."

"Be gentle." He reached into a pocket for a notebook. "I come bearing gifts. Here's the Crime Stoppers info. A seventh grader in Skead spends her time combing the bush for pot farms. She's found three over there already. Diedre Collins. Her brothers are the neighbourhood bad boys. They're over at Cecil Facer for auto theft. She's out to restore the family honour."

"That sounds sad." Skead was about fifteen kilometres from her house, a hilly ride, but easy for a youngster.

"The Collins bunch is a generational gene pool of losers, in and out of jail. Her father and uncle ran a snowmobile chop shop. Hot-wired them at Rocky's and rode them across the lake to their shed. They collected insurance money on a minor house fire, then torched the garage in a propane 'accident' a year later. Seems like whenever a plume of smoke arises, it's at 2006 Kevin Street."

Belle shifted in her chair. That might explain the recent bicycle tracks. Diedre was keeping an eye on her. But suppose her efforts led the angry cannabis planter to Belle's house? She needed to have a talk with that girl. Now that Belle had befriended Micro, another twelve-year-old, how hard could it be?

TEN

Belle met Hélène at ten that morning for a long-trumpeted tour of Costco. "You must be the last person in Sudbury who hasn't joined, and yet you're famous for squeezing a loonie until it shrieks," Hélène said as they stopped at the desk to get Belle a guest pass. Their security was tighter than the Pentagon's.

Belle gestured to the membership board prices. "Fifty bucks?"

Hélène gave a harumph as she shoved the King Kong buggy towards the entrance, and they flashed their ID's. "I can't tell you what I've banked on these bulk buys. And we live so far from town. Stocking up saves time and effort. Not to mention gas at over a dollar a litre."

"I'll borrow a roll of toilet paper from you. And think of it this way. What if everyone refused to pay the membership? They'd have to waive the fee." Belle spread her hands, the soul of logic.

"That sounds quite radical, hardly Canadian."

Belle gestured at the Disneyland of consumerism that welcomed them. "We're too polite. Our national expression is 'Excuse me.' Behind all this, as in American ads, the words are 'But wait, there's more'." She pronounced the last word as "mowa."

Passing the rows of computers, plasma televisions, books,

clothes, exercise equipment, music and even a suspended canoe, they cruised the food aisles. Hélène pushed the cart like a sucking cornucopia, leading her first to the meat, all AAA. Belle blinked at the display as her friend plucked a dozen ribeye steaks of prime Alberta beef. Trailing like a puppy in spite of herself, she drooled over the rounds of aged cheddar and garlands of smoked sausages. Then they crashed the frozen food aisles, a monument to instant meals. Fifteen selections of pizzas. Manicotti by the dozen in three sauces. A mountain of fries. Belle scrutinized a box of brie-and-mushroom appetizers in puff pastry and raised a suspicious eyebrow. "You told me at Christmas dinner that you made those yourself. So that's why you 'lost' the recipe."

Hélène gave a guilty giggle and excused herself to go to the nearby washroom. "Too much coffee."

Following a musical trail, Belle drifted over to a display of stuffed animals. A shaggy sheepdog was singing "Only You", howling at each refrain, paws waving and head moving up and down. She chuckled to imagine Freya's reaction and nearly grabbed it, when she saw the price. $15.95. Expensive for a one-time gag.

Then someone moved up beside her, his voice deep and slightly melancholy. "Cute, aren't they? I was wondering if Micro would like one. He must miss Buffalo."

Dave wore a tweed sportcoat, white shirt and tie and slacks. His wingtip shoes were gleaming. Appearances would be important in his job. She hadn't thought about his need to continue working through all this tragedy. "My mother loved that song," she said. "But to be honest, the toy's more for a younger child." She didn't know whether to pity his naïveté or applaud the gesture. Step-parents had a heavy load.

Hélène hailed them as she returned, embracing Dave in her

usual warmth. "Micro's doing well, Dave. He got an A on his English test."

"How's he adjusting to his new school? Is anyone bothering him? Something I should know about?"

Belle couldn't decipher the cause of his concern. Bothering him? Then she recalled the bullying Ed had told her about.

"He mentioned a friend, Chris, I think. The boy moved to New Sudbury, but they keep in touch. And with this zero-tolerance policy at St. Francis, he seems much happier. You should come for dinner. I'll bet you eat out every night." She pointed at the luscious steaks as if to make him an offer he couldn't refuse. "Tuesday, okay?"

He nodded politely, looking into the distance as if burdened by a cape of sorrow. Creases around his eyes had deepened since Belle had last seen him, and his mouth sagged at the corners. "He has to return home sometime, Hélène. I wanted to let him take his time after...after what happened to Bea, and his staying with you worked well with my being out of town. But in another ten days, I'll be back here with some local projects. Several women have answered my ad for a housekeeper, and to help the transition, I know a good child psychologist who works at the San. He'd see Micro once or twice on a casual basis. Just to get the lay of things."

"It might be an idea," Hélène said, biting her lower lip in thought. "He's had to grow up mighty fast, but he has to face facts. You're his dad, and you love him." She pressed Dave's hand. "It'll make a difference when you're together, two men on a team."

"So are you going to join?" Hélène asked afterward at the cash, sounding like a religious proselytizer. She downloaded twenty frozen entrees, cases of soup and vegetables, and six-packs of Rolaids and Metamucil. No secrets on Edgewater Road.

Belle sighed, deciding never to face this circus again. "Then I'd have to buy a freezer. You know I'm still using the fridge that came with the cottage, circa 1960. Sure, egg rolls are great, but not fifty at once. What if I don't like the recipe?"

Hélène smirked at her. "That's why you should come more often. They give out samples. Free lunch. That should appeal to you."

"I'm not cheap, just frugal. No one can fight a Scottish ancestry."

Later that afternoon, Belle left the office on foot for some chores, noticing that the tall cottonwoods were beginning to blaze into yellow. She crossed the Toronto Dominion parking lot and jaywalked over to the chain pizza parlour at Cedar and Elgin. The tempting radio ads boasted exotic ingredients like eggplant, sun-dried tomatoes and goat cheese. Inside, the colourful picture menu on the wall reinforced the sumptuous choices. A large niçoise for tonight and a Sicilian for the freezer. Twenty-six dollars, but cheaper than eating out. Brekkie leftovers would be a bonus.

"I'd like them unbaked," she said to the teenaged girl, bee-stung red lips and ruthlessly plucked eyebrows with dark follicles sprinkled between like coarse pepper.

Her pouted mouth twisted in thought, and her pigeon-egg eyes rolled. "Uh, we can't do that."

A succulent slice with black olives and tuna sat on the counter under warming lights, seducing Belle's nose. Damn. She didn't want to wolf the thing down. Though she'd been gone from the classroom for over twenty years, she shifted into grammar teacher mode. "'Can't.' Does this mean physically or that you aren't allowed to?"

"Unbaked?" The girl said the word like a disease and cast a glance back to a young man in the kitchen, shovelling pizzas with a long wooden paddle. "Rules. You could ask the manager, but he's not here."

Belle's temper sizzled along with the mozzarella. "Let me get this straight. I'm willing to pay you nearly thirty dollars and use my own fuel to cook the pizza. And you refuse?"

Pushing out the door a nanosecond later, mentally dictating a letter to the *Sudbury Star* about lack of entrepreneurial spirit and independent thought, she collided on the street with a formidable barrier. It was Len Hewlitt, carrying a stack of Styrofoam boxes. His jowls shook with laughter at her description of the pizza fiasco.

"Come over to the office. Plenty here for two."

Tucked behind the St. Andrew's Church complex a few blocks away was Bank Alley, a dark enclave punctuated with Dumpsters. The financial namesake had been long gone since reconstruction in the Fifties. At their approach, a thin man with a cowboy hat turned and scuttled around the corner, followed by a small yellow Lab. A trash sifter, or looking for someone to mug? While in New York, or even Toronto, she might be captured on camera one hundred times in a twenty-minute stroll, Sudbury had few videocops. She felt far safer in the woods with the Deer Prince.

Instead of plate-glass windows, the narrow street had only doors to marginal businesses, Pat's Stamps and Coins, Dragon's Breath Tattoo Parlour, Divine Write Religious Bookstore, and Hewlitt's Investigations. The sign read "Corporate intelligence, surveillance, electronic eavesdropping countermeasures, background checks, DNA." Belle's eyes saucered at the bafflegab, and she gave him a quizzical look.

"DNA?"

He opened the door with a key, frowning at the unblinking answering machine and putting the boxes on a battered metal desk. "Big demand for that these days. Paternity suits. It's all done in Toronto. Takes three weeks and a shit...I mean a carload of cash." One corner of his fleshy mouth rose as he tickled his memory. "Even had a dog case. Purebred Scottish deerhound got knocked up by a mutt next door."

Belle huffed, recalling the time Freya was mounted in her own yard by a dog which could have captured all three prizes in an ugly contest and won a quick trip to the pound instead. Given the morning-after pill, the shepherd had developed an infection and had to be spayed at two. "I don't blame the owner. There goes ten thousand dollars for five pups."

An operatic yowl came from an open door to the rear, and a chocolate-point Siamese streaked out and leaped into Len's waiting arms. When it rubbed its head on his double chin, Belle noticed a black satin patch over one eye.

"Moshe, as in Dayan," he said. "A classy guy for an alley, but I found him with his head caught in a tin can. Poor little fellow didn't weigh eight pounds when I got him to the vet. Worms, infections, the whole shebang. My daughter sewed the patch. She's a whiz."

Belle stroked the glossy fur, mesmerized by the clear blue eye, namesake of her favourite marble. Now she nosed a slight tint of ammonia in the air from an unseen litter box. Len put down the cat and pulled up a folding lawn chair for her. "Excuse me for a minute. Got to go to the back for some sardines and milk. Guy eats better than I do."

While he was gone, Belle peered around. The office was a slice of real estate barely seven feet across, demanding organizational skills and the ability to suck in one's stomach. One shabby file cabinet held a coffee maker, but the focal points were the many pictures on the freshly painted walls: Golda Meir, Ronald Reagan, George Bush Sr., and oddly enough, Yasser Arafat. All signed to Len. A man for all political seasons, it seemed. The desk had a few file folders and a picture in a pewter frame, placed where he could see it as he worked. Curious, she started to angle for a peek when she heard him returning.

Len opened a desk drawer to retrieve a videotape, which he patted like a secret weapon. "Business will pick up soon once word gets out that I solved the gum machine case."

She crossed her legs, trying to get comfortable on the webbing while he rocked in a creaky office model. "Gum machine?"

Folding his stubby hands, he explained. "You've seen those charity bubble jobbies in supermarkets and malls. Nickel City College had a few in the student union area raising money for guide dogs. Someone was breaking them open for the quarters."

"The nerve. And you caught them? On a...stakeout?"

"Piece of honey cake like Mama used to make for Hanukkah. Set up a videocam. Filmed them at midnight. Two freshmen on a beer-money cruise. Pa-bloody-thetic."

"The college is open all night?"

"Sure. Cleaning staff, plus some computer labs." He opened a pack and offered her a cigarette. She hadn't seen an unfiltered Camel since Uncle Harold had died at eighty, a pack-a-day man for sixty years.

"I'm no purist, but I smoke only in bed." She left it at that, and one of Len's unkempt eyebrows rose in polite interest. An old boyfriend once told her, to her youthful shame, that she had no mystique. What a pretentious snob he'd been, president of Mensa at the University of Toronto. Even so, how would she ever know if she'd achieved any? And who cared, anyway?

"Let's eat." Len opened the boxes with a flourish. "Nigari special and California rolls."

Belle admired the artful arrangement of nestled rice morsels. "Sushi. Two decades to make it up from Toronto."

He laughed, passing a hand over his Friar Tuck head. "Should have gone FedEx. Hope it's still okay after all those years."

She tried the barbecued eel, spicy and firm like chicken. The sweet rice was packed around crispy pieces of vegetable, complemented by wasabi and shaved pink ginger. Her eyes watered at the mild green paste that packed the punch of a Patriot missile.

"So how is the investigation going?" Used to dealing with laconic Steve, a man who needed a nut-pick operation to divulge the slightest detail of an ongoing case, she levelled her gaze at him. "Or can't you tell me?"

He took off his thick glasses and rubbed his red, squiddish eyes. "I shouldn't disclose anything, but Dave trusts you and the DesRosiers, so—"

Trusts her? She must have made a good impression, despite her skepticism about private investigators. Enjoying a moment of self-satisfaction, Belle leaned forward. "You *have* found something!"

He opened what looked like a recipe box and selected a handful of file cards. "First off, let's look at the business. Did Bea get along with her employees? Nineteen out of twenty called her a saint. But..." He seemed to pause for effect, gauging her interest. "One guy wanted to start a union. Big-mouthed agitator. The Cesar Chavez of the North. Gimme a break."

Belle nodded. If the mighty unions couldn't crack Wal-Mart, what chance did they have at a small family business? "I can guess. He was fired."

"Yowsa." He snapped down another card, as if telling a fortune. Then he sucked his large, prominent teeth. "Sean Broughton."

"Sounds like a sweet and innocent Irish tenor."

"A real shit stirrer. He tried the same thing over at Weston and got canned there, too. Vandalized a few trucks at Bumble Bea, broke the front window, but they never proved it. I've been making the rounds to check his alibi that morning."

Belle nibbled another piece of sushi, licking a grain of rice from her lip. "Alibis. Not worth the paper they're written on. Friends, lovers, relatives. Everyone can lie."

"You're a bit cynical for a Northerner, dear lady." He cocked his head.

"Born and raised in Toronto."

He rocked back in the chair with a guffaw. "That explains it. We're in the same metro mindset. Now that vandalism. Could be he paid an accomplice. Someone with no connection to the business. A fast and dirty hundred would buy ten minutes from a drifter hanging out at the Coulson."

Belle's eyes widened with growing interest. The lumpen soldier of fortune had some savvy. She hadn't dreamed of a disinterested second party. "I see."

With a sigh, Len pulled a third card. "More people to check, but it's gonna take me a coon's age. I'm a one-man operation, and I can't afford help. Dave's stretched to the max, too, poor guy. His wife's insurance only came to ten thousand dollars. She borrowed on it for renos a couple of years ago, and the funeral cost twice that. You know those Italians. When I go, it's gonna be generic all the way. Maybe I'll even get composted."

Belle blinked, remembering the grandiose viewing at Johnson's Boneyard. She'd been unable to attend the funeral at St. Jean de Brebeuf, Sudbury's stateliest church, but it must have been nothing short of mayoral. Could she help? Micro would never reconcile with his stepfather unless this murder was solved. Placing a hand on the desk, she said, "As a realtor, I drive around town every day. It wouldn't take me much time to—"

"Would you? What a doll." Len leaped to his feet, slightly off balance with his bum leg. He grabbed her shoulder. "Now that you're on board, I gotta good feeling about this one."

As a start, he provided her with the name and particulars of the neighbour, Jean McBride, and they huddled like a football team while he mapped out strategy.

When she got home at six, still soaked from another downpour, a twenty-dollar parking ticket festering in her pocket, Belle found an urgent message from Hélène on her answering machine.

ELEVEN

The DesRosiers' six-year-old grandson in Ottawa had developed a high fever, and doctors suspected meningitis. Hélène and Ed were driving there immediately, despite the poor weather conditions, and would be away until he had passed the crisis. Could Micro stay with her? He had turned pale and quiet when they suggested that he return to Dave. No problem with school. He'd be back by five on the bus and could let himself in.

Though she might need to reschedule a few evening commitments, Belle could refuse them nothing, so often had they come through for her. "He's all packed and will ride over on his bike. We'll drop off the duffle," Hélène said, speaking rapidly as she called out directions to Ed. "I'll keep in touch every morning. And I've included a cookbook. If you run short on food, my freezer is yours. I marked the meatless casseroles."

"Be careful on Route 17. It's a killer." Two women had died near Sturgeon Falls the day before when a semi-trailer had crossed the line and forced their Civic into a rock cut. Sometimes snow could be an unexpected buffer against the cruel rib bones of the North.

Micro arrived at her door not much later, carrying a backpack, breathless but energized with new responsibilities. "Rusty's going to stay on guard at the house," he said as he stroked Freya, curious at the break in routine. "I'll go back to feed her. She drinks out of the lake. Her doghouse is insulated. And I locked my bike under your deck."

Belle sorted out the information, massaging a crease between her eyes that might signal her anxiety. In winter, she would have insisted the dog come along. She showed Micro the sofa bed in the basement rec room, where she'd turned on the long baseboards to chase the chill. Those babies would suck back hydro like pigs at a trough of maple syrup. She pointed out the half-bath nearby and issued the usual admonitions about not flushing paper. "I know," he said. "Aunt Hélène gave me a hassle. It's gross, though."

"If you want gross, try a septic tank full of papier mâché," she added with a grin.

After he had settled in, she gave him a tour of her computer room, its walls lined with bookcases. "Want to play *Grim Fandango?*" she asked. That creative art deco style game with Death as a travel agent had captivated her with its wry wit and salsa music. Then she bit her tongue. Nice subject for a boy with a murdered mother.

"I finished that one when I was a kid. I'm more into *Myst V* and *Dragonshard*. I brought them with me. And I get some hints from the chat lines. Is it okay if I play them?"

Belle did an internal eye roll at the first real problem. She hadn't discussed any Internet rules with the DesRosiers, nor did she have any locking software. Even her Sympatico e-mail brought the occasional spamwich about teenaged babes and their predilections for ungulates. "Sure. Just don't erase anything on my hard drive. And better stay off the net until I get permission from your aunt. You'd grow old waiting for pages to load with my tin-can-and-string phone lines. No high-speed connections out here."

Studying the shelves with an interested gaze, he pulled out a mushroom book, turning the pages. "Crossbones. Way cool. That means poison. My friend Chris's grandmother takes him with her to hunt them."

"Chill" had come and almost gone, but "cool" had mellowed like a fine Bordeaux. "I'm sure she chooses the right ones, but I wouldn't risk it." Micro rushed to hospital, poisoned in the woodswoman's care.

This emergency required a steep learning curve for an only child who'd fashioned a family from a pair of dogs, Nell the Border Collie, who died at thirteen, then Freya. If Hélène had brought a Siberian husky pack, Belle would have had them performing a ballet in minutes. As she watched him leaf through the book, she wondered if dogs and kids were similar, except that kids could talk. Fearsome difference. Her watch read eight o'clock. What was his bedtime? Did he watch much television? That was out, except for Turner Classics. Action pictures, horror or science fiction, not female weepers. How about homework?

"Micro," she began, standing awkwardly behind him as he replaced the mushroom book and selected *The Annotated Frankenstein*, opening the large coffee table book as his grin expanded. She saw a wicked set of eighteenth-century surgical implements, then a full-page dream sequence with gnarly tree roots morphing into a woman's long hair. "I thought that I held the corpse of my dead mother in my arms," one line said. This was no bedside reading.

"Awesome. I did a book report on the monster. All he needed was a friend." Belle smiled to herself at how well he had transcended the stereotype of the Karloff films. He yawned and stretched as Freya mirrored his actions in the doorway, and he focused a bit unsteadily on Belle. "I'm kind of tired. Do I have to have a bath? I'd rather read. Can I take this?"

Belle was absorbing data like a sponge on uppers. She felt her pulse racing, the easy control of a solitary life slipping away. Too much responsibility. What if something happened to him while... She realized that her clenched mouth was making her cheek muscle ache.

"Belle? What's wrong?"

She touched his thin shoulder, deceptively strong and wiry, a man under construction. "Nothing. No bath. Take a shower upstairs in the morning." She rapped her temple with the butt of her hand, trying to recall Hélène's rapid-fire instructions. No one could talk faster than an Italian. "Hold on. We'd better settle something now. How are you going to get to school again? I should know, but remind me."

He answered in a confident, logical flow chart. "A bus lady from the Catholic schools lives down the road. Aunt Hélène already called and told her to stop here. Seven thirty sharp. They'll leave me at St. Charles on Falconbridge Highway, the last catchment spot, and a taxi will take me to St. Francis."

Catchment. She was learning a new word every ten minutes. Belle went to bed wondering what might happen tomorrow, her sense of security sent spinning. Waking at midnight with an anxious bladder, she yanked herself over the edge of the waterbed, reluctant to leave its rolling warmth. Freya was gone, her sheepskin cold. Grumbling, she flicked on the lights, hit the bathroom, then crept down the carpeted stairs to the first floor, tiptoeing to the basement. With a brilliant pocked pumpkin moon gleaming through windows, she could see the dog curled up with Micro in a snoring competition on the sofa bed.

Belle was up at 6:05 a.m. with one snooze alarm, pouring

coffee in the kitchen as the sky reddened petticoat streaks above the far hills toward Outlet Bay. Sailors take warning. Rain trickled down her windows. Water covered her narrow sand beach and was lapping over the second stair of the railroad-tie retaining wall. Two feet higher than in May. Her rockwall was nearly submerged, including Big Marie, a five-foot boulder that had challenged the abilities of the hundred-dollar-an-hour backhoe operator.

Hélène called at six thirty, weary but positive. Their grandson was still in intensive care, treatment pending the results of a barrage of tests. "If he's as tough as you two, he's bound to rally," Belle said before they hung up. Then she realized that she had forgotten to ask about Internet access.

She drummed her fingers on the fridge door. Would Micro drink chocolate soy milk? Eat cheese and eggs and English muffins? No peanut butter or jelly. Not a flake of cereal passed her lips. Cold breakfasts left her the same way. Just her luck that he'd want something exotic like Count Chocula...or Frankenberries. If he was insistent, they could always make a dawn raid on the DesRosiers' cupboards.

She heard the water pump hum into action as the toilet flushed downstairs. Barefoot, Micro came into the kitchen, dressed in long black silk boxers and a black t- shirt, a change of clothes over his arm, his thick lashes heavy with sleep. "Freya wanted out," he said. "She was standing at the door. She's a great dog. A lot smarter than Buffalo. But I miss him."

"Good man. I put more towels for you in this bathroom." Then she raised her eyebrow. "Plenty of time for a shower."

He nodded and padded out. She had forgotten how groggy kids were in the morning. A hyper child, she had rarely slept well, and sometimes her father, the designated dresser, had come in to attach one sock, then the next as she dozed in bed.

That was why she never begrudged him a second of care. When she'd been a baby, he had nearly pinned her chubby thigh to a diaper, but at least he had made the effort in a time when men left nurturing tasks to their wives.

Twenty minutes later, Micro emerged in clean pants and a cotton pullover. Belle crouched at the woodstove in the living room, shovelling out ashes. She looked up with a grin and handed him an insulated gauntlet. "Want to make yourself useful, as my mother used to say? Take this bucket outside to the parking area. Even with all this rain, I can't dump ashes in the bush until they're totally dead. Be really careful not to spill them down the hall or onto yourself."

While she was still crumpling papers, Micro returned to warm his hands by the stove. "You heat the whole place with this?"

She urged the fire into action, adding cardboard, kindling, then a couple of maple pieces, letting her rip. The cascading crackles in the pipe told her that creosote was building up. No time for a lazy-man's controlled chimney fire now. This weekend maybe she'd play it safe and climb onto the roof with her Roto-rooter brushes.

Checking the keys for the draft, she laughed. "Propane is my backup. The furnace goes on until I get this going in the morning. Once I get the stove charged, it's good for the day."

He wiped his face. "It's really warm. No sweaters like at home. You could wear a bathing suit."

Refilling her coffee as he settled at the kitchen table, she asked, "OJ? And what else do you...drink?"

He assumed an offhand look and pursed his lips. "Oh, coffee. Lots of milk. Mom calls it a latte."

Mom calls it. His heart hadn't accepted what his mind understood. She was no psychologist, but she judged this as a normal response. One day at a time.

A toasted English muffin with aged cheddar cheese worked for both of them. Warming milk for the latte and pouring out the juice, she felt strangely awkward, compelled to keep making conversation with her guest, yet wondering if he preferred a quiet early morning as she did.

Noticing the time approaching the magic seven thirty, she stood up suddenly as she remembered another duty. "Lunch? I don't know what I..."

Swallowing the last bite of muffin and blotting his mouth with a serviette, he waved his hand. "No problem. We have a caf at school." As if to anticipate her next question, he pulled out a small Velcro wallet and pointed to a bank card. "I have my own account from the websites I've made. I've saved over two thousand dollars for university."

Belle nodded, impressed. "I hope you have that invested. Savings accounts pay pennies these days with low inflation." She explained the advantages of money-market accounts and mutual funds.

"What's 'liquidity' mean?"

At the office, Miriam had booked off with a migraine, but the phone didn't ring, and no one walked in the door. As she left work late that afternoon, Belle did some studious shopping, having consulted the cookbook that arrived with Micro: *Where's the Meat?* was a sensible manual for parents with vegetarian children. What she needed was *Precocious Child-Rearing for Dummies,* complete with self-correcting exercises. By the time she was home, he was cycling back from feeding Rusty.

"Now about dinner," she began hesitantly as he climbed to the deck, the key to his aunt's house on a string around his neck. "Refried-bean-and-cheese burritos okay? Fresh tomatoes from my garden."

"I can make real rice in the microwave to complete the nutrition triangle. It always comes out perfect. Mom taught me a few tricks in the kitchen." His voice was bittersweet, but that was the second time he had mentioned Bea, a healthy start in resuming his life.

She felt like touching his hand, which rested on the deck rail like an innocent brown mouse. "I liked her very much, Micro. She was a great lady. Not every woman can run a successful business and handle a family at the same time." Too sexist, she thought, adding, "Nor can a man."

"My dad was a doctor," he said with a wistful expression. "I wish I could be like him, help people, but I'm more into computers."

"Computers help people all the time. Hospitals and labs couldn't run without them. And children don't always follow the family profession," she said. Then she explained her father's job as a film booker, and Micro's eyes glinted with flecks of gold in the autumn sun falling behind the purple western hills. "You got free passes to every show in town? Wow! I bet everyone wanted to be your friend."

TWELVE

On Saturday, Belle had a viewing in Mallard's Green subdivision south of town. Since Micro said that his best pal Chris Forth wanted to see the new Vin Diesel action picture, he drove in with her. So far she appreciated three things about the boy: he was quiet, he was a quick learner, and he never complained that he was bored, an annoying adolescent trait. As they bumped over the former rail crossing near the beginning of her road, he asked, "No trains any more? I remember seeing tracks here."

She explained that as competition from truck traffic eliminated unprofitable routes, the rails had been lifted a few years ago, leaving a raised path of dark slag. "This is now part of the TransCanada Trail," she said, pointing east. "That way leads to the Ashigami Lake area and eventually into Temagami, with its magnificent virgin pines." She noticed that he giggled at the last few words, but left him his joke. Explaining the mysteries of sex was not in her job description. "Bikers use it, horseback riders and snowmobiles and quads, too." Purists in southern Ontario, happy to make choices for their northern brethren, wanted motorized vehicles banned, but remote wilderness regions needed both. Sudbury bridged the gap.

She slowed at the dip by Philosopher's Pond, one of many kettle lakes left by the last glacier, and began to climb the steep hill toward the mailboxes. "If you sponsor parts of the trail, your name goes on a kiosk. I bought three metres in Saskatchewan for my mother. She was born in Saskatoon."

His eyes sparkled at the idea. "How much?"

"It used to be less, but the current rate is seventy-five dollars a metre."

"Hiking is neat. My dad took me to Windy Lake, and we did the 10 K trail." Then his voice softened. "That was the summer he and my sister..." He rested his head against the window.

At a bungalow on Churchill Drive in New Sudbury, they picked up Chris, a sweet blond boy, towering over Micro, with a winning smile, the usual baggy jeans, sweatshirt and a Jays cap on backwards. "Nice to meet you," his mother Penny said as she waved them off and a middle-aged woman scissored herself out of a car and limped to the door. Chris explained that Penny was a registered massage therapist who worked out of her home and was studying to be a doctor. "And she's forty-five!" Chris said as his mother groaned and mimed a swat.

Then they took Barrydowne Road to nearby Silver City on the Kingsway, a megatheatre with fifteen screens. Belle had been there only once. She preferred to remember sitting at the top of the second balcony in the old Uptown, one of Toronto's stately queens built in 1920 in the days when the building itself entertained.

The boys were arguing in the back, some obscure point in *Lord of the Rings*. "No, Sauron was—"

"Was not. Don't you remember..."

Belle tuned out the din. One boy, peace. Two boys, all hell breaks loose. Then, despite her efforts, she heard a word which hit like a slap. "You retard!" The van rocked as they shoved each other.

She pulled into Midas Muffler, stopped, and leaned over

the seat, arching one eyebrow until it ached. This last gesture got their attention. "Retardation is a medical condition, nothing to joke about. My cousin Nick has...Down's Syndrome. He's the dearest person in the world."

Chris said with a stricken voice, "But we..."

Micro added, "We're sorry. We didn't know."

"Next time amaze your friends and use a more creative word. 'Buffoon,' 'bumpkin,' 'clod.' 'Jerk' is short and effective." They settled down, probably wondering if she were going to cancel the show. Belle stifled a chuckle. A lie about "Nick," of course, but it brought home the concept. She wasn't guiltless. When she had been their age, the insult du jour was "spastic" or "spas". Her purple-inked diary a la Mary Astor had fifty variations, including "spasmopolitan".

At the theatre entrance, eyeballing the times, Belle opened her wallet and pulled out forty dollars as their faces broke into smiles. "My treat. Play some video games in the lobby afterwards if I'm not back exactly at five." She aimed a finger like a gun. "And not too much popcorn or candy," she added. Setting limits would be expected. She hadn't known Bea, but she'd bet the woman knew where to draw the line in the shifting sands of youth.

The showing at Mallard's Green went well. Belle hosted ten people. Just in time to prevent a major mudslide from the constant rain, the quick-fix sodding and mature mugho pines and junipers from Hollandia Nursery Landscaping had transformed the handsome new brick model with double garage into an established home. Two couples said that they were definitely interested and would call Monday with an offer.

"Yessssss!" she yelled to herself at 4:45 as she packed her attaché case. No problem vetting. One couple drove an Infiniti, the other a Jaguar. They could play off against each other and better the builder's price; $275,000 wasn't chump change. Costa Rican cloud forest on the horizon. A new fridge with a pull-out bottom freezer to replace the shuddering cottage orphan.

She had noticed through the early afternoon that the wind had picked up, blowing plastic bags across the lawn. The day had been overcast, and she had watched a woman walking a brindle boxer and struggling with a broken umbrella. The more sheltered streets of a city gave a false sense of security. As she entered the van and paused to wipe her glasses, she knew Wapiti would be a raging monster if this continued. She felt like buying dynamite, driving to Outlet Bay, and blasting the dam wide open. Tough luck, cottagers downstream. Why didn't man leave Mother Nature alone?

As she crossed town, stoplights cha-cha'd in wild abandon. This wasn't hurricane country, but close enough. Hazel and Connie had rampaged through Ontario decades ago. The radio was reporting flooded camps along the rivers which fed Lake Nipissing. The boys were waiting on the steps of Silver City, pointing at paper cups and wrappers soaring forty feet into the air. Excitement lit their faces, another video game, but with deadly potential.

After they'd dropped Chris off, Micro got into the front and described his favourite "FX," mainly a car chase, which he orchestrated in detail. Instead of listening, Belle was fixated on the road. They swept through foot-deep puddles in Garson as the sewers jammed, sending wings of gritty spray onto the empty sidewalks. After the van hydroplaned as she navigated Radar Road, a cross-draft sent them over the centre line on the high hill of the airport approach, narrowly missing a taxi. Rain spattered the windshield and greased the asphalt. Her wipers were set to max, frantically clearing the water. She glanced over with relief to see that Micro wore his belt. Some mother. She hadn't even reminded him. How many second chances did she deserve?

At the mailboxes at her turn, the deluge was so paralyzing that she paused for ten minutes to let the worst of the storm pass. Micro's eyes were wide as platters. "Is this a hurricane?"

"Near enough. Keep an eye out ahead for me."

As they finally proceeded along Edgewater Road, plastic trash cans from garbage collection day rolled like bowling balls. She bashed one, sending it spinning into the bush. "Should we get out to—" Micro asked.

"Let the drivers beware. We need to get home. I've been watching a leaning cedar for some time. This could be its final hour."

They pulled into the yard as gale-force blasts from the treacherous northwest lashed the bloated lake against her rock wall. Silvery spume flew thirty feet in the air. Micro stepped from the van with his mouth open, wiping his eyes.

"Let Freya out." She walked toward the fatal tree near the property line with the McNairs. Now cracked vertically at the base, it leaned against a smaller cedar, the sole barrier shielding it from the hydro and phone lines which led across the parking lot, over the deck and into the house. Her eyes teared from the buffeting wind as Micro returned with Freya. Even the dog's wise old black brows circumflexed in fear. Always cool in a crisis, she'd ridden out many a storm by hunkering down in a tent with her mistress. Many dogs would have blasted through the sides of the flimsy shelter when a lightning bolt hit nearby.

Belle pointed to the tree. "I've got to call someone to come out and cut this son of a...gun. Take the dog in when she's finished. And we should check your house, too." An odd statement. His house. As if he had always lived down the road.

In a short time, she'd grown used to having him around, like a brother or, she realized, a son.

Inside, sifting the white pages, she punched in the emergency number, rolling through ridiculous menus, chewing her lip as the time passed. The wind roared like a banshee, sucking drafts up the stovepipe and rattling the windows. She heard the door open and close as Micro and Freya returned, the dog's chain collar clinking as she shook herself dry. "Hey, I'm already wet enough, girl," he said with a laugh.

Finally, a human voice answered. "Your number shows that you are in the Sudbury region."

Was this call outsourced to Bangladesh? Furious, she managed even tones. No use letting them think a hysterical woman was exaggerating a harmless predicament. "Yes. Edgewater Road. A fallen tree is threatening my power line. I need a crew out here. Pronto."

The robotic voice seemed to select sentences from a training manual. "Is the tree in question in contact with your lines?"

"Tree in...no, but we're having a terrible storm, and it—"

"Sorry, but you will have to call a tree service. Unless the...not responsible for..." The woman had perfected the art of governmentese.

"But I—"

"Hydro One has over 122,000 kilometres of power lines. Our priorities dictate that—"

Belle hung up with a growl and charged out onto the deck, feeling like the beleaguered captain of the *Edmund Fitzgerald*. The master-suite balcony above her gave feeble shelter in the ferocious gusts. The sweet little fir that she'd saved from the axe when she built loomed up in front of the deck, its branches heaving like a beast. Her poplar grove beside the boathouse thrashed in riotous disarray. To the right, a greenbelt, she wasn't worried. Those trees would fall away from her property. She stared in mute amazement at the valiant rockwall, bracing against waves advancing in huge swells like a relentless army, every seventh whitecap a monstrous blow. Her neighbours had lost their dock and front grass last year. Anyone who thought living on waterfront property was paradise should witness this. Or maybe not. If they did, she'd never sell another cottage.

In a realtime FX, she saw her twenty-foot dock system, from the boathouse to the crib carrying the satellite dish, lifting off as neatly as sliced layer cake. The massive structure was floating free, tethered only by the dollar-a-foot umbilical cord of coaxial cable. Back and forth it rolled as she watched in helpless horror. Into the bay, then toward the boathouse, a lifeless thing powered by the force of ten locomotives. In minutes it would smash the building to pieces. Her insurance company would never pay. God's will. Hydro's will. The mysterious keeper of the dam was probably watching CTV as he enjoyed his dinner.

Micro came to her side, wiping rain from his face. She placed a hand on his shoulder, trying to keep panic from her voice, fighting back tears as she watched her world explode. "What happened?" he asked.

"The dock's old. It came apart. I have to cut that cable and send it away from the boathouse. Go back inside before you get drenched."

She ran down the stairs, soaked in seconds by the downpour, grabbing an axe propped beside the woodpile. Then she stood stupidly, assessing the logistics. Can't chop through water. Entering the boathouse, she rummaged in her toolboxes for the sheet-metal shears.

Standing on the breakfront which overlooked her beach,

she shook her head at the bitter realities, taking off her useless glasses and pocketing them. What seemed possible from the deck looked suicidal up-close. She'd have to wade into freezing water, avoiding at her peril the lurching dock, which could pin her against the rock base and squeeze her like a slug. As the wooden whale returned, moving its bulk in surprising ease, it knocked against one of the huge creosoted beams which anchored the building. The boathouse shuddered like a wounded mammoth. Belle gasped. Another assault would leave a pile of pick-up sticks. For once she wished for the muscles of a man and a warm dive suit. The dock was toast, but the boathouse still stood, the greater investment. She'd call Johnny Salvalaggio, her handyman. Perhaps he could also cut the tree, though without a cherry picker, a dangerous chore in the wind.

Throwing down the shears with a *"hostie,"* she went inside and dialled, finding his line busy. Too much to hope that Charlton Heston's magical Moses hand would gesture across Wapiti and still the waters. Then through the windows she imagined she saw movement on the retaining wall. She blinked and took another look. A small form jumped onto the beach and waded into the bay.

Belle left the house on a run, down the stairs, waving her hands, slipping on the bottom platform and sprawling across the lawn. "Micro! Come back!"

The howling wind tossed her words into her face. The boy's clothes nearly pulled him under as he urged himself toward the cable, the wooden platform shifting to the right. Another barrage of water hit the wall, hiding him for a moment as it crashed down. She jumped onto the sand, wading in, stumbling to her knees on the mossy stones, reaching out her hand. Then she saw the snips flash and flash again. Now detached, the dock floated off, lodging in a rocky shallows, harmless at last.

They walked down the beach and climbed to the grass, huddling like soaked rats. He handed her the snips as she looked at him with a mixture of fury and admiration, searching his face for bruises. The green eyes were cool and clear. "You could have killed yourself...and Hélène would have murdered me." And Dave? His stepson had been parked with a lunatic. This was one story that would never be told, except in a sanitized version. Already she began drafting a conspiracy of silence for their partnership.

He was making a valiant effort not to shiver, losing the battle as his soft lips quivered. She hugged his small frame, and they made their way up the patio-stone path to the basement, where Freya paced nervously behind the glass doors. "I want you up to your neck in a hot bath while I make some cocoa."

His chattering teeth made no reply as they climbed to the main floor. Belle knew how icy that water was. Only in a two-week window at the end of July did she dare swim in her bay. Micro might have suffered respiratory failure from shock the minute the water reached his waist. If she hadn't been in triage mode, she might have pulled a scene-stealing swoon.

The woodstove could wait, damn the cost of propane. She switched on the furnace, heard its ignition and felt the warm rush of air. She dried off and changed into jeans and a sweater. Meanwhile she heard him splashing in the tub, while she hauled blankets and a heating pad to the TV room, making a nest. Tomorrow when she got Johnny for the tree, she'd tell him to arrange for a backhoe to relocate the dock to a burn pile at the water's edge. She should have replaced the monster long ago, but built by a mine foreman with access to "free" supplies, it was full of ten-inch spikes and built with timbers from grandfather pines. It was forty-six years old, a kindred spirit. Still, this was going to cost. Repairs were impossible until spring, when the lake was frozen and the bay dry for a few crucial days.

Micro emerged in his pyjamas, a sheepish look on his mild brown face. Was that café au lait a bit heavy on the lait? "No TV. The dish is defunct." She settled him into the pasha chair with the Frankenstein book and a mug of cocoa. In the kitchen, she whipped up comfort food for soaked vegetarians: tomato soup and grilled cheese.

He adapted easily to her habit of dinner Roman style on lounges. They ate ravenously. After she'd taken out the plates and loaded the dishwasher, she returned to shuffle through a pile of videotapes. *Hitler's Children* might give him a window on teen life in a fascist society where young minds were poisoned early. The timely film of 1942, which beat out RKO's *King Kong* for top grosser, was shameless propaganda. Tim Holt played a young storm trooper struggling with his love for Bonita Granville, his childhood sweetheart. The grim climax pulled no punches and included a flogging in a concentration camp. Swastikas filled the screen, jackboots marched, and children turned in their parents. Too violent? A cakewalk next to the Rings films. Halfway through, she glanced over, surprised to see a tear on his face.

"Want to cut out of this? How about John Wayne in *Rio Bravo?* It's a western," she added, mindful of the age gap. He'd probably never heard of the Duke.

He shook his head, eyes downcast. "I did it."

"Did what?"

"Painted those swastikas at the old people's home."

Belle's spine stiffened as she remembered what Steve said about the vandalism at the Ukrainian Seniors' Centre. "Do you understand what that symbol meant? Do you take world history?"

124

"Not until high school." He sighed. "It was Tom Beerchuk's idea. He bought the spray cans. Called me a chicken. I went along, and painted one, but it didn't feel right. He was a...a...jerk."

Belle felt herself at an unusual loss for words. She tried to put herself in the place of someone for whom wars were a media event, like the charge of tanks across the Iraqi desert. George Bush, with modern psychological noise tactics, could have blasted Celine Dion's version of "I Drove All Night" as the troops moved toward Baghdad while Wolf Blitzer narrated.

She watched him sink into the pile of blankets. Despite his heroics and intelligence, he was a boy new to the complexities of emotional maturity. To him Hitler was a cartoon figure knocking down bodies that popped up again like Wiley E. Coyote. "A swastika meant death to millions and still traumatizes those who starved or lost their families in the concentration camps," she finally said.

Maybe she should introduce him to Jesse, her Jewish friend, who'd escaped Germany as a girl. She leaned back and tried to remember life at twelve. One image came to mind, and she flushed with guilt as childish laughter on dark streets and the feel of a cake of soap returned in fractured images. "I can't be too hard on you, Micro. In seventh grade..." One Hallowe'en, long past the costume stage, she and a thrill-seeking friend had drawn swastikas on car windows. She shivered as the wind battered on. "I'd heard about the Nazis in silly songs. I didn't know the facts." Her weapon was soap, easy to remove, but the result was as cruel.

"Am I going to go to jail?" His voice quavered, and he nuzzled his sleeve.

This was a secret which couldn't be kept. The difference was clear. She went to the bathroom and returned with a mound of tissues. "It's a first step to accept the responsibility like a man. You'll have to pay for the cost of removing the paint, and maybe do some community service at the Ukrainian home. Like raking leaves or cleaning up. But I hope you'll talk to the elders. I can make the arrangements, pave the way."

He pooched out his bottom lip. "They'll hate me."

"Nothing is more lovable than a reformed sinner, Micro." She paused. She was to blame tonight for not keeping an eye on him. "And about the dock. Best not say anything, or I'll get into plenty of trouble, my friend."

He smiled and nodded, pulling up the blankets as his eyes started to close. An early bed was the best idea, she thought. That cold would have sapped an adult with ample body fat. As she got up to turn off the TV, an ear-splitting crack made them jump, and the room went black. Though she feared the worst, Belle put a hand on his arm. "I'll get the flashlights. Power outages happen several times a year here. At least it's not -35°C. And we're not shampooing our hair. And there's plenty of Kraft Dinner."

She felt along the hall to the closet by the entrance where she kept her emergency gear: Coleman lanterns, stove and propane canisters. Flicking on a flashlight, with caution and apprehension she opened the door to the deck, closing it quickly in reflex action, her mind assessing immediate danger. The damn cedar had fallen across the lines and into the yard. Live wires snapped and sizzled red sparks across the deck like a diabolic whip. If she'd been touching the metal screen door, she might have been electrocuted.

Grabbing her coat and keys, Belle fumbled her way to the TV room, the beam playing on Micro's questioning face as she handed him another flashlight. "Get dressed and get your school things. The hydro's down across the deck, and we have to leave by the basement door. We'll head around the far side of the house, and if the van's clear, go down to your place."

Minutes later, holding Freya's collar, she led Micro to the van, a safe distance from the wires. Soon they were at the DesRosiers', and she was on the phone punching menus. Groundhog Day. The same woman answered.

"Me again. Hate to be a nag, but that tree has taken the wires. Your refusal to come out earlier nearly fried three of us, including a child." She gave both addresses and numbers. Crews all over Northern Ontario were in the field. Help wouldn't arrive until morning, if they were lucky.

THIRTEEN

Belle's eyes snapped open at 5:55 a.m. in the strange bed, an innerspring horror, sagging like a swayback horse. The DesRosiers' marriage must be ironclad. She'd been crawling up the sides all night. The bird clock in the kitchen, a different trill, peep or hoot every hour, had kept her awake. Using the number Hélène had given her, she learned that Ottawa had received the tail end of the storm. Belle downplayed their situation.

"Those scoundrels at Hydro One," Hélène said. "We have to pay off the debt they accumulated, giving mismanagement a golden parachute, and they leave us freezing in the dark. I hope you slept well in our bed. There were extra blankets in the linen closet. Isn't that bird clock a scream?"

"You bet." Belle passed over the phone, nodded, and Micro delivered a perfect scenario, excitement without danger, and certainly no boys in icy bays.

The DesRosiers were returning tomorrow, now that the crisis with their grandson had passed. A bladder infection had led to the same blood poisoning that had killed Muppeteer Jim Hanson. Massive antibiotics had stabilized the youngster, and he was eating for two.

After a breakfast of corn flakes, Belle watched Micro shoulder his backpack, his quick stride marching off to conquer the day with the optimism of youth. She'd miss his natural curiosity and winsome presence. "This weekend we can check out a heronry. The birds are gone now, but the nests are still there. Big guys." She spread her arms to demonstrate the wingspan.

"Uncle Ed has binoculars. I'll bring them."

"To get there, we go through an old maple syrup tapping area. You can see the rusted pots and pans."

He nodded in enthusiasm. So many places to take him, things to teach him. Leaves of three, let them be. White pines have five needles, five letters. Solomon's seal, false vs. real. Now she realized, despite Freya's companionship, the delights of being the mentor of an appreciative pupil. One impulse in a vernal wood. "It's a date, then."

She paused about the day's logistics, wondering what mothers of six did. "Here's my cellphone number. I'll stay until help comes, but later I could be out of the office. If you don't see the van at my place, come back here. The repair crew might be on Manitoulin time," she said, referring to the sleepy island community west of Sudbury as she passed him a slip of paper.

A man from Hydro One called around nine to tell her that with luck, they'd be finished by two. "Lucky the pole didn't snap, lady. That would be a hell of a job, digging around in this rock."

When she arrived at work, Miriam was starting a second pot of coffee. "What a storm. Branches are down all over town. A monster in my parking lot just missed the Jetta."

Belle related their terrors of the day before. "You could have been electrocuted," her cohort said, her face paling and her hand on her ample chest.

"You don't know the half of it." Belle took the chance of telling her about Micro's swim.

"Kids!" Miriam said with a wave of exasperation from one long in the trenches. "I've been telling you for years why my hair went grey at thirty-five, thanks to Rosanne and her shenanigans, not to mention my ex-husband. Jack never did grow up. *Calice.* That's part of his charm."

Swinging over to do a routine appraisal for an apartment building on Westmount, a lucrative assignment, Belle worked through lunch, made more calls and was free by three to talk to Jean McBride, Bea's hearing-impaired neighbour. Not totally deaf, she assumed, hoping she wouldn't need an interpreter from the Sign Language Program at Nickel City College. Len had told her that the woman never answered her phone and rarely went out, getting groceries delivered.

Jean's keyhole property, likely one of the original summer camps on Lake Ramsey, lay on the other side of a thick hedge bordering Bea's secret garden. The property to the left was a three-storey apartment building which loomed over the cottage like a colossus, another zoning fiasco or perhaps money greasing palms. Belle walked up the neat pebble path to a Seven Dwarves cottage, lacking only a thatched roof, and darkened by two massive blue spruce. Bird feeders and driftwood sculptures dotted the tiny yard in the midst of variegated hostas, Clintonia blue beads, rose twisted stalk, and lilies of the valley, wisely chosen shade-loving plants. The rounded front door, newly varnished, had a medieval grill covering an octagonal window. She knocked with the little brass lion head...and knocked...and knocked. Perhaps Jean was outside. Belle followed a narrow walkway which led behind the house.

In the minuscule backyard fringed with reddening sumac bushes and their soft purple cones, she saw a tiny person kneeling, dressed in an oversized man's shirt and jeans, digging compost into a vegetable bed, sparing a corner chive patch with its clovery mauve blooms. Belle hallooed as she approached, wary of startling the elderly woman.

"Miss McBride," she said three times, then yelling above the curly silver hair pinked with scalp.

The woman turned, peering up at her with bright eyes set like blueberries in a muffin face. Slowly she rose, bracing herself on the hand trowel. With her knee pads, she resembled a superannuated hockey player. "What's all the noise about? State your business. And no, I don't want to sell. Damn realtors hound you to your grave. That one with the Dolly Parton hair pesters me every May. Who needs a calendar?"

Swallowing a grin about Cynthia Cryderman's perseverance, Belle took a seat on a stump and explained her mission.

Jean's prickliness eased, now relaxed in a wicker chair, knobby hands folded in her lap. "A nice boy, young Michael. Bea sent him over every Friday with a pie. Not much left of that family now. And Dr. Bustamante always made house calls when I had the pneumonia. Dave was too busy to even chat over the hedge. I saw the whole thing happen."

Belle shifted on her perch, working around a splinter. "What whole thing?"

Jean rose, her legs stiff with arthritis, coughing into her hand. "The old pump needs a bit of priming. I'll be back in a jiffy with a pot of tea strong enough to trot a mouse."

Gallop was more like it. Ten minutes later, Belle poured on the cream and waited for the woman to continue. Old folk living alone traded information for entertainment, and she didn't begrudge them fair exchange.

"Now where was I? Cobwebs, be gone. Oh, the accident. There they were on a fine summer morning, sitting peaceful in the canoe, little Molly with a fishing line and Michael helping her put on the bait. She was squeamish like kids are, girls especially. Then out of nowhere, that stupid speedboat." Sorrow creased her pale face, papery as a hydrangea.

Even sixty-four-square-mile Lake Wapiti could be crossed in minutes by a behemoth with GMC engines throbbing under the deck in a hundred-thousand-dollar orgasm. How many times had Belle's canoe nearly been swamped when returning from a peaceful voyage to Flowergull Island?

"Gave the damn fool ten years for manslaughter and other reckless charges. Hear he got out this spring. These parole boards are criminal in their leniency. And what's more, a friend of mine who knows his family says he blamed the poor folk he killed for robbing him of his prime." She barked a laugh of outrage.

While Belle filed another suspect away in her memory bank, she coaxed Jean back to the present with a few gentle verbal prods. The old woman related what she'd heard or seen the day of Bea's death, namely nothing. She'd been in bed with a perishing cold, watching a mind-numbing cycle of talk shows. "Oprah's the only one worth a hill of beans. Yanks had any sense, they'd run her for VP alongside Hillary."

"I agree. Women need their own chance to ruin the country."

Jean clucked her tongue and rapped Belle's knee. "Oh, you."

As Belle thanked her and turned to go, Jean cocked her head and placed a finger on her blunt nose, Columbo-style. "There is one odd thing. Putting away my garden for the winter, I found a bone last week smack dab in my peony bed."

"A bone? Human?" Belle felt a warning frisson. Bones and the bush, yes, often a hundred years old, lost hunters, injured prospectors, First Nations casualties. Bones and the city, no moss there.

"'Course not. Father was a chiropractor, and he made us recognize all 206 parts of the skeleton. We start out with plenty more, but the little guys fuse." She pointed to her knee. "What's this?"

Belle played along. "Patella."

"And this?" She touched her thicker, shorter arm bone.

Belle ceded the game though the answer was obvious. "I give up."

"Radius. Now you've learned something." She ambled to a garbage can, opened it and retrieved a giant bovine knucklebone. "My clever little foxes must have scavenged it up from that Buffalo's dog house. Dirty bugger. Got loose and pooped on my pachysandra." She pointed to the edge of the Malanuk property.

Belle examined it. Whistle clean. But there were gnawed abrasions. Small incisors and large canines. As the sun dipped, she rotated it for better light. One tooth mark was chipped. Didn't Buffalo have a broken incisor? "May I take it?"

"If you're desperate for soup, be my guest. I'll get a bag." The twinkle in Jean's faded hazel eyes revealed a dry sense of humour.

Driving home, Belle wondered if the bone had been heavy with meat, according to her original theory. Would it have been possible to soak it with something to put the dog to sleep for a short time? Was there enough residue for a test? She called Steve on her cell, but voice mail said that he was away for the week. Damn. Another bone to pick. And what about that recently released killer, full of anger and possible revenge? She hadn't even gotten his name. Some sleuth.

When Belle arrived home a bit later than usual, she saw the wires back up and Micro's bike by her deck, endearing symbol of a soul. People too crass to mind their own business always asked why she'd never married, never had children, though the two weren't inseparable. An angled eyebrow usually squelched the questions. Genes and upbringing had worked a tight combination. Her mother had taken eight years to produce her. Not the warm, sitcom type, but a dedicated career woman, she never cooed at babies, never asked Belle "when". Her father would have enjoyed spoiling ten, but it wasn't up to him. Belle also recalled the personal hells her friends had suffered with their little replications: credit card theft, drugs, stints at Cecil Facer Youth Centre, the spectre of pregnancy, even HIV/AIDS. His one indiscretion aside, Micro was a sweet miracle, but how many young princes walked the earth? Then she thought again. "Indiscretion" was hardly the word for vandalism. How easy to rationalize when you cared for someone. Breaking out of her reverie, she noticed thick black smoke pouring from the chimney instead of the light grey trace of a low fire. Had he been fooling with the stove?

Up the stairs she went two at a time, banged through the door, tripping over Freya, rushing on with an aching wrist. In the living room, a soft womp-woof was issuing from the cherry red pipe. The stove keys were wide open, and all of her cardboard, charred history. The cast-iron pot of water on top for humidity had boiled dry. Quickly she twirled the keys shut and waited, her hands shaking as she monitored the burn, eying the extinguisher in the corner. How many years since she'd had it recharged? Without air, the fire soon died. She inspected the twelve-foot pipe for damage, tapping it with a poker and listening like a piano tuner. Safe enough. Then she turned with narrowed eyes. That pot had cost fifty dollars. If it cracked...

She found him in the computer room, immersed in *Lara Croft, Tomb Raider 2*. Jungle tom-toms duelled with the rising blood pressure beating in her ear drums. As Micro mowed down a trio of trolls, she punched off the speakers. He looked up, laughing. "Hey, Belle. Sorry about the sound. I'll turn it down. How about this chain gun? See what—"

"Come, please," she said, and he followed, his face

confused at her clipped tones.

Before the stove, a silent witness, he stood quietly, his face milk-mild except for a nervous twitch in one eye. "Didn't I load it right? I watched you. And I got rid of all that—"

"Micro." She blew out a deep sigh, rolled her head to relax, a weight-room cliché. The temperature was nearly 33°C, Phoenix in Northern Ontario. "You started a chimney fire. The room could have ignited at those temperatures." She pointed to the honey-pine cathedral ceiling, the black pipe joining the shiny insulated chimney that went through the roof. "You and Freya would have escaped, but my house would have been a pile of ashes."

He lowered his head, Freya's gesture when caught eating birch bark or a rotten mushroom. "I'm sorry. We weren't here last night, and there was no fire. I wanted to make it warm for you when you got home. You didn't tell me not to. Is it okay now? Are you going to tell Aunt Hélène?"

"Probably. I'm thinking about it." Only one sentence lingered from his apology. *You didn't tell me not to.* Now there was a concept worthy of a marble inscription. She willed her heart to drop from bass to snare. Surely she'd come out of this a better person, if she lived.

He turned away and said so quietly that she bent to hear, "I brought you something I made in art class."

On the kitchen table sat a brown ceramic bear about two inches high, in credible detail, glazed carefully, its black button eyes glistening.

"It's beautiful," she said, picking it up. He nodded and shuffled to the computer room, where she heard the machine shut off. Belle took another spin on the emotional roller coaster of child care. Now she felt guilty. He'd only been trying to help.

Their dinner of meatless chili and cornbread was punctuated by periods of silence. Hoping to show a positive side of the other night's theme, she played *Edge of Darkness* with Errol Flynn fighting Nazis in Norway. Belle had been fond of the mustachioed Tasmanian devil and his derring-do, even if he porked up at the end and started dating a jail-bait blonde, Beverly Aadland. Who else would title his autobiography *My Wicked, Wicked Ways?* Micro kept quiet, but his body language showed that he followed the action with interest. His small fists gripped the chair arms during the tense chase scenes.

The next morning she waved him off to the bus. "Your aunt and uncle will be home by noon. They can come back for your duffle. The door's always open." She wanted him to assume both meanings.

"Thanks, Belle. I'm sorry about...everything." Did one handsome little lip tremble as he turned to trot off at the bus lady's annoyed toot? That a small boy would be so universally sorry this early in his life left her sure that discipline was a necessary but ever-evolving torture. As the bus pulled away, she remembered that she had forgotten to mention the ceramic bear.

At the office, she called Len about the bone. "I've got it in a paper bag," she said, explaining the details. Steve had told her about the perils of plastic for evidence preservation.

"Good show," he said. "We need to test for residue."

"Surely we should let the police do that."

He roared out a stream of guffaws like a disapproving seal. "You've already contaminated it by removing it from the scene, my dear. Even if something turned up, they wouldn't be able to use the evidence in court. Not to worry. I know a discreet professor of Forensic Chemistry at Shield University. Used her in my last case. She'll do a complete scan for suspicious substances."

"But if the police don't—"

"Have you heard of a parallel investigation? That's what we're doing here. If there's a toxic substance, we can trace the source, for example, find a paper trail. Dave's counting on us."

He came by the office to collect the bone around four, engaging Miriam in conversation for fifteen minutes while Belle finished a phone call.

"Speaking of bones, where did you dig up this rascal?" Miriam asked, wiping tears of laughter from her face as Len perched his ample rump on her desk. He wore a rumpled tweed suit which made him a double for Mr. Toad, especially the umbrella under his arm. "His life sounds like a movie script."

Len apparently took the comment as a compliment as he inspected the bone like a piece of fine china, careful not to add his own prints. "Heavy little guy. Perfect murder weapon."

An avid mystery reader, Miriam said with a smirk, "The fatal leg of lamb. Roald Dahl's classic. The perfect crime." She peered over her bifocals at Len. "You're the expert. Is there such an animal?"

He pursed his fleshy lips in an all-knowing smile. "Definitely. But you never find out about it, so there's the rub, as Hamlet says."

"It's a beef bone." Refusing to join the silliness, Belle crossed her legs at her desk. "Any other developments, Len?" She needed to ask about that killer boat driver, but why not let him set the groundwork?

He related that he had finished interviews at the bakery, including chasing down a Donald Trump wannabe who was eying the choice downtown real estate with an eye to building a luxury condo for seniors. But he was having difficulty locating Sean Broughton, the unionizer Bea had fired. He flipped open a notebook and shook his head as he gave a description of the lowlife. "NFA. That's 'no fixed address.' I tipped a green one to the bartender at the Ledo. He said that Broughton's living out in Massey, frequents the Old Mill, but my beater's at Robinson Automotive again. Your road creamed the struts. They're trying to find me a nearly new set to save a few bucks."

"I buy struts by the case." Belle spread her hands in a universal gesture of sympathy. "I was wondering about another tack. Jean McBride mentioned that the man who killed Michael Bustamante and his daughter is free again."

"Hell of a tragedy that was. So Jason Lewis is out? Wonder if Dave knows?" Len twisted his face in disgust and made a note. "Scumbag. Learning his whereabouts is going to be tough. Parole officers clam up. Bastards like that have too many rights. Maybe I can look around his old neighbourhood, contact relatives short of cash."

"If we can find out the exact date of the accident, I can check the newspaper morgue for the original stories," she said with a hopeful smile, wondering if the *Sudbury Star* had put its back issues onto microfilm.

He caught Miriam's eye and pointed at Belle. "Morgue. Listen to that jargon. She's getting to be a pro."

When he left, Miriam turned to her with a skeptical look. "You're actually working with this idiot? After my experience with Melibee Elphinstone, I think I can smell a con artist with a clothespin on my nose." She was referring to her last boyfriend, who had run a Ponzi scheme defrauding Sudbury seniors of millions of dollars.

"The police investigation is at a standstill. What's it going to hurt? He's from Montreal, and he knows his business. Think big for a change." She felt mildly annoyed that Miriam questioned her judgment.

"Pardon me!" Miriam let her fingers on the keyboard do the talking.

Hélène called at five to say that Micro had arrived, along with his gear, and was already back on the computer. "How was everything? Isn't that cookbook a godsend? Ready to be a mother? It's not too late. Women are conceiving at sixty."

Belle felt a bead of sweat on her forehead. The storm. The tree. The chimney fire, not to mention that confession. He'd have to sort everything out. "Lots of adventures. He'll tell you. Oh, and thank him again for making me that ceramic bear."

"How sweet of him." Hélène's voice could melt icebergs. "He likes you. You're in his every other sentence. Belle said this, Belle did that."

That night, freed of maternal duties, she and Freya slept soundly. The last track on her bedside CD player had been Rachmaninov's sonorous *Isle of the Dead*, where a warm radiance soared and sang, its zest for life struggling against the inevitable before breaking waves softened on the water's surface. Lake Wapiti had returned to perfect stillness in a crisp fall night. The quiet was palpable as a sliver of moon pierced the black velvet canopy. From a deep dream of paddling her canoe through misted waters toward a beckoning island, she crawled back to consciousness to answer the discordant phone, noting by the cool green digital numbers that it was 4:31. Her nose pricked at the perfume of a visiting skunk crossing the groundcover far below in search of a frog. It wouldn't be the first time that she found the grisly remains.

Hélène's frightened voice said, "Micro's gone!"

FOURTEEN

Gulping for breath like an asthmatic, Hélène related the sickening argument earlier that evening. True to his word, Micro had told them about the vandalism at the seniors' centre, and his stepfather had been called. "I've never heard Dave so angry. Usually he's quiet and soft-spoken. Nothing makes him lose his temper," Hélène said. With a bonded housekeeper engaged, Dave had insisted that the boy return the next day, and the DesRosiers had agreed.

After listening to his stepfather on the phone, refusing to say much in his defense other than "sorry," tears streaming down his face, he'd gone to his room with most of a tomato quiche still on his plate. He'd been sleeping soundly at ten when Hélène went to tuck him in. Rusty had barked in her dog house after they'd gone to bed, but since the neighbours were winding down a raucous party and saying goodnight to guests, they had ignored the warning. As for his movements triggering the motion sensor lights in the backyard, their bedroom was on the lake side of the house. Ed's four o'clock bathroom trip for a nagging prostate had sent him in to check on the boy, and that was when they'd found his room empty and his gear gone. His bike was also missing.

Hélène sniffed back tears. "Ed drove off down the road in case he could catch up. And him blind as a bat at night, the old fool. When I get that boy, I feel like paddling him from here to Mattawa, and you know I'd cut off my hand before striking a child."

Belle did some calculations. "It's forty klicks to town, another five to his house, but if he left before midnight, he'd be there now. Maybe we should get off the phone."

"We shouldn't have forced the issue. Three adults ganging up on a boy. But that vandalism caught me by surprise. No thought of the consequences. What on earth could have—"

Belle explained what Micro had said about bullying and how he'd known immediately that what he had done was wrong. "You've carried out your part, providing a place to ease him over the shock. But he belongs with Dave. Maybe after riding around in the dark, cold and scared and hungry as the sun comes up, he'll realize that he has to go home. Maybe he'll even show up at school." With that last desperate suggestion, Belle rolled back into the folds of the water bed, sweat moistening her face as she sipped a glass of water. What choices did a twelve-year-old have? Then she realized that many street kids were scarcely older than that. Micro had nerve, wading into a maelstrom of icy water, the same kind of impulsive action which had triggered his flight.

Hélène related that Dave had called the police, and since the disappearance involved a child, all stops were out. Patrolmen were combing the downtown area, cruisers taking the suburban streets, and the Ontario Provincial Police would handle the roads out of town. If he wasn't found soon, an Amber Alert would be issued, though the province had few of the hi-tech flashing message signs which lined transcontinental U.S. highways, and certainly none in the North.

"Don't panic, Hélène. You'll be there in case he calls in. I gave him my cell number, so that's another possibility." She paused. How far would he travel on a bike? "I don't suppose he could have taken a bus. Gone out of town to relatives. He showed me his bank card. Maybe he got money at an ATM."

"Dave thought of that. Micro has an uncle in Cleveland, and he's going to call him. But no small boy could cross the border alone. That bus idea makes sense, though. The police should contact stations here and in Toronto just in case. I've taken the midnight special a few times going down for Christmas shopping. I've seen younger teenagers on board for rock concerts. And you know our boy. He can talk a good line."

Their last hours together had been clouded with that chimney fire, Belle thought after she'd hung up, sharing Hélène's guilt. Micro must have felt abandoned by the only people he'd loved. For an hour she lay stewing, willing her tap-dancing heart to calm, counting sheep, bears, martens and mutual funds, writing multiplication tables on a mental blackboard and erasing them. As the rubied fingers of dawn raked the sky like a commandment, she went downstairs in a gritty stupor to hit the coffee maker. Action, fruitful or not, was better than stasis. And she had a plan. If she couldn't help find Micro, she could at least keep working with Len's investigation into Bea's death.

She dressed, hauling a wizened lipstick, eyeliner and powder out of a bottom drawer in the bathroom, and took Freya to town. Miriam's pink Jetta was in the lot when she arrived at seven thirty.

"Freya's here again? And what's with that outfit? It's ten years too young for you. Are you auditioning for a play?"

"Very funny. I know that. Just some work with Len." To parry another evil look, she told her what had happened last night.

Her cohort spilled her coffee on the desk. "My God. Where could he be? Riding a bike from your place? Have they checked the hospitals? Maybe he was hit in the dark and is lying unconscious in a ditch." She grabbed a roll of paper towels and began mopping up.

"Don't make it worse. I'm a wreck with hell between me and the end." Those words from the grim poem "How Annandale Went Out" finally made sense. Belle poured her fifth coffee of the morning and sank into her chair, looking again at her watch, unable to concentrate. Were her hands starting to shake?

Miriam tried to sugar-fix things by fetching a dozen doughnuts from Tim's, smaller now, 1960s style, an effort to standardize the size and punish generous franchisees. "Not forty-year-old prices, though," she observed later, munching an oozing cruller. Then she noticed Belle's blank look, her frozen posture.

"Come on now. It's early. He hasn't even been gone one night officially."

The day marched slowly, a few calls, the errant moocher after a free appraisal. After promising updates, Belle collected the dog and left at five, heading down Regent Street to McDonald's. "I feel like getting super-sized, if it's still legal. Big Macs all around. Extra pickle for you."

At the drive-through she ordered, then ate her combo first, serving Freya hers on the asphalt to spare the van's pristine upholstery. The Old Mill in Massey was about forty-five minutes west. The bar had a rough reputation. The dog meant security. She'd leave the windows open in case she made a hasty exit...pursued by a bear...of a man. Len had said that Sean Broughton was six-four and liked to give his hammy fists a workout after a few primers of alcohol.

She travelled busy Route 17, the so-called Trans-Canada highway, more two-lane than not in neglected Northern

Ontario, passing the massive INCO complex in Copper Cliff, then the small railtowns of Nairn Centre and McKerrow, coughing at the Espanola turnoff, where the reeks from the pulp mill wafted over the highway like a nuclear cloud. Hearing a wap-wapping, she watched a Ministry helicopter buzz overhead, a large object in a bag dangling from a cable. She saluted Bullwinkle's cousin. The *Sudbury Star* had carried an article on the relocation of problem elk. Once flourishing in the area, then decimated, a few years ago a select herd had been trucked from Alberta to establish a habitat in a joint project run by Nickel City College and Shield University. Trouble was, they wandered, finding farmers' fields tastier pasture than striped maple browse. A few lottery-losing females had been fitted with vaginal transmitters so that when they gave birth, radio location would be sent. As any woman would understand, reproduction had been lower than expected. Belle squirmed in her seat at the concept.

In the small village of Massey, the Old Mill sat at the bilingual confluence of the Spanish River and the River aux Sables and had once been a thriving granary. Booze had supplanted bread, and now its thick grey stone walls with a rippling riparian overlook hosted a modern watering place. Several Harleys were parked in front, along with pickups in all pedigrees.

Two men admired a truck the size of Vancouver Island. "3500 and a dually? What the hell you haulin', Marvin?"

The bearded older man replied with a grin, "My wife's fat ass. Got us a thirty-five-foot fifth wheel, and we're heading to the Florida Panhandle soon as the hurricanes leave. Broke my snow shovels over my knee and left the suckers in the trash can."

Rolling down the windows for ventilation, Belle aimed a trigger finger at Freya. "No barking. Guard the van." Squinting into the lighted visor mirror, a first, she applied a hasty coat of powder and blush, then liner, nearly poking herself in the eye with the mascara and wondering where her upper lip had gone. Using creative guesswork, she drew herself a kisser. Safer than collagen injections. Then as an afterthought as she got out, she bent down at a puddle and rubbed mud on the license plate. PI mode or what?

Her Levi red-tag jeans, distressed leather jacket over a pale blue turtleneck, and Frye boots would raise few eyebrows. As she entered the front door, malty fumes, the snicking of balls, and the neon advertisements set the atmosphere.

At the semi-circular bar, a glossy surface of varathaned pennies dating back to George V, she ordered a Blue Light. A lonely fifty-inch projection television in the corner was broadcasting the American League playoffs, Boston vs. New York. No interest from the loyal Canucks, mourning over their underfunded Jays and former Expos. The colonial-style tables and chairs seated fifty, but tonight only a dozen people were here, including three men engaged in a serious game of darts in the corner and two young women playing pool. The walls had a moth-eaten moose head and an ancient bearskin punctuated by wrestling posters. As she sipped, she scanned the room for a very tall man. A few grandfatherly types were seated at one table, arm wrestling over a pile of loonies.

She smiled at the woman on the next stool, who was chain-smoking. Ontario nicotine laws hadn't reached the outback. Dressed in a flannel shirt and jeans, she could have been a healthy fifty or a hard-luck thirty. Her braided black hair had beaded ties and a stunning matching necklace with bear claws caught Belle's eye. "Beautiful," she said, gesturing with her glass.

"My grandmother made it." The woman took a sip of rosé wine and shrugged. "Told her she could get big bucks for her craft work in Toronto, but she sells it at the Fall Fair here for peanuts."

Belle introduced herself, shaking a long, slim hand. "Hannah Moon," the woman said. "Don't take this wrong, but you don't look like you belong here. I know all the regulars, especially on welfare Wednesday."

"I'm looking for Sean Broughton."

Hannah's laugh rippled with undisguised mirth, the lines etching her chestnut complexion like fine toolwork. "Aren't all the ladies? Never tried him myself because I'm partial to smooth-faced men, and I don't like liars." She glanced at the Budweiser clock. "Nice to meet you. Gotta get back to the laundromat before the drier fries my undies." She snapped her fingers as an ancient golden Lab emerged from under a table. "Come on, Molson."

Belle waited, husbanding her glass like a canteen in the Sahara. Out of guilt, she bought a bag of beernuts and arranged them in a tic-tac-toe pattern. As she reached for the last, the door opened, and a man ducked on entering. He wore a fleece-lined bomber jacket and dirty wheat jeans. Flicking the coat on to a deer-horn rack, he clumped to the jukebox in engineer boots that looked as if they could kick in a skull and make change on the backswing. His cream shirt with ivory pocket snaps had a bolo tie. He deposited quarters, punched numbers, and the Dixie Chicks' "Long Time Gone" sent their message across the scarred plank floor two thousand miles from the Pecos.

"Hey, Sean," the bartender said, an innocuous weasel eligible for medicare, whose job it was to hear and see no evil.

"Jack and a chaser," Sean replied. He wore his thick red hair slicked back with gel. The semi-goatee with a thin moustache gave him a devilish look, matched by exposed, pointed ears. He

146

tossed Belle an appraising nod, and she picked up his invitation like a ripe plum as they exchanged names.

Her identity du jour was Dee White, an appliance-department manager at Sears. Everyone knew about stoves and fridges. "I was in the Sault all day for a regional conference. Got sleepy driving back to Sudbury and thought I'd take a break. Great song," she added as Faith Hill began "This Kiss". "We need more country stations. 790 has a range of about five miles on a clear day."

"You got that right, darlin'."

She chuckled, lowering her eyes to bolster her mystique. "I've been writing a country song for years. It's not that hard. They use only a couple hundred words. Beauty is truth, truth beauty. That kind of thing."

"'Keep it simple, smartass' is my motto. KISS." His lips puckered. He dumped the shot glass into the beer and chugged it, foam gathering on his thin mouth, covering a half-inch scar at the corner. "But go on. You never wrote no song," he said with a slight Aussie accent, waving his hand at her boast.

In a halting alto, letting embarrassment pose as ingenuousness, Belle began the most recent verse to "Mama's Table":

When the crowd would keep on growin',
Folks would sit upon the floor,
And they'd laugh and talk together
As they came on back for more.

They might have had no money,
Fancy car and diamond ring,
But at my mama's table
They were richer than a king.

147

She was debating making the words "might of" for verisimilitude, but Sean clapped his Whopper-sized hands and ordered another beer for her. "You got guts, girl. And that's a winner. God, I miss my mama's cooking, too. Spare ribs falling off the goddamned bone. Fried chicken make the Colonel's look like garbage." Then he cocked his head as if an idea had occurred to him. "Say now, out in Calgary I know a couple of promoters from the Stampede. Give me your number."

Flattered but wary, Belle scrawled the weather number on a paper serviette, changing the last digit. Time to probe for answers. "So what's your business, Sean?"

"I'm an or-gan-i-zation man. Unions." He'd been born in Australia but had come to Canada at ten when his father got a job in Winnipeg. His work history at meat-packing places out west had ended with the mad cow scare, and he'd only been in town for a year. Gesturing with a truncated index finger, he added, "I was this close at the biggest bakery in Sudbury. Only one more vote."

Belle nodded in sympathy. "So the owner wouldn't budge. I hear you. Bosses are all the same, want to balance the books on the backs of the workers." Clichés were handy.

He pounded the bar, rattling the glasses and signalling for another drink, this time a triple. "She's budging now. Bitch is dead. Somebody whacked her. God, was she ugly. Like a constipated monkey's ass."

Belle hunched over her beer, a sour taste in her mouth. Hearing him disparage a great lady set her blood at a rising simmer, not to mention the trite Mafia slang. "Bumble Bea Bakery? I read about that. Third woman murdered in a month. Gives me the creeps. I'm thinking of buying a gun. My cousin in Toronto has a magna. I mean a magnum." She blinked at her pistol-packing character, accumulating traits by the minute.

He took a self-important breath, expanding his strong chest like a puffer fish. "Cops talked to me first off. Should of seen their faces when I told them I was in the can for a slight altercation over a poker game at the National. Ten days was worth it to clock that sucker after he pulled an ace from his shoe. Anyhow, I told them to check out the husband. For sure he had something on the side."

"Another business?" Belle felt a twinge of interest. Was Dave involved in a shady operation? Embezzlement? Misdirection of funds? Surely not. He worked for many different organizations, and word would have gotten around.

His Mephistophelian brows contracted at her naïveté. "I didn't mean an order of fries. A chick. You watch, they'll turn something up." The triple vaporized as quickly as it had been born, spawning another. Belle took one sip of her beer. In the overheated room, Sean was beginning to sweat, releasing the smell of a cloying, cheap aftershave. Musk was not on her menu. Sweet fern instead.

He invited her back to the trailer where he was staying with a buddy off deer hunting on Manitoulin, but Belle refused, firmer each time, parrying his wandering hands. Finally, she excused herself for the old washroom trick. From down a dark corridor with a twenty-watt dangling bulb, she slipped out the back door and headed for the van.

At home, a message on her machine from Hélène said that the police had set everything into motion. The downtown core had been swept thoroughly and Micro's picture distributed across town on over a thousand flyers. Even a group of street people had organized a rotating posse to watch the all-night restaurants and convenience stores. It was obvious that one long day hadn't convinced the boy to go home. The weather was still mild. 10°C. Another night, with temperatures reaching to freezing, might bring him in...if it didn't kill him.

Hélène had noticed that a sleeping bag was missing from his closet. "This is looking worse and worse. It's as if he knew he'd be staying somewhere else."

"I agree. But at least it will keep him warm. Did he take a tent, too?"

"We only had the old family-size one. Canvas weighs about thirty pounds." She paused so long that Belle thought they had been disconnected. "There has to be a patron saint for lost children. Mafalda has memorized Butler's *Lives of the Saints.* I'm going to call her."

Belle spent longer than usual with her scotch, making a futile effort to concentrate on Buchan's *Prester John,* a 1920s novel about an African uprising and a new black messiah. When she put it down and closed her eyes, sleep evaded her. Once alcohol therapy passed a certain point, it kept her awake. Unable to concentrate, she turned left, then right, pulled up the covers, pushed them back, and finally got up to refill her water glass. Where was he? Cold? Hungry? In danger? Though no one had yet raised the spectre, she was wondering if he was in the hands of someone else who wouldn't call the authorities for all the wrong reasons. And now this implication about Dave. Unwilling to tell Hélène, she didn't believe it for a minute, coming from a jackass like Broughton. He'd fling mud in any direction to advance his cause. After all, he'd said nothing specific. Rolling her eyes at the green numbers, she got up for a third pee, passing the ceramic bear on her nightstand. Was it watching over Micro, trying to tell her something, or both?

FIFTEEN

After photocopying records at the Land Registry office, Belle walked over to Bank Alley to find Len. As she rounded a corner, she saw him talking to that same street person with a cowboy hat. At his side sat a trampish mutt, gazing up at his master with adoration. In a shabby parka and patched jeans, the young man with an unshaven face stuffed something in his pocket and headed off down the block towards the Salvation Army.

Len gave her a broad, welcoming smile. He thumbed a gesture toward the shambling figure, dog trotting along as if it hadn't a care in the world. "Would you believe he was top cross-country runner in the OFSSA finals? Captain of the Sudbury Secondary School team. Schizophrenia hits in the teens. I pass over a few bucks now and then. Guess I'm a softie, because my nephew in Halifax had the same problem. His parents couldn't keep him off the streets. Walked in front of a train one day. Game over. Maybe a blessing for him."

"Sorry to hear that. It's a tricky problem." Belle realized the legal quagmire in trying to force people to take their medicine, live in safe housing, get basic medical care. "How does he feed the dog?"

"Corky gets what he does. Catholic Charities Soup Kitchen. But there's a bag of kibble in his pack. Sometimes he hangs out by the Royal Bank, cadging small change from elderly women. He's one of the few who can tolerate the classical music they play over the speakers to chase off drifters. No big deal, he says. His dad was a music teacher."

Belle wondered how the indigent survived on the winter streets in -35°C, but somehow they did. The occasional freezing death in Toronto and Ottawa hit the headlines, but rarely happened NOB, North of Barrie.

"The kid turn up yet?" he asked, with a worried frown. "Dave called me right off. I missed the news this morning. Don't want to bother him for an update."

"I haven't heard anything. Why doesn't Micro admit he did a stupid thing and come back?"

"Makes me glad I have a girl. They don't pull that sort of stuff. Dave doesn't need this. He has enough on his plate to sink the *Bismarck.*"

Belle cast her eyes at the sidewalk as a patrol car swept down the street, two officers looking left and right. "Maybe Micro has friends we don't know about," she added, remembering Tom Beerchuk. Yet surely he wouldn't seek help from someone he despised, nor would responsible parents shelter a runaway.

Inside, taking their customary chairs, Belle folded her hands with a satisfied smile. "Here's some good news. I talked to Broughton. What a nasty piece of work."

Len stood abruptly, unsteady on his bum leg, his face flushing. A wormy vein at his temple pulsed as his voice rose, and he dropped a lighted cigarette on the desk, fumbling to retrieve it. "Jesus, woman. You could have gotten hurt. I never told you to find him."

Taking a clue from Micro, Belle said with a wink, "You never told me not to."

He shook his head, grabbing an ashtray and dropping back into the chair. "Caught me on a technicality. I thought you were a realtor, not a legal beagle. So go on. Don't keep me in suspenders."

Suspenders. Her father would enjoy that one. She related the Old Mill scene. "In jail that night. Verifiable enough. But he's a real pig. His description of Bea disgusted me. That's why I don't believe his innuendos about Dave."

"I like the guy, too, but if he's been pulling a con, withholding information, it's sayonara. I'm seasoned enough to suspect that anyone might have a secret side." Len tipped back his head and focused his thick glasses on her, eyes bulging like a bullfrog's. "I had a hunch about Leonora Bruce, so I've been tailing her. If you think about it, she stands to gain a lot from Bea's death, maybe get the business in a distress sale. She's no movie star, that banger of a nose and all, but who can say what attracts a man...or woman? My wife and me, for example. Maybe she's working with someone."

Wife? He'd never mentioned one. Had they divorced? Belle left the subject alone. "I talked to her at the viewing. She seemed devastated about Bea. She and Dave embraced, but that's only natural." Or was it?

Raising a seedy eyebrow, Len consulted a notebook. "Stakeout again tonight, the most boring part of my job. With luck, Leonora will turn in by ten like a good girl, and I'll be snoozing at home an hour later."

Suddenly, the door opened without a knock, and into the office walked a statuesque beauty who made a grey business suit look like a *Vogue* photoshoot. Her makeup was subtle and flawless, accenting high cheekbones beneath glittering violet eyes. A delicate scent of jasmine filled the air. She carried a black leather laptop computer case and a designer bag, and her shapely legs stretched from there to eternity. "Dad," she said, then smiled at Belle. "Sorry for barging in."

Len made the introductions. "My daughter, Lillian. She's a social worker at the Canadian National Institute for the Blind." The timbre in his voice spelled PRIDE.

"Pleased to meet you. So are you helping Dad on his case?" As Belle gave a dubious nod, Lillian glanced at the pizza boxes in the wastebasket, shaking her coppery curls, artfully arranged in a high-maintenance style. "Just stopped to remind you about dinner tomorrow. Meat loaf the way you like it. I haven't seen you for so long that I've forgotten your face."

"Nobody forgets this ugly puss. Make that Tater-Tot casserole of yours, sweetie." He squeezed her manicured hand.

After Lillian planted a kiss on his raspy cheek and left, Belle said, "She's lovely," calculating the timeline with curiosity. The daughter seemed in her mid-thirties, yet Len wasn't far into his fifties.

He smiled, touching a finger to the framed picture on his desk, and turned it toward Belle. A couple stood on a beach, palm trees in the background. She had long, reddish hair, cascading in curls around her face, and he was skinny enough to worry about his trunks. No mistaking those trademark glasses. "I was only nineteen when Lilli was born. Mayda and I met on a kibbutz. The hot sun, the shimmer of the sea." He gave a Gallic shrug.

"Your wife is a beauty, too...I mean..." She shifted her feet, hoping he'd rescue her.

Waving off her embarrassment, he lit another Camel and cleared his throat as his voice assumed a faraway tone. "Mayda died in childbirth. Lilli was raised mostly by her aunt in Montreal. With all my wandering, I've been making it up to her for the last fifteen years. Changed our name from Hulitsky. The aunt's idea. Social advantage or something. Didn't matter garbanzo beans to me."

Belle didn't know what to say, insulated from premature deaths. Her mother had been in her seventies when she had died from bowel cancer, like Audrey Hepburn, both members of an earlier female generation which often traded survival for privacy behind the closed curtain until it was too late. Changing the subject seemed wise. "Sorry about crossing the line on Broughton. Micro's disappearance has me on edge, too. Just thinking of sitting safe at home tonight like a useless lump..." She looked up at him with the same winsome expression that had melted her father from cradle to college. "That stakeout. May I come along?"

He flashed a genial smile. "Why not? The old beater's seat hurts my back, and I don't see so sharp at night anyway. If I had a pension, I'd pack it in."

Belle called Hélène to give Freya her supper and let her out, then waited until Len "dressed." When he emerged from the rear of the office, he wore black pants, shirt, socks and shoes. She tried not to laugh. "Is that necessary?"

"Keeps me in the right mindset. I'm not wearing any camo face paint though. It's hell to wash off, and I get odd looks."

They took her van to Quizno's on LaSalle, a new arrival of a popular American chain. Studying the sumptuous menu, they ordered toasted subs and bottles of water. Smoked turkey, rosemary sourdough buns, shaved Black Angus steak. Len floated a twenty onto the counter, then grimaced as he was asked for another fifty cents.

Minutes later, they settled into a dark parking lot at an apartment complex on Voyageur Street near Gagnon Opticians. Len pointed to a large bright window on the first floor and passed her a pair of monster binos. With the curtains open and the high vantage of the sloping lot, they could see into the living room as if watching television. He nodded toward a shadowy ravine and pulled a squished roll of toilet paper from his pocket. "Open-air bathroom. A PI's life story, though I usually use a bottle. Hope you're not too fussy."

She laughed. "A bushwoman can drop her pants anywhere." And pee on her shoe, too.

With his tiny penlight for assistance, they unwrapped their sandwiches and ate ravenously. Blotting her mouth on a serviette, Belle said, "They're good, but people will vote with their pocketbook. Northerners like to squeeze the nickel."

From six to eight, a few cars came and left the lot. Belle saw Leonora get up, leave the room, and return. Windsor the poodle curled up in a chintz armchair. Taking turns, she and Len took advantage of the cover of the ravine. Belle twitched at the scutter of animals, city rats, no doubt, foraging the brush and debris of Junction Creek. Hearing a feral shriek, she wasted no time hustling to the van. The radio kept them company, a CBC program about Canada's lack of competitiveness among the G-7 nations. "How can you compete fairly when half the year you're relocating frozen water by shovel, blower, or plow? We deserve a handicap, like racehorses," she said.

Len nickered in response and lit a tenth cigarette. Then he pulled a tape out of his pocket. "That wholesome government pap is putting me to sleep. I got this at Just-a-Buck. It's a riot. My dad loved this stuff."

She looked at the case. *Wacky Songs from the Fifties.* In the next half hour, they listened to "Transfusion", "The Old Philosopher", "The Purple People Eater", "The Chipmunk Song" and "Witch Doctor".

As the last ting-tang-walla-walla-bing-bang sounded, she was beginning to develop a nostalgia for the foulest rap music. Len touched her arm and pointed to a familiar car entering the lot. "Heads up, or rather, down. Check this out."

Dave Malanuk parked the SUV and walked into the lobby, a large bouquet in his hand. "Damn," she said, wondering how she could ever tell the DesRosiers. "He seemed like such a nice guy." So Bea's husband had been cheating on her. Belle's batting average on character assessment took a major hit.

Thanks to the huge lenses, they could nearly read the lips of the people in the picture window. Windsor made it to the door first, then Leonora. She turned off the television and took Dave's coat, along with the flowers, placing both on a table. Then they sat on a sofa, their upper torsos visible. After twenty minutes and an indecipherable series of hand gestures, there was a chaste hug, and Dave left. "Maybe that's all she wrote, but we'll wait a bit in case he went out for pizza," Len said. "One minute can make the hours worth it."

But Dave didn't return. At ten o'clock as predicted, Leonora turned off her lights. Len stuffed the last butt into Belle's overflowing ashtray. The van needed a steam cleaning after this assault. "Wait until I give that guy a blast," he said, nodding grimly. Then he turned to her, offering a porky handshake. "Thanks. The company was nice. It's a lonely job."

After letting Len off, on the way home Belle welcomed the soothing ebony night rolling over her as she left the harsh city lights behind and sorted out her thoughts. Micro had been gone two days. Hélène had her cellphone number if any news broke. As she slowed for the Edgewater Road turn, her beams lit two red eyes in the undergrowth. She paused until they disappeared. In a duel between moose and vehicles, the odds were even money.

When she got home, she let Freya out again and went to her computer room, where she kept her maps. That sleeping bag had given her an idea. The OPP hadn't seen Micro on the four major highways out of town, but what about rougher secondary roads? They branched in every direction, winding around over two hundred lakes in the region. The phone rang, and she jumped. Eleven o'clock. It had to be serious.

"Belle, I've discovered something else. All my jerky is missing. It was in Ziplocs in the cupboard…" Hélène paused, and Belle heard fear charge her voice. "And what's worse, Ed's .22. I know we should have locked it in a gun safe, but we don't have children around that often."

"Jerky sounds desperate for a vegetarian. And a gun?" Hadn't he said something about living off the bush when they hiked to Surprise Lake? A boy's dream, a parent's nightmare. "Hélène, do you suppose he's camping out somewhere? Bea said he loved to sleep up in his treehouse."

"All the provincial campgrounds must be closed now, but I'll tell Dave. We're in constant touch. He's called all of Micro's friends, too."

In the current crisis, Belle said nothing about the scene with Leonora. Time enough for that to emerge. Then Hélène added, "And the police took the computers, ours and his at the house. It'll be a few days before we hear about that."

Computers. That sounded ominous, though it was probably procedure. "They're just being thorough. That's what we want." As she hung up, Belle wondered if Dave had Chris Forth on his list. Bea would have known all the boy's friends, but not Dave. She'd met the lad and felt comfortable with him. Len would approve of her initiative.

The next morning, Belle reached the boy before school. Filling him in on the latest details, she asked, "Tell me anything you can about what he liked to do, any place that he mentioned."

Chris talked about games, films, toys, the information he'd given the police already when his mother had called them. Then he grew silent.

Belle tried not to rush him. Interrogations were tricky. "Did you remember something?"

The boy sniffed. "Micro said that the best time he ever had in his whole life was the summer when he was ten."

Belle frowned and grabbed a notepad and pen. "Why ten?"

"It was the last summer before...Dave came. He wouldn't call him Dad."

An intelligent boy like Micro could be stubborn, she imagined, her memorable time with him more of a vacation free of rules. Keeping her voice upbeat so as not to alarm Chris, she asked the obvious question. "Why didn't he get along with his stepfather? Did he give you any reasons?"

"Not really. He shut up every time Dave's name came up. I thought he was okay, as parents go. He had a super BBQ at the lake on Micro's last birthday. Loot bags for every kid. That bike was da bomb."

"Da...getting back to that summer, what happened to make it so special?"

She heard silence, then "Oh, yeah. Now I remember. It was a camp. He learned how to canoe, built a lean-to, practiced survival skills."

So the idea wasn't that far-fetched. One hand reached to her throat, fast constricting. Stay in the woods in the summer. With counsellors and tons of food. Not survive in fall when the temperature dipped below freezing. They'd had several hard frosts before he left, but the recent days had been unseasonably warm. It wouldn't last, global warming aside, a concept which made Northerners laugh.

"Do you know its name or location?"

"It wasn't the Y camps, John Island and Camp Falcona. I've been there myself. You could ask his teacher. He said that he wrote a story about it when school started." He paused. "Oh, Miss?"

*

She smiled at the polite, all-purpose name. "Yes, Chris?"

"Is he gonna be all right? I mean, will they find him?"

"My fingers are crossed, and I've never been wrong." Safe enough, as promises go.

After hanging up, Belle was forced to do some hard thinking. Trusting instincts, she called Dave at his office. What she had seen at the apartment wasn't yet the ocular proof of adultery Othello demanded. Len's suspicions were typical for an investigator, but there could have been a sound reason for his visiting Leonora. Dave's secretary told her that he had flown to London for preliminary work on a Thanksgiving telethon to raise money for a wing on the Veterans' Hospital. "Imagine having to run all over the province when your son's missing," the woman said. "But he has commitments, and Dave never lets anyone down. He'll be back tonight."

A call to the DesRosiers turned up no information about the camp. Hélène and Ed had taken an Alaskan cruise that summer and visited relatives in Nanaimo.

"How about the computers?" Belle asked. "Anything yet?"

"They gave it top priority. Got a hotshot from Information Systems at Nickel City College. They accessed the history, or whatever it is. In a chatroom about *Castle King Three,* they found his conversations with Dreamweaver."

Belle drummed her fingers on the table. "Dreamweaver?"

"They all use code names. It's part of the...fun." Her voice quivered with fear. "But there's something worse. The police are afraid that he met someone on the Internet and agreed to join him. An e-mail message arrived here at ten the morning he disappeared. It said: "We're on for nine. CU." That's a C and a U. All these abbreviations mean something. They don't think it's a person's initials. But he didn't read it, because he was already gone, so—"

"Who sent it? Dreamweaver?"

"Someone else. Rapper 219. They're trying to trace it. It sounds to me like a gang or something."

"It's just a kind of music. Every kid wants to be a rapper." Belle wondered about the logistics. "The message could have been a confirmation of an earlier agreement, because 'nine' must have meant night. That night. Why send it at ten if the meeting were in the morning? Any other files? Did they check the history?"

"You know how neat the boy is. Everything else was erased, or deleted, whatever they do."

Belle remembered computer forensics she'd learned on the DorothyL mystery discussion group. "Sometimes deleted data can be recovered."

"I'm sure they'll try everything. One of the officers gave me some brochures for parents to keep their kids safe online. It sickened me." She'd slipped one of the brochures under Belle's door. "Our boys were off at college before computers came around, and the grandkids are too young to worry about. When Micro finished his homework, he was allowed to surf the net, he called it, for one hour, according to Dave. If he was visiting a friend, the game *Grand Theft Auto* was off-limits, for obvious reasons. We didn't set any other rules, just left him on his own."

"I had a thought, but I'm not telling Ed. I know how he'd react."

Belle couldn't imagine where this was going. Hélène keeping secrets from Ed was a new one. They were joined at the hip, steel ball joint aside. "What do you mean?"

There was a pause as Hélène lowered her voice, and Belle punched up the volume on the portable phone. "Ever hear of Psychic Paula?"

Belle covered the receiver and groaned. "The one who tapes handwritten sheets on light poles at all the intersections? Not very classy. Do you believe in that stuff?"

"Don't be so negative. She told a friend of mine ninety years old about a sister dead in 1940. Erma tried to trick her. 'How do I look to you, Betty?' she asked. And the choice part is that the sister had been blind."

"So then what?"

"The voice said, "Don't tease. *Now* I can see you clear as day. And that hairdo doesn't suit you at all. You're not one of the Andrews Sisters."

"It could be a guess. Psychics read a lot from body language and vocal tones. Anyway, I'll go with you." She didn't mention that she wanted to prevent Hélène from getting bilked by a con artist. Her friend gave people far too many benefits of the doubt. She was born to feed and nurture the world, not inquire into its ethics.

Belle hung up and went to collect the brochure, lying in a dark corner where it had been brushed when she entered. She brought it into the living room and sat in her blue velvet recliner, turning on the swing lamp. The cover bore the sinister picture of a hulking man staring at a computer, the screen reading "Kidchat.ca." He was typing: Jgirl15. "I collect dolls too." Apparently twenty-five per cent of children are asked to meet someone they've only met online. Despite the heat pumping from the stove, she shivered.

In the computer room, she logged onto their friendly and comprehensive site, www.bewareweb.ca, which had information about gambling, cyberbullies and kid-friendly addresses as well as tech tools like filters or monitors. Suggestions for each age group called the years eleven to thirteen a "dangerous time". And in both houses, Micro's computer was in his bedroom, not in a safe family area like a rec room. Sadly enough, he fit the profile for abduction in one key way. Since his mother's death, he had felt alone, and he didn't want to return to Dave. Why did he hate the man so much?

SIXTEEN

Micro's school was St. Francis on Lilac Street. Belle knew the principal from a house sale years ago. Jolly Watson was called to the phone late that morning and remembered her. "You were right about not buying too large a place since our boys were already in their teens. When they left for university, Phil and I would have been rattling around that Moonglo castle."

"That's good to hear. This isn't about business, though. I'm a part of the team searching for Micro, I mean Michael Bustamante."

Jolly gave a moan. "God, we're devastated. We had an assembly to discuss the rules about strangers and keep the children calm. Each class made a collage for Micro, and I took them over to his home. Mr. Malanuk thanked me. I remember meeting him and Bea at the Open House when school started. His mother's death, his father's and his sister's before that. What a heavy load for a boy."

"Micro may have gone somewhere on his own. Time is crucial." Belle explained her mission in needing to talk to his teacher. "I know how careful schools are these days, so I wanted to work through the right channels."

Jolly gave a defensive snort. "It's not like the States yet. No metal detectors and private security." She paused as if she were checking schedules. "An essay, you say? That would mean his

English teacher. Lisa Boggs is a sweetheart. I'm sure she'll see you. Can you come around four?"

Later that afternoon, Belle drove to the school, passing the last yellow bus leaving the property. She parked the van and walked through the front doors. The halls were clean and cheerful, with cabinets of achievement awards, plaques and framed pictures of graduating classes. A Thanksgiving bulletin board was filled with cutouts of turkeys and Upper Canada settlers. When she reached the office, the secretary gave her Lisa's room number. "She's expecting you."

Fresh out of teacher's college, Lisa turned out to be a tiny dynamo with fashionable small glasses and her dark brown hair gelled into wings. She wore a short, rainbow-print dress and sturdy sneakers. After shaking Belle's hand, she offered her a chair beside her desk.

"I haven't had a good sleep since Micro disappeared," Lisa said, pointing out a nearby cluster of desks, one of which held a bunch of wildflowers in a retro Coke bottle. "I shouldn't say it, but he's my favourite, more like a teacher's assistant than a student. Always helping the others with infinite patience. If anyone's harmed—"

Belle levelled her eyes at the woman, struggling to push aside the spectre of a molester. "So far we have no solid evidence that anyone else is involved. Micro's initiative may have gotten him into trouble." She related what Chris had said.

Lisa gave a weak smile, her oval face chalk-pale despite the cherry lipstick. "I've been off two weeks with bronchitis that turned to pneumonia. Those supply teachers. Assign work but never mark it." With an accusing tsk, she pulled out a drawer with piles of papers and rummaged through the folders until her nimble hand fixed on one set. "It'll take me weeks to sort this."

They looked at the two-page essay, neatly typed. "Sounds

old-fashioned, but I always have them write about their summer. It's a quick start, and when they read their papers aloud, they can get to know each other."

The essay was spell-checked, though computers couldn't replace the eagle eye of an educator: "Ranger Paul talked to us around the campfire for twenty minuets. He said that beavers had become pests in cottage areas because of too much breading." Breaking the tension, they erupted in laughter. Micro described a normal camp routine, fire building, shelters, plants, animals and especially food. "S'mores are great, but my counsellor Beth made us eclairs on broomsticks over the fire. She wrapped biscuit dough from those tubes on one end, baked it, and put pudding inside. They're good, but not like Mom makes." Belle was interested in the location, and the last paragraph contained a name.

"Camp Sudburga," Belle said, snapping her fingers. Named for the legendary monster whose reptilian neck broke the waters of Lake Ramsey on foggy nights, usually when the sighter had finished a six-pack. "Do you know where it is?"

"I'm afraid not. There are so many in the region." The playground of the North had camps for many purposes, including scouting, wilderness challenge training, Bible study, even one for kids recovering from cancer. Lisa promised to give the essay to the police, but Belle wished she could have kept it to hear his voice again, a little boy who had taken her heart hostage.

As she rose to go, she remembered another name. "Tom Beerchuk. A friend of Micro. Is he in this class?"

Lisa blew out a sigh of relief. "What a despicable bully he was. Very subtle, too. Hard to pin him down for discipline. A little sociopath in training, I'd say. After the first two weeks of school, his family moved to St. John's, Newfoundland. Good riddance."

Driving home, Belle recapped the information. She had doubted Micro had been involved with Tom after the painting incident, but it was comforting to cross off another name. Now he'd face the punishment alone, but she had confidence in him. "Come back, Micro. Nothing is worth what you're doing to yourself and to all of us," she whispered as she crossed the old railbed on her road.

After a bleak supper and an anxious evening, at ten thirty she finally reached Dave. He sounded tired from his travels, but happy to hear her voice. "I have so many people to thank. Neighbours have been bringing casseroles. The school sent collages. The Scouts are going to check the Conservation Area around Laurentian Lake. When I got back the other night from Leonora's... Did you meet her at the viewing? I think she said—"

"Yes, I did. Everything okay on the bakery front?" she asked with a casual cool. What he chose to share about the woman and the tenor of his voice might reveal more than appearances.

"She's a gem. It's her mother. Died in her sleep in palliative care on the weekend. Eighty-nine. Poor lady lived with her all these years. A brittle diabetic who had lost both legs. Don't know how Leo managed. I saw the obit yesterday morning, missed the funeral, but I went over to see her with flowers. I thought I should pay back some of the kindnesses people have offered me."

Easy enough to check. It seemed that Len was off the rails about Dave. Now they could get back to business. When she told him about Micro's essay and Camp Sudburga, his voice gathered new energy. "His teacher had that? Why didn't I think of going to the school? He loves Miss Boggs. Probably opened up to her."

"Of course, we can't be sure, but that sleeping bag, the jerky—"

"Micro never mentioned it, but that's not surprising. Like any boy, he had his secrets. The camp can't be far. Bea kept him on a close rein." His pace speeded up. "It's not that late. I've got a lot of contacts."

He promised to get back to her as soon as possible. Meanwhile, just in case a fast trip would be possible, Belle rescheduled her morning appointments, hoping that the changes wouldn't irritate her clients. All she needed was for the ever-trembling business to fold. On the other hand, if she joined up with Cynthia Cryderman, could she lease a Humvee Two?

Dave called back half an hour later as the eerie warble of a lone loon rippled across the lake. It should be gone for the winter. Perhaps it had lost its mate or was crippled. "Still up? Good news. Bill Desantis works with the Recreation and Parks Department. He knows every camp within one hundred miles." He paused, and she could hear a tissue being generously used. "I offered to take Micro on a canoe trip, a loop in the Elliot Lake area. Showed him the maps to get his interest. He could even bring a friend. It was no use."

Belle drummed her fingers on the desk. Dave needed to take action, not brood over his failures as a stepfather. Clenching her jaw, she managed to keep annoyance from her voice. Some people needed a good shaking. "Where exactly is the place?"

She heard a rustle of paper. "I'm looking at a map, Belle. It's not that far. Over by the Ashigami area to the east. Should we—"

"Ashigami! Whoa, Nelly. This is beginning to make a crazy kind of sense." She helped Dave put it together. The food supplies, the old rail path. "That's why no one has seen him on any local roads. He travelled as the crow flies."

"I talked to the director. The place has been locked up since the end of August. But we're welcome to take a look. There's a key on a hook over the door. It's probably a wild goose chase, but I'm going crazy waiting for news. Should we go tonight? Are you up to it?"

"A bit dangerous in the dark. Dawn's not far off. We should tell the police now, though. They'll dispatch a squad car."

"I called Detective Sumner already. There's been a five-car pile-up on 69 near Britt. A tanker's burning, and a load of cattle spilled onto the road. A regular massacre. No one can go out until tomorrow afternoon."

Belle made a fist in frustration. "Afternoon? Wait all that time? You'd think they could spare one officer. This is ridiculous."

He blew out a long breath. "They've followed several false tips about Micro already. Spotted at a bus depot in Marathon, riding down the streets of Huntsville, at a rock concert in Toronto. It's a nightmare, and you know about staff cuts. They're eleven officers short right now in this brutal amalgamation."

Belle felt like calling Steve and pulling a few personal strings, but she supposed that Micro's flight had cost many thousands of dollars already. "Let's go at dawn, Dave. I've cleared my schedule."

"Why aren't I surprised? I'll repay you somehow for this. You're setting your life on hold for us. That's something only family would do."

"Consider me an adopted aunt. Micro's safe return will be the best payment. We can meet at my office at seven, first light, and take your car. The roads might be rough." She was curious to see how his SUV handled.

Despite their reputation for early bedtimes, she knew the DesRosiers were catching every last hour of news. She called Hélène, who insisted on giving her own update first. "We're safe on one point. Dreamcatcher on the chat line turned out to be a fourteen-year-old girl in Kingston. An honour student."

When her friend heard about the camp, Belle had to hold the receiver away from her ringing ear. "Not that dangerous railbed! Over that high bridge a few miles east? Ed took me on the quad hunting blueberries along there once, and I nearly fainted. He had to tie me to the frame. Even so, I closed my eyes the whole way."

Belle resisted comment on the provocative picture of the older couple. "You have acrophobia, remember? That bridge carried trains. There's plenty of room for a bike."

"I'd go with you tomorrow, but Ed has an eye exam. Those drops where you can't drive."

"We'll be fine. Don't get your hopes too high. I could be wrong." She looked at the clock and calculated her shrinking sleep allotment. "Anyway, I'd better get to—"

"More good news. I got a consultation this week with Psychic Paula."

"Come on. Do you really think that's going to tell us anything?" No sooner had she spoken than she regretted dampening Hélène's parade. "Sorry to sound so—"

"You have your hunches, I have mine. I hear she's a lovely, sincere woman."

SEVENTEEN

In his SUV, armed with a huge thermos of coffee, Dave collected Belle at the office, and they headed out Route 17 toward Ottawa. With a topo map, she explained the logistics of the old railbed, now linked to the TransCanada trail. "He was definitely listening, asking questions. And with those strong legs of his, he could have reached the camp in six or seven hours. Why didn't I remember?"

Dave smiled at her as they stopped at a light beside Chapters. "You're a genius. I'd never have put this together on my own."

Far up the hill she could see the Silver City complex. How far away in time that happy Saturday seemed. Now perhaps they were close to ending this nightmare. But suppose they found nothing at the camp?

They were soon passing Coniston, home of a former nickel smelter. Only a few decades ago, hills of surreal black rock where astronauts came to train for the moonwalk bore witness to over a hundred years of environmental devastation, first from logging to rebuild Chicago after the Great Fire, then from noxious open-pit smelting. Thousands of hectares of soil had washed away in a core area the size of New York City. At last Sudbury was in full recovery mode, green again. The Rye-on-the-Rocks with a lime chaser project had regrassed the area. Then over eleven million trees had been planted in a massive government, corporate and community effort which had earned an award at a United Nations Earth Summit in Rio.

The small community of Wahnapitae sat by its namesake river, farther along, a few rundown motels and Uncle Rick's Flea Market closed for the season. Finally they turned left at a restaurant-gas station on Kukagami Lake Road. For sale again.

Evergreens were the dominant growth on the thin layer of peat over Cambrian granite bedrock. Out of range of the devastation miles west, taller red and white pines soared beside firs and spruce. Occasionally a swamp lake with grey spars and beaver lodges bordered the dirt road. The feathery tamaracks, wetland lovers, an unusual deciduous conifer, added lemon splashes to fall's ongoing postcard. At crossings, painted signs to family camps, Lemieux, Niemi, Cechutti, Schultz, pointed toward thinly travelled paths into the dark woods. Dave braked as an emaciated fox stood briefly in the road, its thin brush drooping.

"Very unnatural behaviour. Foxes are usually wary. It's probably rabid," Belle said. She should have kept her observations to herself. Dave had enough to worry about.

They took the first turn to Ashigami Lake. Twenty minutes later, they saw a large sign with a swimming sea creature grinning in cartoon innocence. Camp Sudburga. A chain lay across the entrance, so they parked and stepped over it. Before them, nestled on one of many bays on twisted Ashagami Lake, was a complex of simple pine buildings. Horseshoe and volleyball grids were laid out, and a baseball diamond waited for summer. They walked toward the main lodge, Belle searching for bike tracks, Dave by her side, eyes down, and gloved hands clasped in mute prayer. The rising wind took a bite from her neck. Without its liner, the Gore-Tex parka wasn't as warm as Dave's sheepskin jacket.

At a muddy spot which had hardened in the cold night, she stopped and knelt, tracing grooves with her finger. "Do you recognize this pattern? The police should be able to match it to the model. Did you buy the bike in town?"

Dropping to one knee and touching the track with shaking fingers, Dave let out a groan of relief. "It seems familiar. I bought it at the Outside Store and put it together myself. If you're right, he could be safe in his bed by tonight." He brushed off his hands, stood and scanned the grounds as if wishing to be in five places at once. "Micro!" he yelled. "Are you here? It's Dave and Belle. Come out, son. There's no harm done."

The stillness of the surrounding woods was broken by the affronted chitter of a squirrel stocking up cedar cones for winter. Belle understood the man's desperation, but if Micro were spooked, he might retreat on to forest paths where they couldn't follow. Still, Dave thought he recognized the tracks. Her heart rate picked up. "Let's search the buildings. He won't be sitting by a campfire. His gear will be inside."

The lodge was a one-storey log building with add-ons. Behind it, smaller cabins for campers and counsellors dotted the grounds along with storage sheds. Dave reached up over the front door and blew out a breath of relief. "Here's the key. Pretty stupid to leave it here like an invitation, though I guess there's not much to take."

"A cottager would rather sacrifice a boat motor or bottle of rye than get vandalized," Belle added. "But it's far from town, and I can't see teenagers driving all over the bush when there are easy pickings closer to home. My road gets a few break-ins every fall when townies leave."

The lodge had a typical musty smell from unheated closure. Passing though the dining room, complete with long, oil-clothed trestle tables for fifty and a fieldstone fireplace at one end, they entered the kitchen. A wall calendar stopped at August. Out of curiosity, Belle checked the cupboards: dry supplies of rice, pasta and flour in sealed containers. Canned goods would freeze.

"No sign of recent use, but Micro's always been neat," Dave said, running a finger through the dust on the counter as the corners of his mouth wavered. "Maybe the tracks belonged to another rider. Let's try the other rooms."

Unwilling to leave until she had touched every corner, Belle paced the room. At the moment of abandoned hope, with Dave already turning to the corridor, something caught her eye. She bent to collect a small plastic bag lodged under the overhang of the sink cabinet. It smelled like jerky, and tasting one shard brought back memories. Dave watched her carefully, his eyes brightening with hope. "He's been here!" she said.

He took the bag, examining it like a talisman, a crease on his broad brow. "I'd like to believe that...but are you sure?"

She smacked her lips. Taste and smell were more powerful memory organs than sight and sound. The flaky crust and sweet tartness of her famous mother's cherry pie had deep roots in her memory, try as she would without success to duplicate it. "Green jalapeño sauce. Hélène's secret ingredient."

As they locked eyes, then headed for the hall, he gestured to her. "You take that room, and I'll look in there."

The two pine-panelled bedrooms were probably maintained for the camp director and assistant. Nothing out of place, but was it her imagination that there seemed to be a depression in the old spring bed, sloppy mattress or not? Had a sleeping bag rested there? Belle tested the window. It lifted easily, and the shutter outside, a sheet of brown, painted plywood braced by a stick in summer, was unlatched. A removable sliding screen sat on the floor. An old stump below made an easy stepstool.

Dave returned, his shoulders sagging. "Nothing."

"Watch this. Why would Micro have known about the key? But he could have come in through here."

He ran his fingers over the sill, brushed a bead of fear-sweat from his temple. "Then where in the name of God is he, Belle?"

The other outbuildings were firmly padlocked, and so was the large boathouse with stacks of canoes, kayaks and paddle boats visible through the cobwebbed panes. The lake rippled with the wind as a trout broke the surface to grab the season's last mosquito.

Dave sat on a picnic table with his head in his hands, fighting back tears as he took out his wallet and showed her a school picture of Micro, beaming into the camera in a white shirt and tie. Dave's hands made fists of stress, and he looked on the edge of collapse in a struggle between hope and despair as he focused his weary eyes on the dark woods. "I'm going to stay, at least until the police arrive. You take the car. I'll get a ride back."

"Well, I—" If he was around, Micro was clearly spooked. And he wasn't going to come to Dave. He'd be more receptive to an officer.

Dave shook his head. "I had another terrible idea. What if he met someone here? That last message."

"Why choose to meet here? It's miles from town." He hadn't mentioned the gun, a dangerous addition to any scenario.

"All the more reason. No one around."

"Or are you saying someone led Micro here...and kidnapped him?" The thought sent an icy charge down her spine. And the location pointed to someone who knew the area.

"I know I need to stay cool, but it's as if my brain's working against itself. All kinds of crazy ideas are flowing in, no matter how hard I try to focus. I just want him home and this nightmare to end." Belle watched him smoulder like a volcano, powerless to act. He stood suddenly, blinking against the sun. "Car tracks at the gate. I didn't look. Did you?"

She placed a steadying grip on his shoulder. "Stay calm, Dave. I know it's hard, but let's think this thing through. There's a much simpler possibility. Yes, he's gone, but not because of our arrival. We would have seen him run, and how could he have packed up that fast? Suppose he came here to live off the land and discovered that his belly hurt after a few days. Squirrels and rabbits aren't easy to kill, even with that .22. He has no fishing equipment. Plain rice and pasta gets boring." She recalled their conversation about aboriginals and how vegetarianism wouldn't have supported a hunter-gatherer lifestyle, especially under extreme cold.

"If he's back in town, he'll be found soon enough." Dave smacked a fist into his large hand in a gesture of confidence. "Maybe I'm way off base on this idea of another person. Thanks for the wake-up call."

Belle nodded as she checked her watch surreptitiously. Closing in on eleven. She needed to get back to the office. "The police will give the camp a closer look this afternoon." She didn't add that from day one they would have been checking the Ontario Sex Offenders' Registry of over four thousand people.

He stood, squaring his shoulders, a catch in his voice. "There is someone else. Micro's uncle, Rafe Bustamante. The boy liked him. I could almost hope—"

"Hélène mentioned him."

"He's an eye surgeon in Cleveland. Rafe came up each summer when Michael Sr. was alive. Bea said they made a great trio. Rafe and his wife couldn't have children." He groaned. "After Bea...died, Micro wanted to go and live with him. Maybe it would have been for the best."

"But surely you don't think he took the boy across the border. That's impossible these days."

He shrugged. "Come on, Belle. You're too law-abiding. With a bribe to someone with a boat, you can enter the States via the St. Lawrence, around Ganonoque, for example. Maybe you're right in figuring that Micro came here, got sick of the rough life, then went back to town and called Rafe collect."

"That would be easy to check. He has a practice, a home. A child can't be hidden."

"I phoned when Micro first disappeared. Seems he's off in Europe on a vacation. Or so his office says. It could be a ruse." Then he coughed as if disgusted with himself. "The man's a professional. This speculation is crazy. I feel like diving into a bottle of rye."

"But you won't, Dave."

"Thanks for the confidence. Sorry for the self-pity. It's not my normal mode."

She thought for a moment, running over all possibilities. "Whatever his plans, he'll need money. Was anything withdrawn from his account?"

"Not a cent. First thing we checked."

A thorough examination by the gate revealed only rough gravel. Winds had blown sand across the road. As they got into the SUV, Belle rubbed her shoulder. She'd wrenched it moving wood from the pile to the deck crib, and it was taking its middle-aged time to repair. "When I get home from work, I'm taking a hike and getting into a nice hot sauna before dinner. Last one of the year."

She listened to him talking on his cellphone, getting patched through to Detective Sumner. "A cruiser's already on the way. And now that they have a lead on where he's been, they're bringing out the Canine Unit. If he's in the bush, he'll be found. No worries. That's what he said. No worries."

Belle met his eyes. "Dogs can work miracles, days, even

weeks later. Things are moving, Dave. And he's still alive. That's the greatest gift."

At the office, the first thing Belle did was call Hélène, but the number was busy. She didn't reach her until four thirty, when she got home early, having left Miriam to man the barricades.

"Dave just called. The magic ingredient in my jerky. How clever of you to remember. And you think he may have left? But where now? Back here by the same route? Why doesn't the boy smarten up?" Hélène asked.

"Any news about the mysterious e-mail?"

"Let me check my notes. I'm not a computer expert, but I may become one." There was a pause while she told Ed that dinner wasn't ready and that he wasn't to fill up on the pickled eggplant. "It was a Hotmail address. The police traced the source."

Belle sat up. "And?" Where would the cybertrail lead?

"A public-usage computer at the MacKenzie Street library. They have six, and there's no supervision."

"So it's local. That's a relief." Better a local predator than one who could take the boy provinces away. She didn't elaborate to Hélène.

"Yes, and it could be another teenager. We don't know." Belle heard the sound of a door slam and Ed's booming hello. "Got to run. Dave's here for supper, and the porketta just went in."

Belle hung up with a few encouraging words she was beginning to have difficulty believing. Clearly, Hélène was still rationalizing. If he'd taken the old railbed again, Micro would be back by now.

She took Freya up her trail to clear her head. Was it her imagination, or did a mosquito dive-bomb her ear? October 8th already, but the few warm days had resurrected another bloodthirsty generation, learning their vampiric trade from first hatch. As they travelled the soft turf, Freya chased a shrew into the underbrush in joyous abandon, receiving a nip on the nose which made her shriek. Her mistress's preoccupation with Micro had cut time from their activities.

Thirty minutes later, restored by the energizing peace of the forest, Belle collected wood from her tarped pile and went out to the little red sauna saved from the original cottage property. Opening the stove, she popped in paper scrunkles, kindling, then dry pine splits for a roaring blaze. After lugging a bucket of water from the lake, she placed it on the lowest tier of the wooden bench. No change room, nor shower. Finnish style without the birch scourges, it smelled like a cedar forest.

Back inside the house, Freya wolfed her meal as usual. With no meat unfrozen, Belle scanned the cupboards and decided to stay vegetarian in Micro's honour for another night. Eating less meat certainly reduced the grocery bill. A can of baked beans with molasses could dress up a raft of whole wheat toast. Easiest way to get fibre short of Freya's Metamucil, even if the Bumble Bea logo on the bread package was a constant reminder of the murder.

Storms aside, fall was the quietest time on the lake. Boats had gone to dry dock, snowmobilers fine-tuned their engines waiting for the big, deep lake's mid-January freeze, last in the region. The air was crisp and cool, and in the privacy of her quarter-acre, she was queen of a vast country, the 180° view of the mirrored lake framed by gentle, graduating hills. Near the North River, on a high island often shrouded in petticoat fogs, a Hudson Bay post had been built in 1820. It had taken nearly another hundred years before Europeans had lived here, working in the lumbering camps in Skead. Because of the difficult access, seventy-five per cent of the shoreline was still pristine wilderness, but that was changing, and not for the better. More people meant more noise, traffic and pollution.

Glad that the boathouse shielded her from the war-torn remains of the dock base, its shattered concrete walkway a reminder of nature's power, she poured a Maudite beer from Quebec and relaxed on the deck with the biography of Pauline Johnson she'd been reading. It told the story of a woman trapped between two worlds. Her father was a Mohawk chief and his devoted wife a shy Englishwoman. After her father's untimely death brought penury to the family, Pauline, a talented poet, took off on endless recital tours across Canada. Her poignant themes dealt with the denigration of a once noble people.

The overproof beer rocketed to Belle's head. One was more than enough. Going back inside, she shook off her clothes, then left by the basement patio doors, ambling barefoot across the sparse grass. Instead of a bathing suit, she wore panties and a towel around her shoulders. With absent summer neighbours on one side and a greenbelt on the other, she enjoyed total privacy. Going topless was legal for women in progressive Ontario, but how many tried it at the public beaches on Lake Ramsey?

Flushes of dry leaves from her prize maple near the shore were skittering in gentle dances. Belle never raked in the fall. From the surrounding forest, others took their place, so why not wait until spring? Savouring the sun, Freya rolled in abandon on the lawn, exposing her vulnerable pink groin, the true sign of a relaxed dog.

Belle's toes curled deliciously in the spongy turf, but as she opened the heavy door of the sauna, heat smacked her like a brick. "Wheew. Take my toxins, puh-lease." Hanging up the towel, she sat on the lowest bench, pulled the dipper from the bucket and ladled water onto the clustered cobble rocks framed in metal on top of the stove. Billowing steam rose in clouds, and for a moment she couldn't see, laughing at the effect. After relaxing for awhile as the temperature edged past 90°F on the old thermometer, she began scrubbing with the raspy loofah sponge, sluicing water over her arms and legs. Fish-belly white for the next seven months, it was the Canadian condition, healthy but as uninspiring as the oatmeal which had fuelled the nation's empire builders.

Stretching in languor, she left the sauna, her skin tingling, gave a quick glance along the lake, and waded up to her thighs, chuffing at the frigid water as she cupped it over her body. She thought she heard a splash as she hustled back to the grass, but being on one side of a point, she couldn't see far along the right shore. A flash of colour caught her attention as a white, black and brown merganser skittered across the water's mirrored surface, followed by his more prosaic, red-headed mate having a bad hair day. Belle chuckled at the performance. "Get going! You have a reservation in South Carolina. If only I could fly."

Back inside, she drizzled more water on the rocks, then lay down to let heat seep into her bones. The cold dip had penetrated to her core. How Micro had managed to plunge in during the storm still amazed her. Suddenly she felt selfish, enjoying herself while he.... She shook off the guilt. Everyone with a lost child learned that falling apart was no option. The time passed while she worked up an appetite, her stomach growling, the perfect sauce for any meal. She thought she heard a noise outside, perhaps a plane on the airport approach. Then the building gave a slight shudder. Blasting again at the new mine a few miles away over the hills? Sitting up too quickly, she felt lightheaded and remembered that she had skipped lunch. She needed to shower off the sweat and start dinner.

Belle got up, a bit unsteady and perturbed at herself for drinking on an empty stomach, and swiped her face with the towel. Then she closed down the fire draft. Heat would remain for almost twenty-four hours once the building had reached max. The large round thermometer read over 105°. She pushed the heavy wooden door, surprised at the resistance. Swollen with humidity? She pushed again. Then again. It wouldn't budge. She kicked it, threw herself against its boards and fell back, banging an elbow on the benches. The door had a tight fit, but it seemed nailed shut. Panic rose in her chest, and she began gasping. The tiny windowless building was a tomb, tough as the old miner who built it. And she had no axe, no weapon to break out. Sweat streaming down her face, her arms slick as they pounded on the door, she began screaming, pressing her face to the seams. Who would hear her? There wasn't another neighbour for half a mile, and no boaters. Struggling not to faint, she heard a whine outside. Freya pawed the wood, curious, then anxious, setting up a mournful howl. With choking breaths that seared her lungs, Belle assumed a tone of command, fighting a terror which might confuse the dog. "Go see Hélène! Go see Hélène! Go!" The dog would sense that her mistress was in trouble. There was no enemy to bite, no intruder to bark at. Only another human could come to the rescue. Would she understand?

Belle repeated the commands, and Freya continued to whimper, leaping at the door, her strong claws scrabbling. Then a yelp, followed by an ominous silence outside as the stove crackled and Belle's eyeballs burned like cinders. "Freya? Are you there? Speak!" Hoarse from yelling, she was sorry she'd called the dog back. Animals needed simple commands. Context and tones counted more than words. Her head was pounding, and cramps racked her belly. She was dizzy and weak, as if she'd run a marathon in Death Valley. This wasn't the way she thought amoral nature would punish her stupidity. She'd be on her snowmachine, bogging in slush on some remote lake or lost in a sudden atmospheric fog on Wapiti, out of gas and without shelter as dusk fell and a joyride turned deadly. Freezing was preferable, but the results were the same. Then she passed out on the floor.

EIGHTEEN

A pantheist who found her temples in the woods, Belle didn't believe in the concept of hell. But she was changing her mind, roasting in the belly of a deep-fat-fried whale. A human turducken. Images kaleidoscoped across her feverish mind, red lava floes shading to black. She watched her father in his gerry chair, gesturing and calling to her.

Then a pounding and a rush of air, but she was too weak to open her eyes. When she tried to talk, her swollen tongue cleaved to the roof of her mouth. Her throat constricted, she saw her father flex his muscles, rip off the lap tray and send it sailing like a paper plate, then rise, his legs oxen-strong. Once he'd jumped into a swimming pool, where her wiry six-year-old body was shivering from cold in the shallows, and lifted her out, hugging her to his warm and hairy barrel chest. Then her ears registered fragmented voices, moving in and out like the annoying static on the CBC. She tried to tune in, but she was out of range. Was she in her van? A crimson cloud blurred her vision.

Suddenly she was lifted into the air, floating, then laved in coolness, blessing its wash over her limbs. The Balm of Gilead. Then cruel rocks pressed her backbone. A chorus of voices, muttering, yelling, assaulted her from all directions. More lifting, her arms and legs dangling like a broken doll. The roar of an engine. Something wrapped around her. No longer hot, no longer cold. Perfect porridge for the three bears. They'd be in their dens now, like she was, snug and cozy. She submitted gracefully to fate. Grace was her hole card. Would she meet her mother at the end of that long, luminous corridor that ushered travellers between life and death? She wasn't ready, but how many people were? Would she return in another form? A pampered dog? A mini-poodle? She thought she heard herself laugh.

When she opened her eyes, she blinked at a strong white light. She could make out no figures, instead a vision from the wrong end of a telescope. "Mother? I didn't want to come this soon." She tried to rise on her elbows, but fell back from a punishing feebleness she'd never imagined. Something pricked at one arm, but if she didn't move, the pain subsided. The rules were clear. Then she closed her eyes and slept pillowed in a peaceful place with no more dreams.

When she awoke again, she saw streaks of dawn creeping through a window. But not her window. Not her spacious, comfortable room with its undulating waterbed across from the framed silhouette of her mother. A light came on. A jolly white-haired man with a big belly and a snowy beard stood by her side, holding her wrist, his soft hazel eyes crinkling. "Santa?"

"I've been called worse." He offered a cherubic smile. "Sorry about the harsh light, but I need to look at you. Feeling better?"

She felt restored, as if she'd had a blood transfusion. Lifting one leg, then the other, she breathed in deliciously. Her systems were working again, power and energy on the rise. Palmers were made of the same stern stuff that had sent their forebears thousands of miles from Inverness to the Holy Land, bearing their signature fronds. He affixed a blood pressure cuff, pumped and waited, nodding approval at the result. "120/70. Good." Then he flashed a penlight into her eyes. *I'm ready for my close-up now, Mr. DeMille.*

"What...happened?" Somehow she knew, but the details were splices of film stuttering across a broken screen.

"Welcome back, lucky lady. I hear you're in the real estate business. You came within a whisker of buying a lot from Saint Peter. If your core body temperature had reached 105°F, your organs would have shut down."

105°F. That was nearly the last image in her memory. On the empty bed beside them, he took a seat. Belle raised her hand. "What's this?"

"Simple fluids and electrolytes. The ice bath saved you."

"You gave me an ice bath here?"

Jim McAlister, according to his plastic nametag, chuckled softly and shook his head. "Maybe 'icy' is more the word. Your quick-thinking friends placed you in the lake. The ambulance would have taken an hour to reach your place. Close to thirty deaths in Canada each year from heat stroke. Usually athletes or the elderly shut up in apartments, but saunas can do an efficient job." He consulted her chart and levelled his eyes at her, clear and honest, like her father's. "No cardiovascular or respiratory conditions. The woman, Mrs. DesRosiers, is it? said you aren't on anti-depressants or neuroleptics as far as she knows, but your blood showed traces of alcohol. That's a bad combination for high temperatures, especially if you're alone."

Belle tried to remember. "One beer, but I guess it was a strong one."

He raised a mildly chastizing eyebrow and cleared his throat. "You must have passed out."

Chunks of memory were assembling like dominoes. "The door! It stuck!" She shifted in bed and winced at a pain in her right elbow.

"Surely not enough to have imprisoned you." He moved

her arm gently, examining the purple bruise. "You're a strong woman. Look at those biceps. Do you lift weights?"

"It's heredity. My father looks the same. Or at least he did." The doctor was so kind, his admonition about the beer so gentle a lecture that she felt near tears. She licked her dry lips as her gaze gravitated to the water pitcher. Nodding, he poured her a glass, helping her shaking hands lift it to her mouth. City tap water she avoided, but now she sipped from the fountain of youth.

Paged by a nurse at the door, he said, "You can have visitors, but I want you to stay one more night. The blood tests look fine. I'm ordering an electrocardiogram to be on the safe side."

He patted her arm and left at eight, according to her watch on a night table, still ticking after its licking in the lake. Belle was vibrating at the idea he planted about coronary problems. "Snap out of it, you hypo," she muttered.

Half an hour later, in came Miriam, who ran to the bed and deposited a box of a dozen doughnuts. Even the luscious assortment pictured on the cardboard couldn't tempt Belle. She needed water more than food. Miriam hugged her fiercely, her Brillo-pad hair surprisingly soft, like the woman herself, who could scare off a mugger but wept at *Dark Victory*. Miriam rarely wore perfume, but a light dust of lilac talcum powder rose from her warm skin.

"Hélène called me last night, but visiting hours were over. I'll take the Auger showing this afternoon. I know your tricks. Drop of vanilla on the stove racks for a home-baked touch." She cupped Belle's face in her hands for an assessment, a worried crease dividing her light grey eyes. "I didn't know what to expect. You *look* all right. A bit pinker than usual."

"Medium rare. I'm okay, just humiliated. What would I do

without you?" Belle tried to sit up for a marginal dignity, but the hospital gown gave "off the shoulders" a new meaning.

"Hélène told me the basics about your accident. She was too busy with Ed to go into much detail."

"Ed?" Belle's blood pressure spiked forty points. "What's wrong with him?" She ran fingers through her short red hair, embarrassingly greasy and no doubt peppered with additional grey. This was no beauty salon, even at two thousand dollars per day.

Miriam stroked her arm, her face stern but reassuring. "You're getting pale as the chicken I stuffed for dinner. Don't fade out on me. It's nothing serious. He had some chest pains."

"Chest..." Belle felt a sudden nausea. Was she responsible for this crisis? Soon she'd need a keeper.

Miriam turned toward the door as a clamour arose in the corridor. Hélène wheeled Ed into the room while he barked directions. Parking him with a sharp look and kicking the tire for good measure, Hélène approached the bed. "You're awake. The nurse came and told me in the ICU."

Craning her neck with difficulty, Belle looked at Ed, fussing with his standard blue gown, trying to cover one large, freckled shoulder. "Ed, are you—"

With the professionalism of one who'd visited many elderly relatives in the hospital, Hélène cranked the bed up and adjusted the IV line. "Dad's fine. A pulled muscle in his rib cage. You know what happens when fat old men mention chest pains. They get every ding dong test tout de suite. Women have to grow their own bypasses like my sister Maria."

Ed grunted. His bare pink feet, totally hairless, bounced on the footrests like newborn piglets. "I haven't had a bite to eat since lunch yesterday. Do they starve people to get them out faster?"

Belle pointed to the box, and Miriam passed it around. Ed's round face broke into a holiday smile as he juggled a doughnut.

Hélène told most of the story, in deference to his gobbles. Freya had arrived on their deck and barked, joined by Rusty until the door was opened. Hearing all the ruckus, Dave and Ed came up from the dock.

"How did you know where to find me?" Belle asked.

"It was Lassie to the rescue," Hélène said.

Ed smacked his lips, red jelly dribbling down his unshaven chin, and reached for a maple dip. "Rin Tin Tin, more like."

"Leave some for Belle." Hélène snatched the box from his grasp. "Freya galloped along the road, down your drive, and straight to the sauna, jumping at the door. We couldn't imagine what could have happened, but we knew something was terribly wrong." She paused for breath, her bright eyes caught up in the drama, laugh lines softening the corners. "Dave was so fast. He ran like a sprinter and had you in his arms minutes before Dad and I could make our way down."

"Dave saved my life?" He'd paid her back in a way she couldn't have imagined.

"Forced the darn door. Said it stuck some wicked. You were out cold." She paused with a grin. "Well, not cold. Then the men put you into the lake. Dipped like a Dairy Queen cone." She looked at the cross on the wall and did a fast genuflection of gratitude. "Or maybe baptism is a better description."

"Call me born again." Belle shuddered to recall that chill. "So that's why—"

"Dave took the St. John Ambulance training. You were burning up. Face red as a lobster."

And without much more clothes, she thought, her helplessness a result of body and mind parting company. She'd never gone under anaesthesia and hoped she never would. Nor would she enter a sauna alone again. Social occasions only. Hélène cocked her thumb at Ed. "Mr. Arnold Schwarzenegger had to carry you to our car, show off his new hip. We told the 911 people that we'd meet the ambulance on the way to save time. We pulled a transfer at the North Star Confectionary on Skead Road. Dad had keeled over by then, so they got a twofer."

"I never keeled," Ed said with a pout. "You're exaggerating as usual, woman. Ought to write a book, the way you make things up."

Belle was tiring from information overload. As her swollen lids fluttered, she saw Hélène elbow Miriam. The women kissed her, and Hélène promised to return that evening with her reading glasses and vitamins. Belle dozed, vaguely registering conversation in the hall, clinks of carts, rolling gurneys and the occasional laugh which relieved the poignant traffic of health care. When she was taken down for the electrocardiogram, she slept through the experience.

Back in her room at last, she felt a cool, gentle hand brush her forehead. A tiny woman in a white habit, bent from a humpback, hovered at her side, an odd plant in her wizened hand. The blood-red garnets in the rosary at her waist winked, the concession to luxury reminiscent of Chaucer's Prioress. "I chose this one especially for you."

It was Sister Veronica, a Cecilianist nun, who preferred the formal habit out of tradition or stubborn individualism. The Health Centre had originally been St. Joseph's Hospital until the amalgamation of Sudbury's three care sites. Of an age known only to God and probably fudged in personnel records, she worked sixty-hour weeks in "semi-retirement" and acted as Crisis Liaison Officer, comforting worried families and collecting toys for sick children and loaner plants for adults.

Every few hours, she cruised the chapel, where she'd met Belle last year, who had been praying that her father would survive a choking incident.

Belle squinted at the strange growth, green cups with pink insides, fringed with tiny spikes which closed over their victims, the stuff of science fiction or *The Little Shop of Horrors*. "A Venus fly trap? I'm not that ruthless a realtor."

Her thin mouth an enigma of dry humour, Sister gave an offended sniff from her patrician nose. "Cerberus is a personal favourite. It's a Darwinian, like you, and it'll provide entertainment...if a bug comes along."

Belle laughed until her stomach muscles hurt. "I'll leave the window open and whistle."

Pushing an errant grey hair back under her wimple, Sister gave her a steely look, as if the fun was now over. "I heard what happened. Everyone's talking about the woman with heat stroke at the beginning of October. Sounds rather foolish to drink like that."

Belle felt her face flush with annoyance at the rumour mill. Did the hospital broadcast bloodwork results over the PA? "God looks out for fools, and I had one beer. One." She described her friends' efforts.

A rare smile of nostalgia broke out on the venerable old nun's wrinkled face, a badger in drag. "Dave Malanuk. I remember Davey from that terrible tent fire. He was airlifted to Sick Children's Burn Unit in Toronto, then came back here for a month while the grafts healed. Sixteen. He was so brave." She paused in reflection. "Very determined. Nothing would stand in his way."

"Maybe that's why he chose fundraising as a career," Belle said. "Never takes no for an answer and makes people feel good about giving more."

"Yes, as I recall, he was instrumental in the drive for our long-awaited MRI machine." Sister Veronica glanced at the gold lapel watch pinned to her habit. Then she excused herself for a grief-counselling appointment as lunch arrived.

"Bring me back a Big Mac," Belle called.

She managed only the jello, juice and oatmeal cookie. What lurked in the other divisions of the tray would baffle scientists. A double chocolate doughnut added to the sugar fix.

At three o'clock, Len arrived with a bunch of red carnations, their fragrance adding a welcome spicy touch to the typical tang of disinfectant. "Dave called me. A sauna, for God's sake. Who would have thought?" he said. "How long will you be out of commish?"

"Getting sprung tomorrow. Have a doughnut."

"Sour cream. Mmmmm." Len took three quick bites.

This was beginning to resemble a party. Guests, food, entertainment. What next? She worked her brain to remember her former life. It seemed like a week since she'd entered the sauna. Was that how coma patients felt? Pulling herself back to the present, she asked, "So did you hear about the test results on that bone?"

"Uh." He struggled to swallow and looked out the window at an air ambulance settling down onto the helipad. "They...I'm afraid they lost it." His voice was subdued, and his pouchy eyes darted back and forth.

She didn't like the sound of this, and her voice rose. "The lab lost the bone? How could—"

"Not to worry. I'm sure it'll turn up. Listen up, I have new information on Jason Lew—"

"What's this about a lab and a bone? Are we talking about some half-baked civilian investigation?" A deep voice echoed in the doorway. In a charcoal trenchcoat, Steve walked in with an armful of reading material. He glowered at Belle as she squirmed like a shady ladybug on a pin, offering a few feeble sentences, reaching for the water in a bid for sympathy.

"You did what? At a crime scene?" His dark brows crossed into storm mode and lightning backlit his black eyes. Len moved from the bed and retreated to a chair, lacing his hands over his belly.

No sense in lying. Pick your battles. Belle struggled to explain herself, choosing words carefully, like playing Scrabble. Steve took his job seriously, so prickly about interference. "It had already been removed by a coon or a fox. We only—"

"It's a good thing you're *already* in a hospital." He gave a cursory nod at Len, whose head and neck were turtling into his torso then stabbed his finger towards Belle. "He's a PI, if that's any excuse. You're a realtor. Do I have to read you the dictionary definition?"

"Sorry, I've got an appointment." Len oozed out.

With an unintelligible curse which might have been Ojibwa, Steve dumped the pile on a table and strode out, leaving Belle like a child caught playing with hand grenades.

She amused herself until dinner by leafing through his thoughtful gifts. *Maclean's, Canadian Geographic,* even a *Storyteller,* Canada's fiction magazine. What surprised her was a hardcover copy of *Fast-Talking Dames* by Maria DiBattista, a comprehensive study of the era of babes, goddesses and working girls who came of age with the birth of sound and ran away with the times. $40.95. Ouch. He never stayed mad, but the tempest had to blow itself out.

Hélène returned at seven, carrying a wide-mouthed aluminum thermos and a couple of whole-grain buns. "Dad was still shovelling rigatoni when I left. Making up for lost time,

since he shed a few ounces. Here's some homemade minestrone."
She placed the reading glasses on the table with a baggie of pills.
"Hope I got the right ones. Just took a general selection from
that big jar in your bathroom. What's this lecithin?"

"Brain food. I'd better triple the dosage. You're an angel."
She pointed to the cumbersome tray with five kinds of mush
in neutral tones. It might have been shepherd's pie, lasagna or
lamb stew.

"Kill it before it multiplies." Hélène trucked the monster to
the corridor where she deposited it like toxic waste.

"The nurse said all meals come from Ottawa in a cost-
saving measure. Buying flats of TV dinners from Costco would
be a hell of a lot tastier and cheap. Take a letter to the Minister
of Health." As she heard a dog bark down on the Lake Ramsey
boardwalk where city folk took their pets, she realized that she
hadn't thought of the canine who had gone the distance.

"How's Freya?" Belle asked.

Hélène shook with laughter, pouring out the soup and
handing Belle a spoon. "She got a top sirloin as a reward. Could
have had a couple of pounds of old moosemeat, too, but Ed
cleaned out the freezer a few weeks ago and took it to the dump
along with a ton of junk in the plow truck. My cousin in Bisco
always brings us a fresh quarter at Thanksgiving."

Belle snapped mental fingers. The ancient plow truck's bed
was half gone, and a culvert humped the road near where the
suspect parcel had landed. "Wait a minute. Was the meat in an
LCBO bag?" Hélène's surprised nod gave the answer. That
explained the arrival of the package. She felt sorry about
having blamed the trapper, wherever he was now, probably
working his fall line at Thor Lake.

"Any new developments on Micro?"

"Best news for last. The bike tracks matched his model.

The Outside Store sold only five of those, and the police have accounted for the others. So he was there, Belle." She squeezed her hand and managed a smile.

After her friend left, Belle picked up the *Sudbury Star* she'd brought. A grow-op in the news again. Members of the Joint Forces Drug Enforcement Unit had raided an apartment on Prete Street. Over two hundred plants were found, each with a value of a thousand dollars. In addition, by-products such as cannabis resin, shake and bud were recovered. This initiative made the personal pot farm she'd seen in the bush look like kindergarten. Two hundred thousand? Her eyes bugged out like Sylvester's before a vat of cream. One good year and either early retirement, or a cell in the North Bay Penitentiary with no more bagels. She was still ravenous, despite Hélène's scrumptious soup. She checked the doughnut box. Empty.

NINETEEN

Shortly before eight the next morning, a huge nurse with chestnut eyes and a Celtic foghorn voice bore down on her with a tray. "Breakfast."

"Wonderful. Can you take off this IV?"

"Not on your life. Think of it as a little friend."

Eager to hear any news of Micro, Belle gulped the juice of undefinable extraction and took the hockey-puck bran muffin to the lounge down the hall. Seated awkwardly on a sofa, she dipped it into her tepid cup of brown water. "If this is coffee, give me tea. If this is tea..." she muttered as the announcer began. "Still no word in the case of the missing Sudbury boy. His father has offered a reward. Details at six." Dave was pulling out all the stops. As if he didn't have enough to worry him, he had to take time out to rescue an idiotic woman. A video came on with Micro opening a present at what looked like an outdoor birthday party. Bea was carrying a monster chocolate cake across the lawn to a group of giggling children in funny hats. With a clenched jaw, Belle wheeled forward to switch off the picture and grabbed a tattered *Reader's Digest*. "Ten Ways to Beat the Gas Crisis."

At high noon, declining the free lunch, with McAlister's blessing she divorced her little friend and cashed in her chips at the health care casino, having broken even by staying alive. Following hospital rules, Hélène arrived to push her wheelchair to the elevator, then out to the covered portico where Ed waited in their Buick LeSabre, its 790 station playing Patsy Cline's "I Fall to Pieces". Had she ever.

"Miriam is taking care of everything at the office. It's Friday anyway. You and Freya are staying with us," Hélène said.

"But I—"

Hélène placed a warning finger on her friend's dry lips, and short of biting it, what could she do but smile with gratitude? "Just for a day. When I'm old and greyer and need a vacation from Ed before I kill him, I'll stay with you, and you can treat me like a queen. Deal?"

She'd been warned about overdoing it, but over the weekend, primed with Hélène's stuffed beef roll and gnocchi, pillowed to death on the sofa with a copy of *Riders of the Purple Sage,* and forced to watch cooking shows all afternoon and American football until bed, Belle felt like a restive racehorse bumped at the starting gate. The second spare room had another torturous mattress, which folded her five ways. At least she scored some emollient for her lips, but she was tossing back their ibuprofen like peanuts.

Monday she returned to work and set the world on normal wash instead of spin. She called Dave to invite him to dinner, the least she could do, but got no answer at his house or office. In the meantime, the day for the appointment with Psychic Paula had arrived.

Tuesday at four, she and Hélène drove down the busy Kingsway and took a perilous road winding up the stark rock face that anchored downtown Sudbury. At the entrance to Paula's shabby stucco house was a shrine to the Virgin, constructed from small bits of coloured glass and cement. In an unusual touch, the statue was polished ebony. Hélène raised an eyebrow, but Belle wondered if it represented the

Black Madonna, a likeness found in many French churches after the Crusades, or whether the motif was New World. Dried bundles of goldenrod, black-eyed Susans and daisies decorated the rustic altar, sheltered by plastic sheets. Farther up the rock face, Belle thought she saw a chicken foot. Or was it a tangled root? Under a broken screen, a crayoned sign was affixed to the front door. "Come in."

In the tiny living room, strange spices made Belle's nose twitch. Curry? Coconut? Cabbage? Lime? Dusty brocade curtains were drawn against the light. "Please enter," a creaky, disembodied voice said, and they parted a beaded curtain into a dining room. In a long white linen dress, a wizened woman dark as India ink sat embraced by a massive high-backed rattan chair, a paisley turban on her head. Before her on a carved oak table was a crystal ball on a lace cloth. Belle struggled to retain a neutral expression.

"Welcome, Hélène. How lovely that you brought a friend."

As a furnace roared into action in the bowels of the house, the fug of oil heat began to move the air, tinkling the dangling crystals of the chandelier. After the introductions, the visitors took two plastic nesting chairs. Paula explained that she would try to channel into one of her contacts in the "shadow world which lies beyond ours."

"You have told me the sad facts of his disappearance. Did you bring an article belonging to the boy?" she asked.

Hélène passed over a FUBU T-shirt. A knot in her throat, Belle remembered Micro wearing it on their last morning together. With the reverence accorded the Shroud of Turin, Paula grasped it with candy-apple-red taloned fingers, closed her rheumy eyes, and suddenly the lights dimmed. An eerie green floated up through the ball like a ghostly protoplasm. Some form of pyrotechnics?

The air was suffocating, patchouli incense burning nearby in a censer hung from the ceiling. Belle shifted in her chair, on the alert for fakery. She could hear Hélène's expectant breathing, felt her own heart's drum. The honk of Paula's broad nose into a tissue gave strange punctuation to the tremulous moment. "Hold hands, my lovies. The circle will strengthen the power."

They locked hands and waited. Hélène's was warm, Paula's cold as raw turkey tendons. Outside, a cat squalled, and a transport's jake brakes shrieked. Paula's breath came in short gasps. "Are you there?" The table rapped twice. Belle blinked. They were still connected. Was a foot control in operation?

"Thank you for answering my call, Ruth. Ever vigilant for your fellow children." She summarized what Hélène had related, how he had vanished in the night on his bike. He had gone to a camp in the bush but had escaped their efforts to find him. The room returned to dead quiet. Minutes passed. Belle felt a sneeze coming on and fought the urge with no success.

"Sorry," she said, managing with a contortion to swipe her nose on her shoulder instead of breaking the circle.

"I sense an unbeliever here," Paula said in a hurt tone. "We must unite our spirits, not divide them."

Belle squeezed Paula's hand. "Sorry. I'm new at this."

After a few agonizing moments, Paula shuddered. "Yessssssss." She whispered sibilants, sometimes laughing, then reduced to guttural groans.

"Rest now. You have done well, little one." The lights came on, and the wrinkles on her face smoothed into a perfect serenity. She withdrew her hands and folded them.

Hélène's eyes widened with hope. "What did you hear? Did you see anything? I don't know how this works."

"Neither do I. That is the wonder of it all." The woman

spoke slowly, forcing each syllable around an ill-fitting pair of dentures. "My contact is Ruth Adams, a wee girl who died in the Spanish flu epidemic here in 1918. I visit her grave in the Eyre Street Cemetery to plant marigolds there each spring, her favourite posie. She tells me he lives. Those in the shadow world have special—"

"I knew it!" Hélène's fingers tightened around a handkerchief, twisting it into knots.

"And I saw green." Her eyelids feathered as she struggled for memory.

"Trees?" Belle asked.

"I suspect not. The aura is very light green, wrong for this time of year in a land of ice and snow. And metal all around. Cold. Hard." Paula pulled a shawl around her thin shoulders.

Metal. What sense did that make? Belle grew impatient. "Are you talking about a cage?"

"There are no...bars. He walks free, but he cannot leave." She covered the ball with a silk handkerchief and bent over in a coughing spasm violent enough to flatten a linebacker.

Belle turned away from Paula. A virulent cold was not the intelligence she sought. "Is he hurt? Hungry?"

The psychic pooched out her dark purple lower lip. "No sign of harm. He has food. His energy is strong, that boy. It reaches out from a long distance."

"So he's no longer in the city? Oh, my God," Hélène said.

Paula gave a vague wave of her hand. "Not that far. A day's journey, perhaps."

While Belle was still pondering the freedom paradox, Hélène rose, bracing herself at the table. "Thank you so much, Paula. You've confirmed my feelings. If Micro had been...had...I would have known."

Belle wondered when the charges would be forthcoming in

this hundred-dollar performance. "What do we owe you?" she asked in a bland voice.

"Not even an undervalued loonie, my chicks." She cocked her head. "You seek answers in unselfish concern. No Doris Day 'Will I be pretty? Will I be rich?' My services are voluntary. If you wish to contribute, please donate to your favourite cause. The Catholic Charities Soup Kitchen at the new Samaritan Centre on Shaughnessy Street always welcomes provisions to succour souls in the harsh winter to come. A full belly is the easiest wish to grant."

As they left, Hélène's face glowed with renewal, and she walked quickly. "I'm going to call Detective Sumner with this information."

Belle pursed her lips. "It's pretty vague."

Hélène turned and gripped her shoulders with passion. "Such a doubting Thomasina. If you were a Catholic, you'd know the power of faith and prayer. What's her motive? Not a cent. Doesn't that prove that she's no fake?"

For once, Belle was at a loss for words. No one denied that sometimes psychics did hit the mark. Other times they gave misleading or useless information, or if they seemed to know too much, became suspects themselves. Metal? Light green? A long distance? Was Paula a true seer, a fraud, or merely a well-intentioned old woman with time on her hands?

She stopped for cream at Mike's Mart in Garson, noticing that Bobby's Place seemed closed. "What happened next door? Bobby get the flu?" she asked the manager as she paid for her purchase.

The woman, a touchstone for gossip in the community, shook her savage red locks. "The legal flu. Pleaded guilty and off to jail once the sentencing comes through. I hope he gets twenty years."

Belle remembered Bobby's handsome smile and generous personality. "I don't believe it. He was far too nice a guy."

The woman leaned forward. "Listen. My daughter saw the tooth marks on his girlfriend's shoulders. It was damn sickening. Choppers don't lie. That's why he rolled over."

Bobby's smile haunted Belle all the way home. Now where would she get her father's meal? The Falcon Hotel was a popular spot. Surely they had mashed potatoes and portioned turkey slices.

That night she reached Dave to invite him to dinner. Life had to go on, and people needed the mutual support of social routines. Hélène and Ed were included, but they opted out, having committed to a fortieth anniversary celebration for Ed's brother.

"I'd love to come. Lord, I need a break," Dave said, then assumed a quiet, self-deprecating tone after she thanked him for rescuing her. "Anyone would have done the same. Your smart pup deserves the medal." He broke off for a sigh. "If I'd been a real hero to Micro, he might still be here."

His reaction to the information from Psychic Paula was similar to hers. "Hélène means well, I know, but most of those people are out to fleece the customers or exercise their egos. Sounds like creative guesswork. Sumner told me not to get my hopes too high. Whenever there's a missing child, Paula calls in on a regular basis."

Leaving work early on Thursday, Belle bought thick filet mignons from Terini's Meat Market on Lorne Street. A package of hollandaise sauce might clog their arteries, but Zocor would be a cheap generic by then. Fresh asparagus from sunny Mexico. Baked potatoes drowning in sour cream, bacon bits, chives from her faithful patch, and a tossed salad with mesclun, prepackaged in California. As Belle set up the CD player with classical selections, Freya barked, announcing Dave's arrival at six, a package tucked under his arm, letting Buffalo out of the rear. From the way the man walked to the deck, the loss of spring in his step, she could see that he was deeply troubled, perhaps even clinically depressed. His smile was forced as he presented the wine, creases dividing his wide-set eyes. He wore pressed dark slacks, a blue cable-knit sweater and polished low-cut boots. His hair needed a trim. She'd set aside her jeans and T-shirt to make the occasion special, choosing beige Capri pants, an off-the-shoulder leopard-print blouse and sandals.

Buffalo roamed the yard and whizzed on two deck posts. Observing the interloper, Freya raised her ruff and charged down, leaping past the dog in a customary bluff. The sheepdog tucked his tail between his legs as he lowered his gigantic head in submission before the Alpha bitch.

They watched the dogs circle, sniff noses and settle into an amicable truce. Dave gave a thumbs-up. "Hope it's okay to bring him. I should have asked, but Hélène said you had a female." His broad shoulders sagged in another message. "He's all the company I have. Mackenzie King passed on last week. Pined away, I guess."

"Bea said your parrot was quite the old man, but I'm sorry to hear that. Anyway, that male-female dog compatibility idea is pure myth." She wheeled the pine table on castors into the sun, its varnished surface set with placemats, cutlery and stemware. "A warm night. I thought we could eat on the deck. Al fresco. No blackflies."

"The weather's been fine since those rains stopped. One prayer that's been answered," he said, firming his lips and then swallowing, his Adam's apple bobbing. He was probably thinking that Micro could survive these temperatures, given shelter. But not for long.

Puffy, gilded clouds, backlit by the setting sun out of sight to the west, gathered in the sky. After handing her the package, he walked to the edge of the deck as if admiring the view, then took out a handkerchief, turning his back in a face-saving mode. She pulled the bottle from the bag and went inside to open it. Napa Valley Zinfandel. 1999. Usually rough stuff which married well with red pasta sauce. 14.9% alcohol. Who let the dogs out? Then she remembered that he belonged to AA. Diving into the bottle again?

He came to the patio door. "Just a soda for me. But tell me how you like the wine."

Perrier with a lime twist seemed a good alternative. "The label mentions dry farming at the highest level. Interesting," she said as they sat down in patio chairs. She knew the small talk wouldn't continue. No one could ignore the elephant in the corner.

"I'm no connoisseur. I asked the guy for the best suggestion to go with beef when you mentioned steaks. A little thanks for your efforts, too. Len told me that you talked to Jean. Funny old girl." Then he levelled his eyes at her, and the lines around his mouth deepened. He pressed her hand gently. "Going out to Massey after Sean Broughton? Bea said he was a hothead. That could have been dangerous. There's a murderer out there, and I don't want anyone in harm's way."

"I seem to be doing a remarkable turn at that in my own backyard," Belle said, stopping the wine in mid-pour. "Listen here. You saved *my* life, mister. Think of it as advance payment for my stupidity in the sauna."

After lighting the BBQ, Belle set dinner in motion. Dave offered to handle the steaks and had them juicy, medium rare with artfully crossed grill marks by the time she'd mixed the salad dressing with white balsamic vinegar and nippy Sicilian olive oil and brought out the courses. She had a fancy buttercream chocolate torte from Laitila's Finnish Bakery waiting for dessert. They ate until a tardy troop of geese winged overhead, stragglers far behind, their honks echoing like hoarse barks.

"Noisy out here," Dave said with the nuance of a smile over his even white teeth. Then he turned his head at the music inside. "Is that Holst's 'I Vow to Thee, My Country'? Bea loved *The Planets.*"

"Yes, it's a cut from *Dies Irae,* a choral collection." Wrath of God. Not a cheerful theme, but the selections were powerful and emotive like the struggles of a man coping with cumulative tragedies. Belle sipped the wine, upgrading her opinion of Zinfandel. Here was the king of its class, blackberry with hints of Asian spices and herbs. When she'd opened the bag, she'd peeked at the sales slip. Thirty-five dollars. Dave was no piker.

He finished the meal, which gave her some satisfaction. Like bruises against his olive skin, shadows had formed beneath his raven eyes. "I've posted a reward for information leading to Micro's return. No questions asked."

"So I heard. That's smart. Good people have already told police what they know, but lowlifes will be motivated by cash."

"I set the figure at $100,000." He looked across the lake, following the path of a plane heading south toward the airport. "Not that I have that kind of money at hand, but Bea put me on the property deed, and the bank has cooperated about a new mortgage. What does a house matter anyway? Without people, it's just a shell."

How Bea must have trusted him. These days many couples marrying later in life drew up pre-nuptials more ironclad than the *Monitor* and *Merrimac.* She gave a slight cough. "Do you still intend to sell?" She didn't mean it the way it sounded and hoped he wouldn't think her an opportunist.

"A smaller place would be ideal, maybe a condo if Buffalo can have a yard. That Laurentian Village on Paris isn't bad. Not this year, though." He clenched his jaw, moving a small muscle that revealed his ongoing tension. "When Micro comes back, I want his home, his room, to greet him, not a moving van."

Belle didn't mention the publicity surrounding the chamber of death. It would take a while before tongues stopped wagging and the John Street property resumed its stature as a prime piece of real estate.

"I'm glad to talk straight to someone about my son. You're Micro's friend, and that's golden." He cleared his throat. "Hélène and Ed are good people, but they skirt around the worst possibility, that he's in the hands of a pedophile. I can't stop thinking about that message on the computer. Every day that passes makes such a hideous idea more of a possibility. Even Sumner had to admit that."

Belle swallowed back a sigh. The mind spoke what the heart whispered. "I'm sure the police have been very frank. But there have been cases where children were recovered safely." In Florida, a baby thought dead in a fire had emerged as a six-year-old, having been stolen from her crib by a family acquaintance. Her real mother had seen her at a children's party, recognized the resemblance, snipped a lock of her hair on the pretext of removing gum, and found the DNA match. Fairy tales come to life. But how did that apply to Micro?

He rubbed his scarred fists and leaned his head back, muscles rippling in his strong neck. "I miss the little guy so much. You see, I couldn't have kids of my own. I was married in university to a corporate lawyer who insisted on a vasectomy. How blind and trusting we are at that age."

Belle thought of her first real love, the class valedictorian at Scarborough Collegiate. He had asked her out on many double dates before they went to the semi-formal. After that, nothing. Was it normal to have to ask a boy to kiss her goodnight? Years later, she wondered if he'd been gay. "I know what you mean. Hindsight is twenty/twenty." She polished her glasses on a serviette.

Dave kept opening fresh pages in his soul. It was almost embarrassing, but she owed him a sympathetic ear. "Then after I divorced and found Bea all these years later, I would have had it reversed, but since she was over forty, I didn't want to put her or a baby at risk. Micro and I had our challenges getting used to each other. That's normal enough. We would have worked it out."

She switched back to action mode instead of dwelling on fears and regrets. "Have you heard from Len lately? Did they find the bone?" She told him about the run-in with Steve at the hospital.

Dave blew out a contemptuous breath. "The cleaning staff sent it to a Dumpster, and it's at the bottom of a landfill, for all that matters. Sounded like a hare-brained scheme from a television show. I think we'll soon part company. His bills are mounting up with no results. What really ticked me off were his innuendos about Leonora. Leo was like a sister to Bea, for God's sake. He's such an owly guy that he probably still doesn't believe me. Maybe his job calls for it, but I hope I never get that cynical."

Their professions were at opposite ends of the spectrum. Sipping her wine and wishing he'd brought a case, Belle kept quiet. Dinner had been calm and reflective, and she feared the bad feelings that would emerge from her spying on him at the apartment. Apparently Len hadn't mentioned her tagging along. *Merci, mon ami.* "What about that man who drove the speedboat? If anyone had a grudge against your family, he did…in his self-serving mind, of course. Len said he had news, but I didn't get the details."

"Jason Lewis? That smug bastard destroyed a family and left beer cans floating in his wake. Bea told me about her victim impact statement. When that woman got charged up, good night nurse." He shook his head in admiration. "Everyone in the courtroom except for Lewis was in tears, including the judge and defense counsel."

Belle refilled their glasses. "Nothing can bring them back, but it must have brought…closure." Until he was released and came calling? Sometimes the law forgot the dead and their grieving families.

He gave an optimistic smile. "Detective Sumner told me that they've been in touch with the Vancouver police. Lewis has a cousin out there, and his truck was seen near Kamloops. They think he might be working up north in the lumber industry, in a place where they don't ask many questions. He'll be found eventually, and if he's responsible for Bea's murder, they'll have to lock him up to keep me away from him."

Suddenly a dull ringing came from the yard. The dogs pricked up their ears. In slight confusion, Belle went to the edge of the deck. As she homed in, she laughed in embarrassment. "My cellphone. I left it in the van."

Dave scanned the high hills of yellow birch and maple on the ridge behind the house. "Can you get a signal out here?"

"Normally not. But you've heard about Falco's Nickel Rim South development around the airport."

"I saw the new roads when I drove in. Nearly four hundred million dollars over the next five years, they say. Plenty of jobs. It's going to recharge the community."

"They put up a tower last week. Spinoff benefits. It will squeeze the bears and moose, though. Crown land's no protection for them when mineral rights are leased. I just hope the water quality doesn't suffer when they start crushing ore," Belle said. "Pardon me. I'd better get it. Business calls." She took the stairs two at a time and finally snagged the phone on the tenth ring. "Palmer Real—"

A small voice froze her like a slap in the face. "It's Micro. I can't...long... He's..." There was a garble of static and something about his head aching. Then a click. She realized that she had stopped breathing.

TWENTY

She whimpered, staring at the phone as if it were a lifeline severed by an axe. No bells and whistles on this toss-away model. No last call or call trace. Leaning on the deck railing, Dave looked at her in mild confusion, shading his eyes against the light from the setting sun rippling through the trees. Her legs weakened, and she slumped into the van seat. Sprinting, he came to her side, putting an arm around her, strong and comforting. How could she tell him how close Micro was, that his son lived in this toy of plastic and circuitry?

"What's wrong? Not your father, I hope. Hélène said he was in a nursing home."

Good and bad, she thought. Alive, but under someone's control, their worst fear. Tears of joy spilled down her cheeks, and she wiped them on her sleeve as she explained the few precious words she had heard.

"My God! At last!" He pumped his arm in a triumphant gesture. "How did he manage to call? He's a smart one. But a man's got him? 'He,' you said? What was that about his head?"

Had she dreamed all this? Dave needed to slow down, so that she could remember every word of the call. "It was aching. But he didn't explain. The connection was cut."

"Bea told me he used to have headaches as a kid. A sinus condition. Thought he'd outgrown it, but with this stress..." His voice trailed off as he eased the phone from her shaking hands. "I know the police numbers. Judy will be on this in a heartbeat."

"Judy?"

"Detective Sumner. At first I was doubtful about a woman handling the case, but she's been super."

After Dave left, spinning his wheels in the gravel drive and nearly clipping the garbage box, Belle called the DesRosiers with the news. Hélène could barely talk for crying. "They're coming out to take my statement," Belle said. "Paula was right."

Yet according to the bittersweet saying, it wasn't despair that killed, but hope. As two ravens swooped mock battles in the air, Belle returned to the deck and considered the wine bottle. A glass or two left to toast her brave friend. Micro had survived two weeks. He could survive another day, or another, but how long? She only hoped that he'd been able to hide his call from his abductor. The thought of the boy punished for his brave attempt to escape turned her to ice, and she hugged herself as a wind rippled the waters. But why keep him without claiming the reward? Because his value wasn't in dollars? The thought turned the wine to vinegar on her tongue.

Detective Judy Sumner, a woman in her late thirties with curly brown hair, trim and muscular in a light wool suit and low-heeled shoes, arrived an hour later and sat on the deck, warming herself with fresh coffee as the temperature dropped. Belle had to respect the fact that the detective had come so far so fast after working hours, and so she had prepared a brief time line of events, turning on the deck lights before she sat down.

"It's strange that he called here first," Judy said later with a quizzical look, entering notes into a pad. Her makeup was understated, a blush of peach on her full lips and a touch of mascara accenting almond eyes. Tiny rose quartz studs gleamed in her ears.

"He and his stepfather don't get along. Could be his aunt's number was busy. Still, you'd think in a possible life-or-death situation, he'd have called 911. Kids know that."

"It's clear that he trusted you more than an anonymous person. And this case has broken all the rules from the beginning. We know that he ran off on his own. Now apparently he's in someone's hands. It's a parent's living nightmare." She stood, checking her slim gold watch. "Let's hope he'll call again. Will you have that phone nearby at all times?"

Belle hugged the unit to her chest. "On my pillow. Charged and ready to go."

Saturday, Belle took a walk down the road to where she knew she'd find the *Sudbury Star* in a neighbour's drive. She shot a look up and down, cocked her ears for the sound of a vehicle, then knelt, slipped off the plastic wrapper and read the lead story. "Missing Child Calls: Mystery Deepens." The article quoted the Police Commissioner as saying that she'd put her job on the line if Micro wasn't found. Belle noticed that she omitted the word "alive." Every available officer, the OPP, and a task force of Mounties were sweeping the province. The reward had sparked hundreds of calls, screened by a host of volunteers working out of the old Cambrian Foundation building downtown.

After replacing the paper neatly, at a loss to pass the dragging hours, do something normal in a time when every day brought a fresh hell, Belle turned to yard chores. Drain and put away the hoses. Dig the last faithful carrots and beets. Mindless work. She couldn't concentrate. Even two lucrative house sales fluffing her bank account hadn't cheered her. She kept hearing that small, disembodied voice and struggled to analyze the few paralyzing seconds they had connected. He wasn't crying, but he had a headache. Was he injured, sick, feverish? If he'd been wet and cold, pneumonia was a possibility, but she'd heard no cough. Still, he had remembered her number and appointed her his saviour. If only there'd been a minute more between them, even fifteen seconds. She patted her sweatshirt pouch, where the cellphone rode like a joey, and whispered, "Micro, you are always, always in my thoughts. Don't give up."

Near the sauna, emptying cold stove ashes into the bush, she noticed Freya sniffing something, her tail up in abnormal interest. Rotten mushrooms and rabbit pellets were her favourite hors d'oeuvres. She walked over with a stern look, remembering the sharp and effective obedience-school phrase. "Leave it!" The dog dropped a small triangular piece of wood, which Belle inspected. A rough wedge with faint red smears and a slight smell of fish. Perhaps that's why the dog had nosed it. Her eyes tracked from the red of the sauna to the piece of wood as her brain's synapses snapped a path. "Good girl. Any more of these?"

In fifteen minutes, Belle found three similar chunks in the tangled verge of the yard. An inspection of the sauna door showed marks at the edges, but along with Freya's frantic scratches, hard to tell. She sat down with a shiver, recalling the slight movements of the building, which she'd taken for a mine blast. Had someone shut her in with these wedges? Though she'd declined to take high school physics, she reasoned that each push from inside had deeper set the triangles. Yanking the heavy wooden handle with a man's muscles, Dave probably hadn't noticed the small pieces in his panic. The effort had flung them away from the door, and perhaps the wind or small animals had moved them again. Yet why did they smell of fish? Or was there a carcass in the weeds on the shore?

After striking out at the Police Department, she called Steve at home, breaking a personal rule. Janet answered, her

Munchkin voice prim and unwelcoming. Why couldn't she understand that Belle was not her competition? She suspected that Steve kept their occasional lunches from his insecure wife. "Hon, it's...that woman."

She'd bet a pocketful of toonies that Janet hadn't called him "hon" since Mulroney was PM. Some clatter later, Steve picked up the phone with a "Yo."

She eased into the subject. "Sorry to bother you at home. That call from Micro has me chewing my nails. Any news on the reward?"

"The snakes are coming out of the woodpiles. A couple hundred already. We're stretched to the max following them up." Either his hot mood at the hospital had cooled, or he and Janet were sailing smooth waters for a change. His marriage was a barometer for his moods. "Call me a pessimist, but I would have bet the farm that he'd never be found alive. In ninety-five per cent of abductions by child molesters, the victim is dead within twenty-four hours. We need a credible tip to tell us where he's being held, but even then, his captors could have him on the move. It's possible that they've been waiting for the reward. We'll know soon."

She sighed in desperation, filling him in on Paula's vision, despite his implied dismissal. "Anywhere in Canada with lots of metal and a light green colour."

"Forget that hocus-pocus. I have a feeling he's close, though. In a couple of cases, the children were tied in basements on the same damn block. If he has the guts you describe, maybe he can get away again."

"I never thanked you for the magazines and book. Sorry about the scene at the hospital." She paused before disclosing her own discovery, struggling for the right words so that he wouldn't think her a fool. "There's something else." She described what she had found near the sauna.

His voice was skeptical, but at least he listened. "Don't expect anyone out for a couple of days. If that's all the evidence you have, this has the priority of a cat up a tree. But seriously, assuming it wasn't an accident, what the hell are you doing that someone would want to hurt you, or shouldn't I ask?"

"Nothing, but..." She related the pot farm incident. "I need to find Diedre Collins. I can't imagine that she's behind this, but I've seen her tire tracks in my drive, like she's monitoring me. And remember, out there somewhere is the angry owner of the pot farm she destroyed. I'm on that path several times a week. They might think I did it. People have been killed for less in Toronto. Twelve different grow-ops were raided in the same high-rise."

"It's not rocket science. Stay off those trails for now. And you haven't talked to her yet? I gave you that info a long time ago. Be careful what you say, and make sure a parent is present."

"I should have followed up, but other things are moving rather fast, Steve."

"Are you sure about what you found? Micro's disappearance has your imagination on overdrive. Those pieces of wood could be scraps left from construction. You're always dinging your mower on rocks or debris. I changed that blade for you last summer so that you wouldn't hurt your little hands."

"Little...imagining. Why you—" She could hear a singsongy voice calling him to a meal.

"Gotta go, but one last thing. About that PI guy, Len. Leave him alone. I had the buzz from Montreal that he travelled on the edges of biker gangs."

Belle smiled to imagine chubby Len on a motorcycle, but that picture in Israel portrayed a younger, more vital man. "Naturally, he worked undercover with the Sûreté."

"Every bad apple in Quebec tells his mamère that."

"He's been busting his...bum for Dave, even working nights. You told me how you have to cross the line sometimes." She felt her anger building, but reined it in.

"Is your hearing failing at your advancing age? I said 'draw the line.' This isn't a De Niro film. And what has he turned up? Dick-all. Malanuk will be well rid of him."

Monday's long-overdue trip to the bush brought Belle a welcome change to recharge mental batteries as the brilliant foliage ran its final diorama before the leaves fell. She would be driving north towards Timmins for two hours, then east nearly the same distance to Bobber Lake, where she was meeting the owner to list his camp. In Northern Ontario, there was no direct route. A huge square comprising the Chinaguchi and Temagami area, including the magnificent Lady Evelyn-Smoothwater Wilderness Park, sat in the middle. She could have travelled busier Routes 17 and 11, the other two boundaries, but quieter roads gave her more pleasure and relaxation.

As always, preparations were critical. Dressing comfortably in soft corduroy pants, a denim shirt with Micro's bear close in the breast pocket, and heavy Aran turtleneck sweater, she took her Gore-Tex coat, wavering, but at the last minute zipping in the fleece liner and popping a pair of gloves and a toque into the pocket. She drove in blue sneakers but packed hiking boots, remembering the times she "walked the line" with property owners who wanted to show off every bramble and puddle. Her car carried the typical emergency gear of matches, candles, chocolate and a blanket. Finally, she made sure her cellphone was charged. Technology had cut the risk of travelling remote areas, but often help was hours away, unless a rescue helicopter could land nearby. Considering the mute bundle of circuitry, she rubbed it like a genie's lamp. "Micro. Call again. Find a way."

Ready to roll, she opened her desk to search for a topo map of the area, folding a selection into her jacket pocket. Driving bush roads, often no more than deteriorating logging and mining tracks, had taught her that knowing your location was crucial. Many citizens leased remote patches of Crown land, a cheap attraction. Anyone could afford to put up a shack for fishing, hunting or trapping and be Lord of the Blackflies.

A call to the weather line brought no response. Was nobody home in government these days, in more ways than one? As she stepped onto the deck, she saw the thermometer reading only 6°C. Perilously close to frost, the first time in a month. The opposite shore was in fog, stitches of the dark low hills peeking through. Threads of vapour rose skyward, as if the lake were on fire instead of reluctantly yielding its stored warmth to the cooler air.

Having "reserved" the night before, she dropped Freya off at Hélène's in case she had to stay overnight, and was offered a mouth-watering breakfast of buckwheat pancakes, eggs and lean deer sausage. "Buckwheat's good stuff for you," Ed said, as he drowned his plate in maple syrup.

Belle checked her watch as she finished the last morsel, blotting her mouth and getting drowsy from the carbo hit. She got up to pour another regular coffee Hélène had made for her. "I hate to leave town. I keep thinking that any minute we'll hear—"

Ed cleared his throat, and Hélène put a hand on her shoulder. "I know. Dave can't be far from a breakdown. A human being can take only so much. I've lit a candle to St. Nicholas every day. He's the patron saint for lost children."

"Call me in the late afternoon, whether you're staying over or not. That route's dangerous," Hélène called as Belle pulled from the drive. Belle tooted, and her friend's waving form grew smaller in the rear-view mirror.

Stopping at the mailbox pavilion, Belle opened a letter from Joyce Fitzgerald, a distant relative, who had once sent her genealogy information logged from the Latter Day Saints' database. The letter said that it seemed that they shared a great-great-grandfather, William Palmer, married to a Mary Chalmers. "We are wondering about William," Joyce wrote. "In the 1871 Ontario census, that name appears only once. The background is described as African, his religion Baptist." Using the Ontario Cemetery Finding Aid website, Joyce had located a place where a William and a Mary Palmer were interred and was tracking down the inscriptions on the tombstones. Lakeside Cemetery in Sarnia, a huge burial ground on the Michigan border. Belle made some fast connections. Did that ethnic origin explain his son Reuben's enlistment in the Civil War? And Reuben's son Thomas, Belle's grandfather, who'd died the year she went to university, had a broad face, a deep tan and lustrous curly white hair. If Thomas Palmer were a quarter African, a quadroon, that made Belle's father an octoroon, and Belle a...? What a sign of the times that there were once such fine distinctions. Mary Chalmers, of obvious Irish ancestry, marrying a former slave in the early 1800s, would have been a singular woman, braver even than Bea. William could have crossed the border to Canada through the Underground Railroad. She remembered reading about Black farming settlements in frontier Ontario. Knowing her father, when she told him this information, he'd say that it explained why he'd won Charleston contests in his teens. Poor Henry Morgan would get his ear worn off listening to his new blood brother.

Checking her watch, she looked left towards the short distance to Skead and decided to double-up on her tasks. Steve was right. She needed to set this Collins girl straight. A few minutes later, she entered the former logging village of three hundred, passing St. Bernardine's, where Hélène worshipped, and parking at the small general store, which, except for Tony's Marina, was the only business. A boy barely in his teens was restocking the video rental shelves.

"I'm looking for Deidre Collins. Do you know where she lives?"

"Just missed her. She should be walking toward Kevin Street. Poor kid. Someone stole her bike a couple of weeks ago." A tongue ring made him click when he talked.

Belle exited the store and drove a few blocks until she approached a lanky girl toting a quart of milk. "Diedre?"

The girl's freckled face, thin and suspicious, narrowed into an expression of sheer terror. "Leave me alone. I know who you are."

Despite Steve's caution, Belle got out of the van and walked over, hands up in an unthreatening approach. "You don't know. That's why I'm here." She stood in front of the girl, noticing her patched parka and jeans worn at the hems, less from fashion than want. A pair of dirty white runners were on her feet, one toe duct-taped. A scab on her chin completed the image of a tomboy, or could it mean abuse? Suddenly Belle felt like a bully.

"You left a note on my van and damaged my wiper."

Diedre smudged a hand across her runny nose. "You can't prove it."

Belle sighed. "True enough. But I didn't put those pot plants in the woods, and I certainly didn't harvest them. I just walk there."

The girl's tiny button eyes narrowed, and she flipped back her braids. "That's what they all say."

"I'm Belle Palmer, and I sell real estate. Anyone in Skead will tell you I'm no law breaker, or ask the police. You must have better things to do than ride by my drive."

The girl gave a bitter laugh. "My bike's been stolen. Why

do you think I'm walking now?"

Belle gave her a half-smile. In some strange way, the plucky girl reminded her of herself at that age. "I might be able to use someone for snow shovelling this winter, cleaning off my woodpile from time to time. Interested? I'll pick you up."

The reply was tenuous but promising. "Maybe. The only job for a kid over here is the paper route, and that's taken. But I'm going to ask Sergeant Rick if you're okay."

Satisfied that Diedre hadn't been involved in the sauna incident, but concerned that she might be a target of someone more dangerous, Belle resumed her trip to town. She stopped at the darkened office to collect her file and a contract. Parking at the TD bank to make a withdrawal, she saw a local eccentric, Marty Melnor, dressed in woollen monastic robes covered by a thick velvet cloak, her elongated head exaggerated by a silken turban over a bronze buzzcut. Belle had met the forty-year-old woman at the magazine rack at Black Cat Too, a local bookstore and café. From literary conversations in the Café Matou Noir in back, she'd thought Marty was a professor. Then she learned that the former librarian was on a disability pension for a bipolar condition.

"How are you, Marty?"

"No complaints. Yourself?"

Belle gave the so-so sign, then turned to notice the familiar cowboy-hatted man seated on a bench sipping a coffee, the dog snoozing at his feet. Belle caught Marty's eye and inclined her head. "I heard about his situation. So young. Sad, eh?"

Marty's unashamed unibrow rose over a teardrop-tattooed eye. "Allan Ritchie? He's doing fine these days. Got him a nice room at the Park Hotel down the hall from me. Drives an old Honda Civic, too, instead of walking. Says he found a part-time job at Bingo One."

Len would be glad to hear about Allan's turnaround, Belle thought later as she picked up 144 North, notching the bedroom communities that ringed the city. First Val Caron, Francophone Chelmsford, Dowling, then Onaping with its ski hill.

She passed Cartier and Benny, defunct railroad depots fast becoming ghost towns. At Halfway Lake Provincial Park, she drove open-mouthed by the remaining destruction of what weather experts had called a microburst. A few years ago, the violent storm had cherrypicked its way through the popular spot, turning hundred-year-old trees into matchsticks, leaving campers in shock and awe.

Then the bush got lonely fast, and gas stations were rare. Prepared for the absence of radio signals, she plugged in a tape of classic musicals and began tapping her toe to Roz Russell croaking "One Hundred Easy Ways to Lose a Man" from *Wonderful Town.* The line about correcting the boyfriend's grammar made her grin. Yet for some elusive reason, the name Ritchie kept tickling a corner of her mind. Her cousin in Etobicoke was Barb Ritchie, but where else had she heard it recently? In her reverie, she didn't notice that a giant transport had barrelled up behind on the narrow two-lane and was attempting to pass. His downdraft nearly sent her blocky van careering onto the soft berm into a rock cut spray-painted "Yves and Danielle 1988." She pulled to the side a hundred feet later to let her heart still. The adrenaline rush shook her leg with palsy. No room for error on these roads. She didn't want to be driving them after dark.

Thirsty from breakfast, she took a bottle of water and unscrewed the cap, enjoying a long drink. Allan Ritchie. Didn't someone with that name buy the old brewery Cynthia mentioned? That didn't jibe with what Len had told her about Allan's homelessness. Did he have a trust fund, family money as the realtor had hinted? She put down the bottle and wiped her mouth. Maybe Steve was right about Len's shadowy past. Were the two working a con about Micro to extract money from Dave? A hundred thousand wouldn't be chump change for either. She shook her head. The timing was wrong. The brewery had been purchased before the boy disappeared. Len was a comical figure, but she trusted that two-eyed, two-armed flying purple people eater.

The maples splashed peach-melba tones against the buttery birch leaves. A huge aspen shot fountains of golden coins in her path. At intervals, the conifers opened to ring lily-padded swamps or the occasional lake. In the summer, these places provided free camping. Yet it was Paradise Lost. She could see remains of garbage, burn piles and broken glass at some sites.

She wasn't going as far as Mesomikenda Lake, but it wasn't a place she'd forget. Ten years ago with her friend Jim Burian, she'd canoed a route which ended by traversing that long body. A violent storm had hit during their last hour of paddling. The sky had dropped a black velvet curtain as thunderheads loomed. Seconds later, a deluge of water filled the canoe, and they had barely made shore, no gentle beach, but a steep climb with packs. Unable to raise the tent in the wind, they had sheltered under a tarp, fighting hypothermia, while, tied to a branch, the canoe filled with water. With more nostalgia than horror at the selective memory, she wondered if Micro would like canoeing. Several islands an hour's paddle from her home had level campsites and would make an easy... Then she pounded the steering wheel and concentrated on the road. Entertaining happy thoughts about him was as useless as expecting the worst.

At eleven she reached Route 560 and headed east to Shining Tree, centre of an old gold mining area. On an Ojibwa canoe route between Temagami and Mattagami, the town was named for the profusion of gleaming white birches. It was a fur-trading post by 1905, and in 1911, a rich metal find had brought miners from all over the country. When a fire had burned out the undergrowth, explorations were expedited. The lode measured fifteen by a hundred miles. In 1933, the *New York Times* had called it the biggest gold rush since the Forty-niners and the Klondike. Now the old roads and trails were used by quads or snowmobiles. She crossed small streams, then the CN rail tracks before passing a few tourist-supply businesses and a liquor outlet. Belle was getting concerned about the time, but she'd play it as it laid.

Gowganda was a pretty little settlement on the Montreal River. Then she continued in the direction of Elk Lake, taking a cut-off north at an old two-storey abandoned house, weathered to grey, its tin roof bleeding rust. Originally the front entrance would have sported a braced porch and balcony, but it had rotted away, leaving above an eerie "suicide door," as Alice Munro had termed it in one of her matchless short stories about small-town Ontario.

Reading the expensive routed sign for "The Bilbo's," she winced at the ubiquitous apostrophe error, but it was not a realtor's role to correct clients' grammar. The humpbacks in the grassy road punished her undercarriage. At a few deep mud puddles, the all-wheel-drive repaid its cost.

At last, she reached a tidy A-frame on Bobber Lake, an oil-drum diving raft the only sign of people around its azure depths. High on a dead spar, the wide nest of a long-departed blue heron testified to its supply of fish and frogs. A tall, wiry man with huge ears and a handlebar moustache, Eino Bilbo offered her a delicious shore lunch of crispy lake trout with tangy whole-grain mustard and fried potatoes, which nearly made up for the trip. She gave the camp a tour, changing to her hiking boots to walk the lines, to admire his raspberry patch, and to list the place at a reasonable $30,000.

Her watch read two p.m. Eino scratched his grizzled jaw. "Hell, you'll never make it back to Sudbury before the sun sets. You could bunk here, or if you want a head start, there's a motel in Shining Tree. Food's good, too."

With those last magic words in mind, Belle opted for the conservative side, and an hour and a half later, pulled in at the Three Bears Camp.

"My, yes, we're always busy," Serena Johnson, a pudgy woman in the office said. "Bear all fall and moose for another few weeks. Grouse year-round. December we'll get the snowmobiles. Makes a change from Windsor, where I was raised in the banana belt."

Wearing a thick Scandinavian sweater over Farmer John's, Serena showed Belle to her cabin, northern-style with pine panelling and heaps of colourful Hudson's Bay blankets. She turned on the electric baseboards below a paint-by-number picture of Lake Louise. "Frost tonight. You'll be cozy in no time." Gesturing to the TV, on which sat an ashtray in the shape of an elfin catcher's mitt, she said, "Satellite. Tons of movies. Got us a hot tub and sauna at the lodge, sixty-inch TV at the bar and grill. And when you're hungry, tonight's the moose stew special with dumplings, soup and salad. All homemade. My husband's the genius in the kitchen."

Belle took a long, hot shower. Thoughts of Micro crept back unbidden, especially after the news about frost. For the sake of sanity, she pushed them aside. Her throat was dry from the trip. Wouldn't a cold beer go down well? And what about some scotch to take to bed? She'd forgotten to bring a supply. No way was she paying by the shot, though. Palmer family rule. What about that liquor outlet on the way in?

Later, she tuned the TV to a numbing number of programs, appreciating the peace of her recent media fast, and checking only the Weather Channel. Ugly stuff coming late tomorrow. Possibly white. By then, she'd be back. She looked at her watch. Only four. Drive to the LCBO, come back and relax in the hot tub. Cancel that. No suit. She'd brought along H. Mel Malton's *Dead Cow in Aisle Three*. The antics of the witty puppeteer who lived in a cabin with her dogs in cottage-country always made her smile.

As she drove west and stopped to fill up at a self-serve Petro Canada station, wincing at the frontier surcharge of an extra fifteen cents per litre, she found a signal and dialled Hélène to tell her not to worry. The line was busy. Her father also needed to know that lunch would not be a go tomorrow. He should be watching *Judge Judy,* complaining that she was a bossy shemale next to wise Judge Wapner. Though he didn't have a phone because of his long distance shenanigans a few years ago, an aide would bring the portable model residents used.

"Nurse's station." God bless the towers, knitting the North together. There was a delay of a minute after she explained herself, then his voice came on, mellow, resonant, fifty years younger than his flagging body.

"Pardon? You can't come Tuesday, Tuesday?" He paused, and she heard a polite bark. "Yes, Puffball. Dinner's ready. A piece of meatloaf has your name on it. Gravy, too. Don't tell Nurse Debbie, the old battleaxe."

"I'll be there Wednesday, Wednesday instead," she said, imitating the double language he sometimes used.

"Got a letter from Mary LaGrotta today. We need to remember her birthday. December 3rd." He was referring to his girlfriend in Florida, a lovely, zaftig Italian woman from the Life-Goes-On group who had made him laugh like a teenager as they chatted daily on the phone in those happier times.

"Sure. I'll get a card. She loves flowers. We can wire an assortment." Using the word "we" made him feel included, as he should be.

"Perfect, perfect. Any sign of that boy?" he asked. Last week over lunch, she'd finally filled him in on Micro's disappearance when he'd asked why she had looked so sad. Children in trouble were a painful subject for him. He didn't understand a world in which it was even possible. "Doesn't make sense. Runs off. You find where he was hiding, but he's gone. Then he calls you. What did he say again?"

Belle warmed at his healthy interest in the case. Charging the minds of the elderly kept them active. She dreaded the day when his intelligent blue eyes would stare straight through hers to an emptiness from which he'd not return. "He said he had an aching head."

"What? Speak up. I can't hear you. Where are you anyway? Out of the country?"

"Of course not. I'm up north in Shining Tree. He said he had an..." Something caught in her throat, and she cleared it with a cough, then bellowed. "An aching head!"

"No need to yell. I'm not deaf, like the fossils around here. Aikenhead's Ancient Ale. Every time I had to get the old LaSalle and drive a can of film up to Parry Sound because they were going to have a dark house in the Strand Twin Theatres, I'd put in at the Brunswick Hotel. Always ended up in the lounge with a pack of travelling salesmen. Bunch of practical jokers. But why is a boy drinking beer? I thought you said he was a nice—"

"What's that about ale?" Belle's heart doublebeat, and she placed a hand on her chest.

"Aikenhead Ale. Haven't seen it since St. Laurent was PM. Uncle Louis."

TWENTY-ONE

Promising him on her mother's ashes that she would bring lunch with double ice cream, Belle sat back on the seat, trembling as she sifted through several topo maps of the region. She selected the one named for its largest landmark, Opikiminika Lake, with a dirt road to the southwest as Cynthia had indicated. It passed the lake, crisscrossed the hydro pole lines, bridged rivers and creeks on its way south. Then it ended where a cluster of dots and a grid indicated a building site. A rail spur linked it with the Ruel stop on the CN main route to the west. The vast wilderness to the south boasted over eighty lakes and virtually no inhabitants, leading south to the Thor Lake region, where her favourite marten trapper had gone.

Aikenhead. It was giving her an aching head, too. What did the old brewery and Allan Ritchie have to do with Micro? Was she spinning the world's most irrational theory? Did Len lie to her, or did Allan lie to him? Was either man keeping the boy at the brewery in a scheme to extract that hundred thousand from Dave? If so, why hadn't contact been made? And why buy the place, for God's sake? All she could hear was his small voice, static in her ear, then a sickening click that shook her to the core.

For a moment she thought of calling the police, or at least asking Serena, the woman from the hotel, about the exact location. Then an old man gassing a rattletrap pick-up noticed her consulting the map and strolled over, unlit cigar in his mouth. He tipped back his ball cap. "Help you, lady?"

"I'm trying to find an old brewery, Aikenhead's."

He drew his finger along the same road she'd located. "That's her, all right. Hear the place got sold. After all these years. My grandpa used to work there. Mines closed and lots of fellows needed a job. Free keg of beer at Christmas. Damn good stuff, too. Old German recipe. Not like today's sissy swill."

"How's the road? Any washouts?"

"Good clear to the end. I got some partridge there a few days ago." She nodded her thanks, and he moved off. "Gotta hit the trail. It's the Kap by midnight, then on to Thunder Bay to see my new granddaughter."

She headed west a few miles to the logging road, then stopped and scrutinized the map with more care before folding it into her coat pocket. From her observations, the road snaked into the bush for fifty kilometres, passing Opikiminaki Lake, then a series of creeks, Little Meteor, Meteor, Raven before heading west into a flat area where the brewery was located. The forest closed around her like a cloak, opening only at occasional interstices with the hydro lines. In almost an hour, she passed no one.

She drove on, eye on the clock, calculating how much time she had to turn back safely before the sun fell below the horizon. At one point, she braked at a swamp to watch a cow moose forage for pickerelweed, the beast's slack jaws dripping with water as her head rose. Beside her, a spring calf watched the van, twitching its ears in nervousness.

Her stomach made moans of protest to her stubborn mind, and she wondered whether she should give up and head for a home-cooked meal at the Three Bears. She might have been totally mistaken about the meaning of Micro's words, yet someone had bought the old plant. The road had been narrowing, with no clear place to reverse. Suddenly, it ended with a sharp right turn, the shambles of mossy split-rail fences marking an entrance. An old painted sign lurching into a ditch caught her attention. She stopped and got out. Surrounded by beaked hazel bushes and tall grass, it bore the image of a family crest, a maple leaf above a rampant moose. "Aikenhead Brewery. Serving the North Since 1920. Ten miles." The days before metrics. She lived on the cusp, accepting centigrade, starting to think in kilometres, but baking with cups and spoons.

A track led into a grove of birch backlit by the sun setting in the western sky. From the crushed bracken, a few vehicles had travelled it recently. For a moment, she wished she had Steve or Dave by her side, someone to sort this out. Curiosity as much as concern for Micro led her on.

Big deal, she thought, excusing herself as she pictured her saner friends' disapproval at a questionable excursion to a remote place so close to twilight. A quick look, and out. Surely there would be a parking lot, some vantage to scope out the place from afar without being seen. Running alone into danger was such a cliché for a woman, and she weighed each moment that Micro might be suffering against the odds. She turned on her cellphone. Signal clear. No worries now in an emergency. 911 would bring an OPP unit from Shining Tree. The overhanging willows and pin cherry trees brushed her van as she turtled forward, her blood pressure rising steadily. From the depths of a lemony aspen stand, a "Hoo HooHoo Hoo Hoo" echoed, and she saw a dark form perched on a branch. The great horned owl who guarded her property would watch over her.

At last, slipping along soundlessly across a sandy patch, she reached a large clearing with no visible vehicles. What remained of a dirt parking area was now peppered with scrubby poplars and birch having taken root over the decades. Surrounded by shattered glass and shards of scrap metal sat a derelict car, Capone vintage, tires rotten and its windows gone.

The massive, incongruous red-brick brewery reached three windowless stories, a castle in the wilderness. Two large, round white exhaust stacks bearing the Aikenhead crest rose a hundred feet. Several outbuildings lay in stages of decay, doors sprung and windows splintered like ravaged eyes. A ziggurat of wooden barrels faded to grey had tumbled at random, the broken staves poking up like supersized fries. Her neck muscles ached from tension as she inched along, craning her head. The warble of a raven picking at paper led her to lean out the window to notice the fresh remains of a chocolate and marshmallow pie wrapper. Her breathing quickened, and her foot trembled on the gas pedal, braced for a fast and dirty exit.

Although a couple of broken-down boxcars sat at the end of a railway, a shiny new hydro mast connected the building with a pole. She thought about Paula's vision. Commercial green paint was common in plants. And a brewery would be filled with metal structures. She bit her lip in frustration. Either this was all coming together, or she'd need intensive psychiatric therapy for an imagination gone wild.

She parked the van behind an industrial-sized garage and took a two-foot Maglite from behind the seat as a cold wind swept across the lot. Putting on her coat, she walked toward the complex, ready to bolt at any movement. It had a delivery area at one end, leading to three sets of giant doors where she could make out the words, "Nature's Pure Spring Water Makes a Superior Beer." Cynthia had mentioned a spring. This *had* to be the place Allan had bought. If her theory about Micro was wrong, what did she have to fear? If it was right, she was his only chance.

Belle walked the perimeter, trying several doors with no success, knowing it would be foolish to call out before she could assess the danger. At last she climbed concrete stairs to an office entrance. A shiny, unsnapped padlock was hooked on the staple. She removed it, pulling the rust-streaked door with a creak that made her cringe, advancing warily. It led to a dingy reception area, nothing more than a few wooden chairs, two desks with black rotary phones and assorted file cabinets with a 1955 wall calendar displaying a cheesecake picture of Marilyn Monroe. She crept along down the hall, opening each door with the delicacy of a surgeon, some rooms empty, the last two with metal bunks, dressers, clothes on the floor, new *Playboy* and *Penthouse* magazines, beer cans and full ashtrays, a makeshift dormitory. Her sense of fear sharpened, but it was too late to turn back now. No cars in the lot didn't mean she was alone.

Then she parted a double set of doors, gazing up open-mouthed at twenty copper vats, each reaching two storeys inside the vast warehouse. Instrumentation panels of complicated controls, dials and levers monitored the brewing process, but they weren't making suds here. Some of the glass was cracked, and levers were missing, yet the plank floor was as spotless as if it were swept daily. The atmosphere was oddly humid, and a strange herbal aroma teased her nose. From somewhere she heard the dull buzz of fans. Each vat had a plywood door installed into the side, and a web of wiring and plastic tubing snaked down from above. Entering one round incubation chamber, she blinked at the sight of hundreds of green baby pot plants, scarcely six-inches high. Sprinklers joined massive light systems on the ceiling.

A grow-op. And on a potentially gigantic basis, or getting there fast. Had Micro stumbled onto something in town and been taken here? Then it wasn't a case of a molester after all. Where was he? She swallowed against the possibility that he'd already been moved far away, or worse yet, left in one of a million hiding places in the bush. Cold sweat trickled down her back, and she felt her knees tremble.

Beyond the brewing area was a bottling facility with dusty cases of empties, labels and caps beside a broken conveyor belt. The next door led to a storage room for wooden packing boxes with the brewery's stencilled name. She passed a small bathroom and noticed fresh shaving supplies on the sink beside an old can of Bab-o, still useful after half a century.

Then as she tiptoed farther down a hall, she heard the faint cadences of a familiar song and froze in her tracks. "Clap Hands Til Papa Comes Home." She could still see Bea nodding her head at the sweet and gentle rhythm. How the lovely song must have sustained him. She had to take the chance. Time had run out. "Micro?" she called, her words sticking in her throat.

"Belle! I'm here! Down the hall."

Galvanized, she ran like a sprinter as his voice led her along a dark warren of halls with only the flashlight to point the way. At last she came to a frosted-glass door which opened onto a staff changing room. Flanks of rusted metal lockers stood like sentinels. Frantic, she stumbled over a bench as she pushed down one aisle. "Where are you?"

"In the bathroom!" he cried. And she rounded the corner into a room with a set of sinks, urinals and toilet stalls. He was sitting on the floor beside a storage chest, leaning against a pale institutional-green wall, his hands tied to a heavy water pipe. Metal grills crossed the filthy windows. No bars, yet a prison. Paula was a true seer, and the soup kitchen was getting a Christmas bonus...if she lived until then.

"My God. I thought I'd never find you." In her haste, the Maglite fell to the cracked linoleum, where it rolled out of sight under the chest. She hugged his small, tense body, gaining strength at the palpability. "So how..." Her hands fumbled with knots on the harsh polypropylene ropes which had made cruel abrasions on his tender skin. Bruises to the elbow purpled his arms.

"Please hurry, Belle. I'll tell you everything later. They could be back any...ouch."

"Sorry. I pinched you." Her hands shook from tension, her fingers uncooperative, as if she wore oven mitts.

Finally free, he stood and shook himself to urge blood back into his limbs. Despite his ordeal, he seemed strong. The boy inside was another matter. His sweet green eyes had changed, older perhaps, having seen things best unimagined. "How did you find—"

"My turn to call the shots. I've got the van. Let's blow this chipstand." A Canadian expression if ever there was one.

He gave an involuntary giggle, then covered his mouth as they retraced her steps through the complex until they reached the main corridor. The darkness made travel slow. Damn. She'd forgotten the Maglite. As they reached the office, the outside door opened, and Allan Ritchie stood there, tipping back his greasy cowboy hat, a toothpick dangling from his cruel, angular mouth. Instead of the shabby clothes he'd had in town, he wore a new leather jacket and clean cargo pants. "Lookee here. A visitor. Girlfriend of yours, little boy? Must like 'em on the tough side."

As Belle bit her lip and the lights came on, he reached into his jacket and brought out a blue steel automatic, which winked under the fluorescent wands above them.

"Run, Micro!" she yelled, and they took off down the hall toward the vat room. Why had those lights come on? Were they on a timer, or had someone else arrived? Seconds counted. If they could reach the van, they were out of here, foot to the floor. Micro could alert the OPP on the cellphone before they travelled a kilometre.

As she pushed into the huge warehouse, a stumpy, familiar figure blocked her way, his face expressionless, except for a flicker of sadness in his saggy eyes. Len Hewlitt held a large fire axe and cocked his head as a warning. Before they could backtrack, Allan strolled up behind them.

"Nice and easy. Nobody gets hurt. Get back to where you been."

Len said nothing as he followed. In the bathroom, Allan passed the gun to him. "Spread 'em, ladies," he said. "Got the rifle off him at the camp, but the little bugger had a weeny pocket knife I missed. Isn't that right, smart ass?" He gave the boy's head a mocking cuff.

Then he patted her down, enjoying the job a bit too much from the grin on his feral face, pitted with acne scars. She could smell stale tobacco smoke and a wisp of rye. "Hey, what's this junk?" He pulled the ceramic bear from her pocket and tossed it into the corner. She held her breath against his discovering the precious topo map folded in the breast pocket, but he finished, giving her bum a caress. Her jaw clenched. She doubted the van would be there if they ever got out, and should they take to the woods, they couldn't travel blindly. For some perverse reason, she remembered her wallet in the glove compartment. Two hundred dollars and credit cards. Invitation to a crime spree. Go see what the boys in the back room will have. What did it matter now?

Micro coughed as dust motes played in the dying sunlight,

submitting to the ropes as he slumped against the wall. Tears welled in his eyes though he turned his cheek. She swallowed back a painful lump, thinking of his long days in captivity, then this botched rescue. Hope lifted its pretty head only to get a slap in the face.

She was placed on the opposite side of the room, lashed to another heavy pipe. "It's obvious what you're doing here, but why did you take Micro? Were you trying to get the reward?" She drilled daggers at Len, who wouldn't meet her gaze. He pulled out a handkerchief and blew his nose with a honk. "You damn liar, Len. I trusted—"

"Shut up, bitch," Allan said, kicking her thigh as he checked his watch and addressed Len. "Rael and Jean-Paul will be here with more wiring for Vats 5 and 6. Dave's bringing a load of clones." Then the door closed behind them as the weak October light surrendered and the room darkened.

Dave. The dots didn't even need connecting. She saw Micro scowl at the name. Yet why draw patterns in the past when their short and brutish future was the only question? A plan needed to be made. What was the routine here?

"Jesus, I'm thirsty," she said. Would they remain like this all night?

"There's breakfast and supper, mostly soup and bread or beans, and water from the taps. At first, they just left me tied in here." He inclined his head toward the strong grills on the windows. "But I got to my knife and made it to the bunk room a few days ago. Allan's cellphone was there."

"Your call." What that bravery must have cost him when he was caught. Why hadn't she realized what he meant by "aching head"? "You told me enough. I wasn't thinking straight. What happened?"

"I heard them coming and made out like I was running for

the door. They didn't know I used it until later. Allan bragged that Dave had fixed it up, fooled you with a story."

"And how I bought it. Sinus headaches instead of Aikenhead." She blew out a contemptuous breath at the gullible idiot she'd been.

He straightened his shoulders. "The first night I was locked in a supply closet with a pile of rags for my bed."

"God, how did you stand it?"

"My tree house is pretty small. I pretended I was a soldier. They have to go through lots of bad stuff, and they don't always get food."

"At least they left us our coats. It's cold in here." She leaned against the wall, hot tears flooding her eyes. Belle turned her head to cover her stupidity and shock at the truth. She'd been led by the nose on a ludicrous wild goose chase that wouldn't have deceived a five-year-old.

Later, a light went on, and a man in his twenties brought in peanut butter sandwiches. Swarthy and full-chested, he was clean-shaven, short-haired like a military recruit, and dressed in hunting grey camouflage, an impressive Bowie knife on his belt. "I'm Belle Palmer. Who are you?" she asked. Perhaps if they exchanged names, personalized the situation, he'd be less inclined to harm her. Harm her. Now there was a concept. She was headed for a rendezvous in the belly of the beast.

Contracting his heavy eyebrows, he put a long finger to his full lips. Instead of untying them, he fed them with patience and offered cups of water, which dribbled down their chins. "Dere will be someone come later for your bathroom break," he said softly, a thick Quebecois accent in his consonants and a fist-fighter's bump in his long, pointed nose.

After the door closed, Belle turned to Micro. "How many are there?"

His round eyes blinked as he calculated. "Len, Allan, this Rael guy and Jean-Paul, a fat man. He's really mean. Calls me bad names and picks his nose. He smokes the product, too."

"Product?" What a little sponge he was. "Right. Anything else I should know?"

"Sometimes I hear more voices. And there are at least three or four cars with different engine sounds."

"Sharp ears. How did they get together in this business?"

"They act like they're friends of Len. Talk about places in Montreal a lot. Girls and bars. That kind of stuff." He paused, and his tones growled like a young cougar. "And Dave. Dave's the boss. He runs everything." With a bitterness beyond his years, Micro told her his suspicions that his stepfather had hired one of the group to kill Bea and make it look like the work of the serial killer. "I don't know which one. It doesn't matter. I just hope she didn't—"

Belle gave a warning "shush" as the door opened. A blond neckless man in faded work pants and shirt with rolled-up sleeves, revealing a cobra tattoo on his blubbery arm, arrived to oversee their efforts in the toilets. Jean-Paul barked orders and pointed a revolver, leaving no leeway which might be exploited. Manhandling them, he reeked of stale sweat and clouted Micro on the temple when he didn't move fast enough.

"What about later?" Belle asked, mindful of her midnight pee.

"Forget it. Need one before morning, and you can crap your drawers all I care. You're out of here tomorrow anyways. Nighty night. I gotta date with a bottle of rye."

As all but one of the lights were shut off and the door closed, Belle braced herself at his ungrammatical but dire promise. To their captors they were mere liabilities, pieces of meat for disposal. She had to be upbeat but straight with

Micro about the long odds against escaping. They would be freed again, with luck in this oaf's custody. He seemed the dullest of the lot. Probably learned to read from a case of beer. But without a weapon, how could they seize the moment? Then she remembered the heavy Maglite and twisted her head to glimpse its shadowy image under the cabinet. Nothing could clean a man's clock like a couple of pounds of D batteries. How could she reach it? Timing was crucial. A non-renewable, get-out-of-jail card.

"I'm going to be completely honest with you, Micro. After what you've been through, you can take it. But I must know everything. Tell me why they kept you alive." she said. Then maybe I can imagine what's in store for us.

He swallowed and gave a small sniff. "Dave owns the house now, but selling it takes a lot of time. Mom left me her half of the bakery. Leonora made an offer, but there could be a problem without a lawyer's approval. Something about a trust agreement."

"How did you learn this?"

"I heard Dave on the phone before I went to Aunt Hélène's to stay. I didn't know what it all meant."

"So if you were found dead..." Bad word, but what could shock him now? "Why does he need the money so soon? He seems set up enough here to start raking in plenty of cash, given the right connections."

Micro shook his head. "To buy the brewery and the equipment, he borrowed from some people Len knows. Really dangerous people, like in the movies. They don't want to wait. Allan and Rael were getting nervous."

Len. That sweet cat, Moshe. His lovely daughter. She wanted to strangle him, feel her fingers squeeze his flabby jowls. "Have they hurt you?"

"Len's the one that kept me alive. He keeps telling Dave everything has to be perfect, something about crossing 't's and dotting 'i's. They feel pretty confident, because the police think a ped...pedo—"

"Pedophile, a child molester."

"That's the word. See, when I disappeared, Dave got on a computer somewhere and—"

"He sent the e-mail?" Belle sat up and tugged at her bonds. Often people twisted their wrists and presto. She got rope burns.

"Jean-Paul laughed about it. Said Dave plans to drop a few more clues. Then I'll be found, my bike, too, somewhere far away." He pounded the back of his head against the wall. "I helped him set it up. If I hadn't run off—"

"Stop blaming yourself. Sure, it was a dumb idea. I could have told you living in the bush on your own was impossible." At the word "dumb", his sweet face fell, and she apologized for her lecture. As thoughts of their captors returned, she hoped Jean-Paul's date with the bottle included the others and would leave them all running on empty. She told Micro one plan. There wouldn't be time for another.

Belle's restive sleep was a series of troublesome naps that long night's journey into day, cramped and aching from the awkward position. She had no access to her watch, and when light slithered through the grimy windows, shining grate marks across the floor, she woke up to what might well be her last morning on the set of *20,000 Years in Sing Sing* with Spencer and Bette. She wouldn't go without a fight, and she knew that Micro would battle at her side. They had nothing to lose.

Soon after she and Micro had reviewed their roles in their command performance, Jean-Paul walked unsteadily into the room, bracing himself against a wall. "One at a time to the toilets. You first, girlie. Hustle!"

She made eye contact with the boy. Step one. Despite her fear about the next critical moments, she almost laughed out loud at the archaic term. *This girlie has a big surprise for you, J-P.* He had no gun, trusting his bulk to easily overpower her. As he fumbled with her ropes, a stale, sweet alcohol smell seeped from his large pores. His face was unshaven and flaccid, the bulbous nose sprouting hairs and his bulging eyes beeswinged with red veins. *"Tabernac* on toast. Granny knots are a bitch. You've been pulling at them."

Belle knelt, moaning in her best theatrical fashion and taking time to rub her wrists and knees. Nine hours without motion made the charade easy. She shot another glance at Micro, and he winked. *"Dépêche-toi.* Ain't got all friggin' day," Jean-Paul said, reaching for her arm.

"No! Please! I have to go first!" Micro yelled on cue with a pitiful wail. Jean-Paul frowned as he looked at the boy, his ox brain pondering the logistics. Belle reached under the cabinet, seized the Maglite, and hid it behind her as she stood.

"Wait your turn, you." As Jean-Paul shook his hammy fist at the boy, she brought the heavy light down on his head, hitting him once more for good measure after he fell. Blood spatter splashed her pants. In a minute, Micro was free, and they tied the man, gagging him quickly with his own shirt before he came to.

She plucked up the ceramic bear, kissed its nose, and asked Micro, "Perfect so far, but we can't afford one mistake. What's the safest way out?"

He snapped his fingers. "The loading ramp. They bring in supplies there. It leads out back."

Moving with speed and caution, they made their way to the vat room, slipped out a door and down the metal stairs. Belle scanned the parking lot, knowing too well what she'd find. The van was gone, probably on its way to a chop shop in Cornwall. An old Honda sat there, probably Allan's. They ran over and checked the ignition. No keys. Frantic, Belle didn't need to examine the topo in her pocket. There were only three ways out. The road, the railroad spur or the bush. Allan said that men were on their way. It was sixty klicks back to town on the road. Could they hide in the bush if they sighted a car? Door number two, the railway spur led to the main CN line along the Vermilion River. On such an exposed route, they'd be easy targets.

"Belle, look!" Micro pointed to the far end of the lot, where a panel truck crunched gravel, followed by Dave's Santa Fe. Suddenly the vehicles increased their speed, heading towards the frozen pair. A window opened on the passenger side of the SUV, and shots rang out, dinging the rocky ground. More bursts echoed from a shotgun in the truck, shattering the bushes.

A familiar voice, revealing the iron fist inside the velvet glove, yelled, "Cover the rail line! They're trapped." Two hundred feet away, she imagined she could see Dave's contorted face behind the windshield, an icon of trust, now a gargoyle.

"Into the woods!" Belle grabbed Micro's hand, and they zigzagged to the perimeter, shielded by clumps of willows and faded goldenrod.

They leaped the remains of a rusty wire fence and soon disappeared into the thick forest, following a game trail, then a ridge, the paths of least resistance. With at least three men, Dave was close behind, directing their pursuit with hoarse calls. They splashed through a stream, climbed on all fours to a hill of lustrous sugar maples. These venerable trees, a greedy species, blanketed the ground with their wares, leaving little undergrowth for concealment. She urged Micro to veer left to where a landscape of bushy striped maples helped their camouflage. Suddenly she tripped over a root, and her glasses flew off. As she struggled to her feet, she reeled in her nearsightedness at the vivid fall colours, a kaleidoscope of red, yellow, orange and green. Frantically she scanned the ground, a disorienting blur. Then a voice said, "I have them, Belle" and handed her the life-saving lenses.

Ten minutes later, they stopped behind a large granite outcrop to catch their breath. Luck and brains had been on their side. Running had caught the men by surprise. Dave probably thought she'd beg for her life, a foolish action. To set up and protect a project like this, what did a few people mean against millions of dollars? Had it all been set in motion when Dave had seen the opportunity for a copycat killing? How Len must have laughed when he'd talked about Broughton hiring a drifter for vandalism at the bakery, just like he'd engaged Allan. And the sauna incident. Len himself, skulking along the shoreline? With Dave rushing to the rescue from an attack he'd orchestrated. That fish smell on the wedges. Hadn't he and Ed been down at the dock? Angling for bass, he'd had scales on his hands when he pulled out the pieces of wood and tossed them into the grass. What a twisted mind lay inside his charming exterior.

They set off again, ducking their heads and scrambling forward. Belle tried to keep a bead on distant trees for directions, fearing that in the well-known phenomenon, they might circle back towards the group. Micro was panting, but gamely keeping pace despite the weakening confinement. His heavy basketball shoes slowed him, but they were warmer and sturdier than runners. The waterproof jacket over his sweatsuit had a hood, which he'd soon appreciate. She was glad she had zipped in her coat liner and added the gloves and toque. Hiking boots would have helped, but she'd changed to sneakers at the motel.

Suddenly they heard a distant barking. Micro turned, his face creased with stress as he bent over, his chest heaving. "It's Buffalo. I'd recognize him anywhere."

Through the capricious nature of sound through leaves, they heard Dave yell, "I've got the dog, and he'll find you. Stay where you are. You'll die out there anyway." At least he hadn't thought them stupid enough to believe a promise that they wouldn't be hurt, that the lucrative enterprise would be shut down, and everyone would fold tent and go home, crossing fingers and promising not to snitch.

Micro opened his mouth, but Belle closed it with her hand. "Is it a bluff? Could your dog lead him here?"

Micro gulped, then nodded. "He's my friend, but Dave took him to obedience school. He'll do what he's told."

She pointed downhill to a brook, and they splashed along a few hundred feet in the time-honoured method of eluding captors. Buffalo wasn't a tracking dog, and a leash would slow Dave. Still, it was a matter of attrition. A boy and a woman in her forties were no match for the strength and speed of men. Behind them came distorted cries and the crashing of branches.

After countless minutes of breakneck bushwhacking, with dead reckoning serving as compass, Belle and Micro took refuge in the embrace of a hollow cedar sarcophagus, blackened by a lightning strike. Her nose inches from the trunk, she could trace the regular patterns of scorch, smell the dry resin of the wood. The dog's yelps came closer and closer. Her heart drilled into her ribs as she held Micro in her arms, but she knew they could go no farther. His eyes were wild with fear as he pressed his cheek against her chest. She held her breath, praying to all the forest gods, when a grey and white bundle of fur bounded out of the bush with a woof.

TWENTY-TWO

He broke his leash. Good dog," Belle whispered as the animal placed his massive paws on Micro's shoulders and covered his face with loving licks. A frayed piece of cheap cord hung around the animal's neck. She stilled the boy with a hand gesture to listen for the crunch of feet on dry leaves. Only silence as deafening as the bush can be, punctuated by the twitter of chickadees. Then the rollicking animal sat quietly, expressing his happiness groin-first in the sincerest form of flattery.

She had few worries about Dave tracking them now. Even she couldn't have retraced their steps in the errant leafmeal and fall debris. She patted her chest to make sure of their one tool, the precious topo map. They had to find a safe place to study its whorls of hills and maze of watercourses, locate a landmark, make a plan to stay far enough away from the gang and eventually walk out. But without a compass? From the middle of nowhere? Maybe it happened in fiction, but such a feat pushed optimism to fantasy. Soon, judging from the sky darkening to pewter, they'd need shelter. The Weather Channel at the motel had predicted freezing rain turning to flurries, an evil combination in either order.

As they headed for a hill with heavy conifer coverage, somewhere to get their bearings yet stay hidden, she was glad that their coats melted into the surroundings. Hers was green, his tan. That protection also meant that hunters could mistake them for game, perhaps the dog, too. Meeting someone could save their lives...if they weren't shot first. Was it too much to hope that in all these thousands of hectares that they would blunder on a party chowing down around a campfire? She licked sweat from her lips.

Convinced that they were out of range of their pursuers, she spread out the map, starting at the brewery cluster. Her eyes swam with contour lines, trickles of creeks, height numbers on hilltops. All she knew was that Dave and his men blocked the way north towards Shining Tree and west to the tracks. East was a large chunk of swampland. Her mind working like an overcaffeinated chipmunk's, she scanned the horizon for a landmark. No sense taking one step without knowing exactly where they were.

"Did you miss me, Buffy? Give me five. Give me ten." Micro and the dog patted paws. Did he really understand the present danger?

Then, across a far ridge, she saw the tips of metal towers marching south like friendly giants. The pole line. Land would be rough-cleared for a hundred feet to facilitate access for repairs with Hydro's tracked vehicles. Wasn't it about time that Ontario's white elephant did her a favour?

Under a spruce, they huddled against a cruel wind which pummelled the heights. As she pored over the map, Micro looked at her with such clear and perfect trust that she steadied her voice, swallowing a lump of fear. "We might have a chance. That's the pole line three hills over. Once we get there, it's..." She counted the squares, each one kilometre according to the scale. "About twenty-five kilometres to Thor Lake. See those dots at McKee's Camp?"

His eyes widened, and he nodded with enthusiasm. "Lots of dots."

"Lots of dots are good. It means people and safety."

"Then can we catch a ride home?"

She forced a gentle smile. "It's only a railroad stop. No roads. But I know a trapper who should be there, and even if he isn't, we can flag down a train." Or could they? Surely in a matter of life and death...

"We studied Thor in mythology last year. He was a cool guy. Is the lake named after him?"

It took them a punishing hour to negotiate the heavy bush across the steep hills, hung up by deadfalls and scrabbling through alder groves which tugged at their clothes. Over, under, or around, three simple but time-consuming actions. Their faces and hands were scratched when they finally reached the pole line and stared down its interminable path toward the horizon. Twenty-five kilometres. No walk in the park. The land was cleared, but it was hilly country carved through rocks, and from her hiking experience, they might make fewer than two kilometres an hour. McKee's Camp was too far for tonight.

At least they couldn't lose the trail, a critical advantage. Each fall brought bulletins about missing hunters. Some survived, some didn't. Her arm ached from carrying the heavy flashlight. When darkness came... She didn't want to think of that, nor would she tell him that they'd spend a night outdoors. "Let's go, Micro."

"I'm hungry," he said later as they crossed the meandering trickles of the Wapiti River. In a rich irony, the tiny canoe in *Paddle to the Sea* could reach her lake faster than she could. Her mother had read to her at bedtime from that timeless children's book, and she'd imagined the little carved man bobbing his way across thousands of miles.

"Me, too." Her empty stomach churned acid on the

burning reserves that were fuelling their flight. His face was flushed with effort, as was hers. Fall was a bad time to forage. In spring they could have nibbled raw fiddleheads or tender cattails. Summer would have provided blueberries, raspberries and blackberries. Thinking about the juicy fruit reminded her that the bruins should be in their dens by now, storing brown fat for the winter. That didn't mean that they didn't stretch their legs now and then, another worry, especially with a cub, which denned with its mother the first winter to learn its trade. She shook off the image, preferring a bruin over Dave, the Dark Man, and his rat pack. Humans had more on their minds than a meal, a hidden agenda with the basest intentions.

The wind buffeted them in the exposure of the pole line, and she pulled her toque over her ears. She noticed that Micro's hands were shaking. "Take my gloves until the next rest, and put up your hood even if you're sweating. Heat loss will drain you faster than hunger."

Her watch read four p.m. in the waning fall light. They would have to stop soon and make shelter. Under a fir tree perhaps, the branches bolstered with overlapping birch bark strips, an impromptu hut. An uprooted cedar with a snug rootball hole might do the job if a bear hadn't commandeered it. No fire would warm them. Her matches stayed with the emergency kit in the van, wherever it was now, a cherry of a deal at only twelve thousand klicks. For a moment, she wished she were a chain-smoker with a ready Bic to flick. But Allan would have discovered that item in his groping.

As they walked, she'd been scanning the area for edibles, but the barren land offered nothing. On a rest break, she led him into the nearby forest. Even a token mouthful would give them heart. "Look for berries or mushrooms." She told him about boletes, an edible fungi with a spongy base instead of gills. As they passed a rotten clump, melting into the peat, her stomach lurched.

"Gross," Micro said. Nearby were a few young ones, which she pocketed.

She knelt to gather a handful of reliable teaberries, which wintered over and were more palatable in spring. Her old friend Anni had said that they gave strength and energy. But they were scant, only one or two per bush. "Taste these," she said, waving him over. "There used to be a chewing gum with this flavour."

His eyes wavered, but he ate them in confidence, then presented a yellow mushroom with telltale white encrustations of the fatal fly agaric. She tossed it into the dried ferns and grabbed his collar. "You didn't eat any of that, did you? It's poison."

His face bore traces of hurt and confusion, a wicked scratch on one cheek. "No, I wanted to ask—"

"Sorry for panicking, my friend. I should have known you were too smart." She placed an arm around his shoulder and squeezed. "Wash your hands in the next creek."

"Hope we get there soon. I'm thirsty," he added.

Drinking from a lake or stream would be a crapshoot in all definitions. Even dogs could contract giardia. In their fast-collapsing time frame, though, beaver fever would be the least of their worries. The painful but non-life-threatening condition took several weeks to emerge. Dehydration would stop them with the power of a sledgehammer. It was all a matter of calculated risks.

At the next sizable stream, she gave reluctant permission, and they knelt and slurped along with Buffalo, beasts of the field. Belle sluiced water over her hot face. She could smell rank sweat oozing from her underarms. "Our ancestors didn't have bottled water, and they survived. We'll have to trust our genes and pray that the microbes are swimming the other way."

He swiped his mouth with his sleeve and smiled, fast to forgive her recent alarm. "Nanny of the Maroons used to hide in the hills when she led the freedom fighters in Jamaica. She was Ashanti. That's African. Some say she had magic, but I think her troops were using guerrilla warfare. They disguised themselves as bushes and trees."

Her eyebrow rose in interest. "A female general. I'll second that. What does 'maroon' mean?"

"It's another name for a runaway slave."

A slave. Like her great-great-grandfather might have been. She explained the recent discovery in her genealogy.

"Really? How can you find out for sure?"

"Some records from that period have been computerized, but most have to be searched on-site. The Ontario Archives in Toronto is a good source. I have my great-grandfather's birthdate, so I can send away for his birth certificate, learning more information about his parents. Until then, it's a family mystery."

"Oooooooooo." He made a creepy universal sound for the paranormal and waved his hands. The casual conversation had lifted their spirits. Refreshed, they set on with a collective will. Even Buffalo ran circles like Freya did when excited and happy.

In a valley farther on, a swamp full of stumps and fallen logs bordered the pole line. Belle was heading over to a tempting crimson flash in a bush when suddenly she noticed that Buffalo had tracked something down into the weeds. There was a huge splash, and with horror they watched him swim into the water. A large dark snarling object rode on his broad back, nimble black hands gripping his fur. Frantically, the dog paddled forward, his front raised like the prow of a sinking boat. Dogs drowned this way, she thought, powerless to help.

"Can't we do something?" Micro clutched her arm, his misty eyes gathering despair.

They weren't fifty feet from a hot bath like last time when he'd waded into the lake. Getting soaked would send their chances to zero. She explained with quiet authority, "You can't go after him. Buffalo will have to deal with this. Make a lot of noise."

As they yelled and clapped, the raccoon leaped onto a grey cedar spar which pierced the swamp. A yellow stream of urine rained down onto the dog, a final insult. Trailing noxious brown muck, Buffalo climbed back out of the water and performed an undulating head-to-tail hula, then tried to rub against Micro's legs.

"Get off me. You stink like a big old rotten egg," the boy said, leaping away with a grin.

"The least of our worries," she added, her heart rate slowing. Despite the reek, she checked the dog for wounds, but his thick coat had protected him.

At the water's edge, she examined the late arrival she'd spotted, highbush cranberries. They picked a cupful.

At five o'clock, the sky an ominous battleship gray, Belle looked again at the map. From her reckoning, they were traversing Oxo Creek, which led to Nipper Lake. "Are we going to stop and make a campfire?" Micro asked.

"I don't have any matches or lighter, and the fine points of rubbing sticks I never mastered," she answered, massaging her painful leg muscles. She pointed to a tiny dot. "This could be a cabin." Or it could be the remains of a building from two turns of the centuries, either burned or abandoned. Topos weren't updated very often, for reason of considerable government expense.

Micro pushed back the hood on his jacket and wiped his forehead. His voice wavered as he looked at her, his eyes losing their lustre. "I guess I can't go much farther."

She knew it was bruising his young male pride to confess that, and she felt the same. The last meal had been a twenty-four-hour memory. She'd noticed him struggling to hide a limp an hour ago. "How are your feet?"

He sat on a flat rock and took off his shoe and sock, flashes of misery crossing his face. "It's only a blister. No problem."

Ugly, broken and weeping serum. "I've had my share of those. They can really hurt. I promise you we'll stop to find shelter in the next hour."

Her sneakers were soaked and filthy, and one foot ached from a heel spur. A cold, light rain began to fall, the turn of bad luck she had dreaded as they walked a rickety balance beam. Hypothermia brought confusion and certain death. Belle searched with fatigued eyes for the thickest possible cover, but here the land had flattened and gone to birch and poplar. Two hundred metres ahead she saw the dark green of protective conifers. "Another five minutes."

Dripping wet and bone-weary, they crested the top of a hill of feathery white pines, looked into a valley, and yelled at the same time. Nestled in neon-red sumach bushes, a small cabin sat at the edge of a shallow lake full of bulrushes and reeds, perfect moose territory. Beside it, a golden grove of quaking aspen whispered sibilants in the wind, their leaves rippling like a football crowd creating a picture. "In Xanadu did Kubla Khan..." she said, her voice trailing off as she knelt in the soft cover of fallen needles.

"Xanawhat? Who's Kubla?" He knelt beside her, shivering, his words stuttered, a sure sign of danger.

"An old poem about a palace, written by a talented man with a substance-abuse problem. This looks just as beautiful." She could see a tarped stack of wood on the porch. Surely inside would be matches or a lighter. They were saved. For now. And now was what mattered.

Coming down the hill, their knees buckling from exhaustion, they passed a building with a crescent moon carved into the door. "Do they keep their lawnmower there?" he asked.

She stifled a snicker. "An outhouse. A bathroom. No indoor plumbing. No electricity either."

"Looks cold," he said, one brow rising. "Are there snakes?"

"All gone to hibernation. Ontario doesn't have any poisonous varieties up here. Just the midget Massasauga rattler farther south."

As a rush of energy thrilled her muscles, she began to walk faster, water squelching in her shoes. It was an unwritten law of the bush that people in serious trouble could break into a camp. On the porch, she found an axe beside the tarp and snapped the old padlock on the door. Micro caught up, and they entered, shaking off the rain. She closed her eyes and took a deep breath. Maslow's Hierarchy. Get warm. Find food. Sleep. Under pressure, life simplified itself.

The building had only one room, about twenty-by-twenty feet, easy to assess at a glance. Two rustic camp beds. Rag rugs on the floorboards from a time when nothing was wasted. A woodstove, table and chairs. A kitchen with a sink and handpump.

"We'll take care of your foot later. Making a fire is job one," she said, fixing on the stove, a homemade version using an oil drum. It looked like it could warm a mansion. A wooden box held pine splits. The cabin had been used this summer, according to the dates on the *Field and Stream* and *Outdoor Canada* magazines on a barrel table. She passed them to Micro. "Crumple up these pages one at a time. No cheating. Then add the kindling. Get the driest wood you can from the porch."

"Any cardboard?" His smile sent a signal that he was better already. How quickly the young revived.

"If your preparation is careful enough, we won't need it."

While he busied himself, she found matches and a long BBQ lighter on the counter. Passing them over when he returned with an armful of pine and maple, she began to hunt for medical supplies. In an alcove, a dry sink had a bucket hung below the drain, a disposable razor, and a shaving cup with soap and brush. What stared back at her in the silvered mirror had hair plastered to its head, a scratch on its nose, and muddy streaks on both cheeks. "Hello, sweetheart," she said. "Come here often?"

In the metal medicine cabinet, she found an ancient first-aid kit with a blackened bottle of World War Two-vintage iodine. No sissy painless sprays for them.

From the crackling sounds which tickled her ears, Micro had the blaze going. She returned to find him placing two lanterns on the table along with a tin of fuel. "I found these in a cupboard," he said.

"Excellent." They shrugged off their sodden coats and hung them by the stove. "We're on a roll. Sit down, and let's check that tootsie."

He plopped onto a bed and pulled off his shoe and sock, yipping as the tender skin blisters ripped away.

"Ouch," she said, brandishing a pad. "But don't worry. I have just the thing. Moleskin."

"Yuck. Like from a mole?"

Chuckling, she placed strips of the pliant material over his heel and wrapped them with adhesive tape. "Soft like a mole." Then she pulled out the iodine. "This stuff's going to hurt, soldier. We'll only cover the major scratches on our face and hands. You paint me, and I'll paint you."

Soon after, still smarting from the cruel applications, each one uttering not a whimper, they put their soaked pants over a wooden chair, then pulled two more seats close to the stove, drinking in the warmth like cocoa. The place would be a bakery in twenty minutes. Where was Buffalo? Then she noticed him making himself small and cozy behind the stove, nose under tail. He'd take hours to dry, poor fellow. The downside of hair.

While Micro poked at the fire, adding maple once the pine got going, she prowled the cupboards. The owner leaving so recently was a promising sign. She took down canisters and opened them, coming up with what she expected. A chocolate bar would have been too much of a bonus.

He came to her side, peering at the collection. "Is there food, Belle?"

She arranged her treasures on the counter. A bag of flour, brown sugar, salt, baking powder and a can of bacon drippings. "Nothing else? How can we eat that? Are you going to make bread?" he asked, a crease between his brows.

"Bread without yeast." She laughed and chucked his dimpled chin. "We're going to set a world record for eating the most bannock in an hour."

"Ban—?"

"Where are those cranberries we picked? Check our coats." She worked the pump. Nothing. "There's a bucket under that dry sink. Get water from the lake to prime this." Willing as any man expecting a meal, he went out in his underwear and T-shirt.

Bannock was a lifesaver, nourishing and portable. They could eat their fill and make pounds more for the next day's travel. She found a bowl, measuring the ingredients by eye, adding extra sugar for energy, and saving the plump berries for last.

When he returned, with several arthritic squeaks, the pump plunged into action. Belle found a kettle to boil water. It looked clear, but no telling what might lurk in the aquifer. A couple of teabags from the pantry helped the taste, slightly metallic from iron deposits.

With darkness fast arriving, Micro filled and lit the lamps under her direction. Then Belle patted the batter onto a greased griddle. They waited, their grins spreading in a wordless communication, drips of drool at the corners of their chapped mouths. Savory aromas filled the air, and the dog joined the group, coming to rapt attention and raising a paw. She felt nauseous from hunger.

"Eat slowly," she said as she slid a golden cake onto his enamel plate, her hands shaking from low blood sugar. "Finish this one and wait a few minutes. I went to too much trouble to have you vomiting."

He explored the heavy pancake with a fork, the berries jewels in the crown. His light brown cheeks, streaked with iodine warpaint, filled like balloons. "Goobgh."

Belle had abandoned the concept of grace before meals when she left home for university, but she brought from her pants pocket the ceramic bear, one ear broken. She touched it gently as she placed it on the table and watched Micro smile. "Something is watching out for us in the forest."

"Really? Like an angel? A ghost?" He raised his arms and flapped them.

"A spirit. Remember the Deer Prince?"

"Now I'm glad I touched his nose."

As she enjoyed the carbohydrate fix, savouring the tart berries that exploded in the mouth, Belle explained her philosophy that all creatures shared the wilderness and had to respect each other.

"Have you seen a bear?"

"Lots of them. Nearly every day when I walk the flats in May and June. They're hungry, foraging on fresh spring grass before the berries ripen. I avoid the dense forest until August, because we can't see each other until it's too late. They need lots of room to run away."

"And they do? Always?"

She spread her hands. "Here I am to tell the tale. Noise helps, like with the coon. Some people wear bells or carry whistles. I sing. That's enough to scare King Kong." Recreating the woodland scene, she thought of Freya. Thank God she was with the DesRosiers and not waiting in a dark house for a mistress who hadn't returned to give her dinner. She mashed a couple of the cooling cakes and served them to Buffalo, giving him a pan of water as well.

She noticed that they hadn't mentioned what had sent them to this remote place. Perhaps that was good. They needed strong, positive thoughts to reach Thor Lake. Micro had finished all of the bannock, and he pushed back his plate. "I feel better, Belle. That was great."

"I'm proud of you. Any other kid would have folded." She could swear he blushed at the praise.

"Nanny of the Maroons, meet Alexander Bustamante, first Prime Minister of Jamaica," he said, shaking hands.

"Yes, your mother told me about him." How long ago, and how many life lessons since?

He gave a burp after patting his stomach. The cabin was home, and they were content for the moment, their clothes finally dry. "No bath?"

After draining her mug, she tossed back his teasing smile. "I think not. We'll splash off in the lake tomorrow morning."

Above the table, she saw a drugstore wall calendar and

thumbed it forward. Was today October 13th? She traced it with her finger.

"Important day?" Micro asked.

"My mother's birthday."

He blinked, his thick velvet lashes almost girlish. What a heartbreaker he was going to be in a few years. "She'll be worried about you."

"She died some time ago. Cancer."

"Not your father, too?"

"He's in a nursing home, but he's fine." She explained how he had given her the clue about Aikenhead.

"Won't he wonder where you are?"

"He doesn't know anything's wrong, and...and we'll be back tomorrow." There, she'd said it. Was it the big lie?

"Do you miss your mother? What was she like?"

Belle sat back and tried to put a long history into a few words. In a law-enforcement motif applied to her family, Father had been the good cop, Mother the bad. Father praised the As on her report card, Mother speared the lone B. A legal secretary who could have been a Queen's Counsel had she been born later, her mother had been an immensely talented woman, gardening, sewing and drawing. She just hadn't been a cuddler, nor did she coo over babies. Not until she was nearly seventy had she become nostalgic during Belle's yearly visits to their retirement home in Florida. Belle still recalled the last time she and her mother had hugged. Terry Palmer had been frail from chemo, her spine shrinking with age, a grey-haired child to her daughter, but spunky enough to tell Belle that her mashed potatoes needed garlic and should have been whipped with the mixer. "Maybe that's why I never thought about having—" She noticed that his eyes had closed.

After cleaning up, she turned out the lamps as they settled

into the bunks with satisfied sighs. Buffalo snored on Micro's bed, emitting pungent farts at intervals. The army-surplus blankets were raspy but thick. She nosed mildew on the lumpy pillow, letting a drift of smoke lead her towards sleep. She needed to think, plan more than a day ahead in case... Then she erased the blackboard of worry. What they would find at McKee's Camp on Thor Lake, they would find. *Que sera.*

She lay like lead, wide awake, her recovering muscles twitching with intermittent galvanic shocks. Her brain refused to accept the rest it needed, so she reviewed Micro's story, trying to piece his fragments with hers. The men hadn't laid out the complete scenario for the boy, just enough to speculate. Dave had hired a hit man for Bea, hoping to piggyback onto the two other murders, tossing in the missing payroll for motive. Was it Len? Allan? One of the Quebec crew? For all his duplicity, she didn't see her chubby ex-friend as a cold-blooded, hands-on murderer. Dave's next step was pure brilliance: hiring crafty old Len to search for the killer. She seethed as she recalled how he'd shared selected information, sent her on fool's errands, made suggestions about Leonora, Sean Broughton and Jason Lewis, even about Dave, the mastermind himself. Micro's running away had given them a lucky break. Of course, Dave knew about Camp Sudburga, and he'd found the boy easily. By the time he and Belle had arrived, Micro had been relocated to the brewery. Orchestrating his death would have taken some planning, but it would have come. Presiding at yet another funeral would have been Dave's finest hour.

She reviewed her actions in Shining Tree, doubting that a rescue team was on the way. Only the geezer at the gas station had heard her questions about the brewery location, and he'd been en route to Thunder Bay, a day's travel to the northwest.

Finding her overnight bag and a few clothes, the motel would sound an alarm, but with what results? They might think she'd been abducted.

She dozed off but sat up suddenly at an eerie call in the night, quickly answered by another, and for a moment she thought she was in her own bed. Then she felt the hard mattress and turned over, pounding the heavy pillow. One dawn she'd seen five wolves cross the ice. Usually they were very circumspect beasts, a threatened species. What were she and the boy? Prey or predator? Mice scuttled under the camp. Micro groaned in his sleep.

Later she heard him get up to go outside. "Take the flashlight on the table. Don't bother with the outhouse," she called. "It's probably full of spiders." In return she heard a squeak.

Finally, in the glimmers of the tardy autumn dawn, she awoke with a start as a roar blasted over the cabin.

TWENTY-THREE

For a gut-wrenching moment, she wondered if they'd been tracked, if Dave had fixated on the pole line, too, instead of believing them hopelessly lost in the woods, waiting for death. She peeked out the window, craning her neck to make out in the clearing sky a white plane, Bearskin Airlines, the red-eye from Timmins, heading due south to Sudbury. Taking a deep breath, she reminded herself that she wasn't co-starring in a Bond film with swooping Apache helicopters, hi-tech all-terrain vehicles, and rocket-propelled suits. Travel was slow and dirty in the North. The bush respected foot travel or canoe. Even in winter, with ponds and lakes frozen, snowmobiles couldn't manage the rough terrain she and Micro had breached in their first agonizing hour.

The stove was dead out when she got up, leaving her warm bed with reluctance. She found a knapsack and plastic bags, and packed the bannock, several lumpy pounds. After this orgy, she'd probably never eat it again, but it would serve them well on their cold march.

At the noise, Micro got up, stretched cat-like as if he had no worldly cares, and ran a hand through his curly hair. "Morning, Belle."

"Morning to you. One guess what's for breakfast."

"Yum, yum," he said, laughing as he pulled on his pants. Then he took Buffalo outside for their ablutions.

Belle scanned the small cabin for whatever might aid the journey. If...when she reached civilization, she'd pay the owner for their life-saving bed and board. She poured the water in the kettle into a plastic juice bottle and added it to the pack. The lighter and a bone-handled knife on a belt rode along. Two brown, durable canvas jackets hanging on the wall attracted her eye. They'd make good overcoats.

Micro returned, passing a hand over his wet forehead. "It's snowing."

She looked outside. "Only moisture in the air when the dew point freezes. See where the blue's coming back? Enough to make a Dutchman a pair of trousers." How many times had her father said that? Would she hear it again?

They went to the lake for a wake-up splash, kneeling as they cleaned their faces, arms and hands, laughing at their painted iodine streaks. Back inside, while she pored over the map, they munched the cakes she'd set aside. She moved her hand down many squares to a long, thin lake intersecting the pole line at the southern end. Slowly she counted, each half inch a punishing demand on their energy banks. "Thor Lake's getting closer. We've done thirteen kilometres. Twelve to go."

"I rode three times that on the railbed." Micro pointed to the dense, sculpted lines across the route. "What are those?"

She gave a rueful smile, fingercombing her hair, in need of a wash like the rest of her. Would she rather be fed or clean? No contest. "Height indicators. We have more climbing today. How's your foot?"

He pressed the heel with cautious fingers. "It's way better now."

Wait until you start walking again, she thought.

Finding a pencil and a paper bag, she left an apologetic note on the table and secured the cabin door by looping twine from a utility drawer around the handle and tying it tightly to a nail. The door would stay shut, protecting the interior. They buttoned the bulky canvas jackets and set off, led by the giant towers which marched across the landscape like Quixote's windmills. Stuffed with bannock, she felt more like Sancho Panza.

Over the next hour, the day brightened as the clouds parted to reveal a pale cerulean sky. Minus 10°C at a guess. Easy breathing, no catch in the nose or throat. Thanks to the double coats, they stayed toasty.

"I'll take the pack," Micro said, hoisting it at the next rest stop, a rocky outcrop which resembled giants' chairs.

The heavy frost made the leaves crackle as they walked, their breath puffing in the cold morning air. In a customary game from her hikes, Belle closed her eyes on a level spot. She could identify the leaf by its crunch. Thin poplar and birch were louder than thicker maple or leathery oak. From a spruce grove, Buffalo flushed a pair of clumsy, flapping grouse, which fluttered into the high branches. Their white, chickeny meat made Hélène's grouse fingers one of Belle's favourite treats. The bush was an endless party for the dog, accustomed to walking city streets, but it frustrated Belle to see food escape her useless hands.

As they advanced down the line, she wondered if her decision to leave the cabin had been wise. The land was open enough that they could have built three small fires in the universal distress signal. No one was looking for Micro here, but had her absence triggered the OPP into aerial action? No signs of a yellow rescue helicopter reached her ready ears.

On they plodded, up to a bald knob, down across creeks, around a smooth mound of rock. She pointed out the glacial grooves across the dark basalt.

"I heard about those. A couple miles high, my teacher

said." He followed the striations with his eyes. "North to southwest, right?"

As they approached a meadow, three deer foraging on dry grass sprang towards safety into the woods, lithe and sleek with white tails, facing a winter which would thin their herds and leave Darwin's best. Where would she rank at the end of the day? While she planned no Palmer additions to the gene pool, Micro deserved a chance.

They hiked through an old burn of jack pine skeletons, witness of a lightning bolt. Fireweed, pin cherry and other sun-loving plants had begun to reclaim the territory. Burns were part of nature's clean-up. Otherwise these species couldn't prosper. Only when man encroached and the sacred word "property" came under threat were the blazes perceived as bad. Every summer she saw thin wisps of grey in the distant hills framing Lake Wapiti and smelled smoke on the wind. Once a filigreed, blackened birch leaf had dropped from the sky into her hand, an eerie postcard.

When they stopped at noon for lunch, Belle reopened the map, creased and beginning to tear from hard travel and moisture. Pray God they wouldn't need it much longer. "I'm thinking we're here," she said, tapping a square. "Another two hours and safe at last." And surely they would be. Yet how many times had an adult lied to a frightened child to make him feel secure? She remembered her ruse en route to Silver City with Chris about the use of the word "retard" and decided to come clean.

"I have a confession." She told him about her fabricated cousin.

"That's okay. You taught us some better words. The substitute teacher had to look up 'bumpkin' in the dictionary." Micro munched his bannock, portioning some for the hungry dog. Buffalo had lapped at each creek, but their water was nearly gone, and the food was salty and dry.

"We're crossing into Lampman Township from Frechette. That's Harrison Lake," she said from the promontory, exposing unbroken wilderness in all directions. "Avery Lake's over there." She pointed east to a large body of water with jewelled islands.

"All these places have names, but no people?" he asked, a flash of wonder raising his neat eyebrows like tildes.

She pictured the last hundred and twenty years of the region's history: hunters, trappers, loggers and government mapmakers. "I guess someone walked in and planted a name on a hill, a creek, a lake. I do the same thing in my territory. Remember Surprise Lake?" She laughed. "Of course, it's not official."

"It should be," he said, considering the map with a serious expression and spreading two lithe fingers like a compass. Before she could grab him, with an impish grin he scrambled a few feet up the metal hydro tower and pointed northwest to two azure pools as he hung like a chimp. "There's Belle Lake and Micro Lake beside it."

"I'm the round, fat one, eh? Get down, you rascal, before you break a leg. I'm not pulling a travois, let alone constructing one from my clothes."

At three o'clock, they glimpsed the upper end of long, narrow Thor Lake. The last few kilometres took them along the shimmering water's east side. "Do you see anyone?" Micro asked, a trust in his voice which opened fresh wounds in her heart.

His gait had slowed, and he was limping again, as she'd feared. She cleaned her glasses, blurry with sweatfog. Far across, she imagined small buildings, but the trees were thick. Was that a movement near one shape or a trick of light? Her nostrils flared at the ever-so-faint aromatic cedar perfume of woodsmoke, a quick and easy fuel in early fall. To add to the fun, intermittent cramps niggled at her belly, a twenty-four-hour warning of her monthly biological clock. Men had it lucky. She shuddered at the thought of scratchy moss in her pants.

At the lake's terminus, they left the pole line, Belle kissing her hand in thanks, and crossed the narrow Vermilion River on a rustic bridge. From there they began hiking a well-established trail along the west side of Thor. Her muscles were screaming from lactic acid build-up. They were both an hour beyond the end of their resources. If the place was deserted, she was determined to drape herself over the tracks Perils-of-Pauline style and wait for CN. What if the trains ran only once a week?

Then she heard a melodious sound, silver in the air, rising and falling like a symphony. The guttural snarl of a chain saw. Picking up the pace on the magic of sheer grit, they followed it through the woods like Looney Tunes characters floating inches above the ground, past several cabins into a clearing. Beside a woodpile, dressed in lined jeans, a red wool checked shirt and pink knit cap with ear flaps, a familiar figure was chunking up a huge cedar log.

Belle made a wide circle to move slowly into his sight. She didn't want a Texas-style massacre if she startled him and he lost control of the machine's formidable twenty-inch blade. "Hello. We meet again." She bent to brace her arms on her shaking knees.

At first, his tanned, creased face registered confusion. Then he broke into a roar of laughter, switching off the motor and putting down the saw. Reaching under his hat, he scratched one ear. "Jesus, Mary and Joseph on a snowmobile. You followed me after all, or are you on some survival exercise?" He looked at the panting dog. "That's a herder, not a retriever, so you can't be hunting."

Sitting on a chopping block while Micro, once again a curious boy, wandered to the water's edge with Buffalo, Belle told him about their trip. Telesphore Rochette, Ted, extended a beefy hand, which she shook with more delight than meeting the Queen.

"By God, the radio's been talking for weeks about that boy. Heard something this morning on the short wave about a woman missing up by Shining Tree. Picked up by a stranger, they thought. You came all that way?" He put his hands on his hips and stared at her until she wondered if her face were dirty as well as striped with iodine. Probably. And who cared? She'd earned her smudges.

"Every motherloving kilometre." She rubbed her sore legs, the muscles stiffening. Steve would have relayed the news to everyone. But not her father, not yet. He had more savvy than to panic an old man.

"So you broke into Jon Saari's camp? He's a good guy. Lives in Coniston. Buy him a bottle of rye."

"He'll get a case of Gilbey's finest." She pumped her fist.

He looked down to the lake, where Micro was skipping stones. "The lad's a fine one. Yours?" In an old-fashioned gesture, he cut his eyes to her ringless hand.

"Just friends." So much more than that. They'd been to hell and back together. Belle heard a chattering and noticed a metal pest trap holding two furry babies. She gave him an ironic smile. "Are squirrel coats back in fashion?"

He shook his finger at her joke. "Meet Abbott and Costello. Their nest was destroyed when this rotten cedar fell. Killed the mother, too. They can't live out the winter on their own. I'm taking them home for my granddaughter to bottle-feed until spring. Do they ever like canned milk."

So the trapper had a soft heart, another human contradiction.

Barbecuing Elsie, Babe and Chicken Little, who was she to lecture?

"Hey, Micro," she called. "Come look at this."

He returned from the water and stopped Buffalo from nosing the cage. "Wicked!" he said, reaching toward a squirrel head poking through the wires.

Ted and Belle exchanged eyerolls. "Watch your fingers, son. They bite, and they're covered with fleas. Gotta dose them with powder from the pet store."

Ted took them into a nearby cabin, where he had a pot simmering on a cast-iron cookstove. Placing them at a table, he served that morning's beaten biscuits with a tasty rabbit stew. She noticed with a smile that Micro abandoned his vegetarian principles to dig in faster than a starving tick. She couldn't have pried him from the plate with a crowbar.

Ted poured himself a coffee. "I'm getting picked up tomorrow. Train only runs south three days a week. Got my quota, and I'm taking the wife to Victoria, where her sister lives. She's been bitching at me for years. Would you believe that it hardly snows there? Damn bulbs come up in February. Close as you get to Florida in this crazy country."

Before dusk fell, she and Micro grabbed bars of soap and towels, and headed for the lake, scrubbing off their well-earned sweat on either side of a rocky point. From his kitbag, Ted had managed to find clean shirts for them. Belle didn't think she'd ever wear that fragrant sweater again. Or maybe she'd frame it.

The trapper offered them his cabin with twin beds and made sure the stove was set for the night. "Sleep well, explorers. I'll bunk next door."

The next morning, after a breakfast of oatmeal laced with brown sugar and canned milk, Belle was outside with Micro showing him a small velvety mass on a maple tree. "It's a rare Hebrew moth egg case," she said, stroking it gently. "In the spring, it'll hatch. The markings look like letters."

Coming up behind them, Ted laughed like a loon and slapped his leg. "Never thought I'd find someone fond of tent caterpillars," he said, pointing farther up to cottony black masses in the branches and the desiccated remains of an army glued to the trunk.

"Ick," she said, wiping her hands. Nature loved to play tricks.

Around ten o'clock, the conductor of the Budd car, an independent engine unit used in remote areas, was amused as Ted loaded his seventeen-foot aluminum canoe, squirrel cage and packs of pelts into the baggage car, along with Buffalo. Two other people had arrived from a "stroll," he said with a wry wink as he peeled off a few twenties for their fare.

In the passenger car, seating two dozen, they made themselves comfortable along with a group of unshaven but jolly canoeists for the hour-long trip to Capreol, north of Sudbury. For those who couldn't afford a bush-plane flight, this no-frills railroading was a cheap and convenient way of reaching the wilderness. While Belle and Ted sipped from a thermos of coffee, Micro stroked the rabbit pelt that Ted had given him for a souvenir.

The toy train stopped at the Capreol depot. From the siding they watched a gleaming Via Rail express bound for Vancouver roar by, complete with luxury dining car, bedrooms and bubble-topped viewing car. She wouldn't have traded a place on it for the quick phone call she made to Hélène, setting a record in speed talking.

In Ted's truck, the canoe on top, Buffalo in the cap with the gear, Belle found herself jammed between the "men," so she made room by resting her arms on the back of the bench seat, knitting together a strange family. "I don't approve of your killing anything but beaver, Ted, but I owe you more than train fare. Come for dinner the next time you're in the neighbourhood. Champagne and steaks are on the menu."

"I won't be working out that way. Some sneaky bugger springs my traps." His craggy face broke into a smile. "Happy to be of service, madame. What goes around comes around."

"What do you mean?"

He made the turn toward Radar Road and set an even eighty klicks across the flat farming area. "When I graduated high school, I tried to kayak the Albany River by myself. Broke up in a Class Five rapids. More nerve than brains. Stumbled into a native fish camp after a week. I lost twenty pounds."

They reached Edgewater Road by one o'clock. Belle leaned over and honked the horn the last hundred feet to the DesRosiers' drive. Hélène rushed out, her face flushed with tears and smiles.

"Dear Lord," she said, as Micro ran to her arms. Buffalo and Rusty started sparring over an old soup bone. Stumping down the steps, Ed gave Belle a bear hug which took her breath away. He smelled of bacon. Then she knelt to bury her face in Freya's familiar fur. "Home again, girl. I think you should put me on a leash."

After introducing Ted, they went inside for coffee royales, though the sun wasn't within a mile of the yardarm. Hélène took her aside in the kitchen as she pulled out the Seagram's. "Let's not mention Dave and the whole mess. Micro's been through enough. This is a celebration."

"So as you said on the phone, Bea wasn't the third victim of a serial killer," Belle said. "Did they—"

"He's in custody. A young handyman who worked for cash,

scoping out opportunities. No records or receipts. Then he'd return like he was making a flower delivery. Psychic Paula gave the police the crucial tip about his license plate. They found some of the stolen items at his apartment. Everyone in town's breathing easy, I can tell you."

Belle took one sip of the potent coffee and picked up the phone to dial the police. "I've been waiting long, uncomfortable nights to do this."

Hélène added with a frown, "If you left your wallet and cards in the van, you'd better call VISA, too."

"And I need some..." She doubted that Hélène, a hysterectomy in her past, retained any supplies, but her daughters-in-law often visited.

Detective Sumner got on the line through a patch, wasting no time. A fortified OPP unit would be assembled at Shining Tree to raid the brewery. Police were issuing all-points bulletins for the men, starting with Dave and Len in town, she told them when she returned to the group.

Micro was tapping at his computer, catching up on games. She could hear muffled beeps and bangs from his room. Ed and Ted relaxed in conversation in the recliners by the stove. "So you're a trapper. I was a plumber, but that outdoor life always..."

After Hélène pulled her famous manicotti out of the oven and poured glasses of knock-three-times black-market wine, Belle was glad to get home to her waterbed. She noticed with a smirk that Dave had left several worried messages on her answering machine, setting up another alibi. She hoped he would soon get an intimate view of Sudbury's free civic housing.

EPILOGUE

Steve relaxed on the blue leather sofa in Belle's living room, shoes off and his size tens up. Her van had been located in a sidewalk car lot in Montreal and would be on a flatbed coming home tomorrow.

Between sips of coffee, he gave her chastizing looks beneath his black brows. "Why in the hell did you go alone to that brewery? You should have called 911 first. One of these—"

"Stop the lecture, Mother. Would they have taken me seriously? How much time would have been wasted? If I hadn't checked out Aikenhead on that very day, Micro would have been wearing a toe tag instead of moleskin." She rapped her head. "I felt like such a fool not realizing what he had said on the phone. Guess I listened to my emotions, not my brain."

"What's new? You're damn lucky Rochette was at Thor Lake. Big strong man saves your butt."

"Hey, I had to get there. Two days in the bush living on bannock. Give me credit." She tossed him a mischievous glance. "What's the news on the rat pack?"

He held up his fingers. "There are six of them, and more on the periphery, mostly Len Hewlitt's friends from Montreal drug gangs. They needed all kinds of expertise for those sweet little greenhouses. Plumbing, wiring and heating specialists, plus dormitory accommodations to be built for the caretakers. That operation was going to be the biggest in Canada. Ten thousand square metres. The returns would have been exponential. Within a year, they would have been doing five million dollars' worth of business, going international immediately. Charges range from production of a controlled substance, possession and possession for the intent of trafficking."

"A thousand a plant sure beats Royal Doulton. I'm thinking of changing my profession."

"They were going to use the old rail spur. Buy a few used units. Gives a whole new meaning to the name Budd car."

Belle laughed for nearly half a minute, stopping short of wetting her pants. Steve did have a sense of humour, or was this a one-off? "When is the government going to wise up and legalize the stuff? Think of all that hefty tax revenue filling the coffers."

"Pot tax for potholes."

"Stop it. My stomach hurts from laughing." Then her eyes saddened at the tragic side of the case. "What about Bea's murder? Dave didn't do it himself, but—"

"Plea bargain is the concept du jour. Hewlitt's fingered Dave for hiring him to kill Bea."

"Len killed Bea? I can't—"

"Didn't have the stomach for it. Gave the dirty job to Allan Ritchie on a subcontract while he waited outside. Drugged the dog first with that famous bone of yours."

"Aha. When I tried to tell—"

"Every now and then a blind squirrel finds an acorn. And the choice part is that Dave got to pay Hewlitt with cheques for his PI work." He fingered quotes around the last two words.

"So I wasn't totally wrong about the man." She recalled with some strange fondness their evening at the stakeout, that zany music, the jokes and the excitement of discovery. The fact that she had been a total patsy dampened the jolly memories. And pawning off the job didn't make him more ethical than the actual murderer, just cagier.

"There's also a conspiracy charge for the three of them. As for the kidnapping, technicalities are tricky. Dave was Micro's guardian, so we might be talking child endangerment and certainly abuse. No bail for anyone, and after Dave's trial, they'll all be away until the Green Party takes over Parliament. Too bad we don't have capital punishment."

"And don't forget attempted murder for me, the human pot roast."

"Allan Ritchie again, yakking like a parrot now that he can't feed his crack habit. He parked a van with a car-topper at the public launch and rowed to your place along the lake. Dave told him to scare you off."

"Me and my big mouth, telling him about my sauna plans. But scare me? That's a crock. What if Freya hadn't run down the road?" She finished her coffee and placed the mug on the glass table, noticing the coat of ever-present light ash, the price of wood heat.

"Claims he would have called you on some pretext, or gone to your house to invite you to join them. Sorry I blew you off when you told me about the those wedges."

"A rare apology. I accept. So was it all about money, then?" She recalled Sister Veronica's description of Dave's single-mindedness. Apparently that trait had led him in other directions.

"Not exactly. Seems Dave had some inspiration from Len's daughter."

"Lillian? Are you saying—"

"You got it. They'd been having an affair, well before he married Bea. Lady likes to spend money. BMW. Caribbean vacations. In a few years, they would have had enough for several luxury homes where the rich congregate in places a damn sight warmer than this."

"But the CNIB? It's hard to believe that ordinary people with ordinary jobs get involved in murder. And she's gorgeous."

"Are you still that naïve? Tune in Court TV and meet the real world." He grinned as he patted Freya.

Belle showed him a postcard of Jacobs Field. "Micro wrote. He's living in Cleveland with his Uncle Rafe. Can't wait for baseball season to open. The Indians have better odds of making the playoffs than our Jays."

"You must miss him. Sounds like you made a good team, little mother."

"Don't push it. He'll come back each summer for a couple of weeks to stay with Hélène and Ed. I have a lot more to show him in the woods. And he wants to visit the Ukrainian Seniors' Home again."

"So you and the DesRosiers did get in contact with the Restorative Justice people I suggested. How did that work out?" The group consisted of dedicated lawyers, judges, counsellors and volunteers who sought to build a bridge between criminals and their victims. Though Micro had not been charged with a crime, they had bent the rules to accommodate his case.

"Micro repaid the removal costs with his savings. Then, until he left for the States, he spent an hour after school reading to the residents or writing letters for them. Had his cheek pinched so many times he looked like a kewpie doll. And he learned to make perogies and cabbage rolls."

"He's a strong kid. Lost his father, sister, then his mother."

Belle felt a tiny throb in her chest. "He's designing my business website long distance, using some fancy Flash program. Virtual house tours. Ain't technology wonderful?" His rates were more reasonable than those of professional designers. Was she guilty of soliciting child labour?

After Steve left, she went to the hall closet and retrieved a black plastic box with her mother's name. She took it outside to the flower beds beside the house on the sunny side where a small patch of earth nestled in the inches of November snow. Setting it down, she pried off the square cap with a shiver, unsure of what to expect. Little finger bones? Melted gold fillings? No, her mother had teeth hard as rocks. She peered in, opening a twist tie around a plastic bag. Nothing but a few pounds of fine, innocent bone meal. Humming "Onward Christian Soldiers," Terry Palmer's favourite hymn, she scattered the ashes against the trimmed bases of the climbing roses. The earth was frozen, and it was the wrong time of year, but this gesture was long overdue. She replaced the burlap covers, snugging them around the thorns.

She stood in satisfaction. "You always wanted to be six feet tall or a rose. Now you can be both."

Headed for the garbage box, she stopped and with a gimlet eye, examined the simple container. Cremation was becoming a popular option, and no one she knew was getting any younger. The label would peel off with a little soap and water. She tucked it under her arm and headed back, ahead by a cool fifty dollars.

BUSHWOMAN BANNOCK

3 cups flour
Pinch of salt
2 tablespoons bacon grease
1 teaspoon baking powder
Water as needed
Cranberries, raspberries, blueberries, anything in season

Combine all ingredients except berries, and knead well into a stiff batter. Add berries gently and form into patties 1/2 inch thick and heat in a cast-iron pan or seasoned griddle. If you are cooking outside at a fire, the pan can be leaned gently toward the fire, baking the top first.

LOU ALLIN sings two national anthems, having been born in Toronto but raised in Ohio when her father followed the film business to Cleveland in 1948. His profession explains her passion for celluloid classics, which shows up frequently in her writing.

Armed with a Ph.D. in English Renaissance literature, Lou headed north, ending up at Cambrian College in Sudbury, Ontario, where she taught writing and public speaking to Criminal Justice students for twenty-eight years before recently retiring.

Her first Belle Palmer mystery, *Northern Winters Are Murder,* was published in 2000, followed by *Blackflies are Murder* and *Bush Poodles Are Murder. Murder, Eh?* is the fourth in the series. *Blackflies Are Murder* was shortlisted for an Arthur Ellis Award in the category of Best Novel. Lou can be visited online at www.louallin.com.